Axe to Grind

The Road to Rocktoberfest 2023

GABBI GREY

Copyright © 2023 Gabbi Grey

All rights reserved.

No part of this book may be reproduced in any form or by any electronic or mechanical means, including information storage and retrieval systems, without written permission from the author, except for the use of brief quotations in a book review.

This is a work of fiction. Names, characters, places and incidents are either the products of the author's imagination, or are used fictitiously.

References to real people, events, organizations, establishments or locations are intended to provide a sense of authenticity and are used fictitiously. Any resemblance to actual events, locations, organizations, or persons living or dead is entirely coincidental.

NO AI/NO BOT. We do not consent to any Artificial Intelligence (AI), generative AI, large language model, machine learning, chatbot, or other automated analysis, generative process, or replication program to reproduce, mimic, remix, summarize, or otherwise replicate any part of this creative work, via any means: print, graphic, sculpture, multimedia, audio, or other medium. We support the right of humans to control their artistic works.

No generative AI was used in the creation of this book.

Edits by ELF.

Cover by Natasha Snow.

Ed

For ten challenging years, I've been the lead guitarist for the band I formed with my best friend Axel. Grindstone is on the verge of making it big. Which is why I'm livid when our manager brings in some snooping, scandal-chasing documentary producer to film our trip to Rocktoberfest. We're about to hit the biggest stage of our career, and I'm worried this rich jerk, who has destroyed other celebrities, might uncover the secret I've kept hidden for years. I want to just ignore him, but as attraction sizzles, I start letting down my guard. Giving in to these urges might mean distracting him from his mission and getting him on my side. That's the point. Right?

Thornton

I want to bring Ed and Axel down for what they did to my sister. I've managed to insinuate myself into their inner circle as a documentarian, and I'm this close to pay dirt. Using seduction to uncover the last of Ed's secrets might be tacky, but what red-blooded man would turn down what the bisexual rock god is offering? But as we find stolen moments to try to slake the need, I'm having second thoughts. If I don't avenge the wrong done to my family, I won't be able to live with myself. The promise of sex shouldn't be enough to stop me. But as I sink deeper into a relationship with Ed, I must decide if my need for revenge is worth destroying any hope of a future together.

Axe to Grind is a book in the multi-author Road to Rocktoberfest 2023 series. Each book can be read as a standalone, but why not read them all and see who hits the stage next? Hot rock stars and the men who love them, what more could you ask for? Kick back, load up your Kindle, and enjoy the men of Rocktoberfest!

Dedication

Laurel

Kaje

Renae

Wendy

TL and the other Rocktoberfest 2023 authors

Contents

1. Chapter One — 1
2. Chapter Two — 9
3. Chapter Three — 16
4. Chapter Four — 27
5. Chapter Five — 33
6. Chapter Six — 40
7. Chapter Seven — 49
8. Chapter Eight — 58
9. Chapter Nine — 65
10. Chapter Ten — 74
11. Chapter Eleven — 81
12. Chapter Twelve — 90
13. Chapter Thirteen — 98
14. Chapter Fourteen — 106

15.	Chapter Fifteen	114
16.	Chapter Sixteen	123
17.	Chapter Seventeen	132
18.	Chapter Eighteen	140
19.	Chapter Nineteen	147
20.	Chapter Twenty	157
21.	Chapter Twenty-One	166
22.	Chapter Twenty-Two	175
23.	Chapter Twenty-Three	183
24.	Chapter Twenty-Four	194
25.	Chapter Twenty-Five	203
26.	Chapter Twenty-Six	213
27.	Chapter Twenty-Seven	219
28.	Chapter Twenty-Eight	232
29.	Chapter Twenty-Nine	241
30.	Chapter Thirty	249
31.	Chapter Thirty-One	258
32.	Chapter Thirty-Two	267
33.	Chapter Thirty-Three	275
34.	Chapter Thirty-Four	280
35.	Chapter Thirty-Five	290
36.	Chapter Thirty-Six	299
37.	Chapter Thirty-Seven	306
38.	Chapter Thirty-Eight	314

39. Chapter Thirty-Nine — 322
40. Chapter Forty — 330
41. Epilogue — 337
42. Sunrise — 344

Chapter One

Ed

"No fucking way." I glared at our manager, Pauletta. "Final answer."

She placed her hands on her hips and glared right back. "I know what's best for you." Her dark-brown eyes flashed fire. "Who's been with you since day one?"

I clenched my jaw. "You."

"Who's been here to pick up the pieces?"

Jesus. "You." Although I'd done a fair amount of picking up myself. The role of protector in the band came naturally to me—and I often stood up when others might get plowed over.

Like now. I paced across the small backstage space, nearly tripping over some cables.

Pauletta held up her hands in that placating gesture that always softened me. Even as I fought against it, my resistance weakened a fraction. I loved the woman, and going against her wishes grated. No lie, she'd been with Grindstone from the beginning—when Axel and I had been a garage band, begging for gigs at every venue we could in Vancouver. She caught our act one night and had seen promise.

Nearly ten years later, we were at the top of our game. About to play Rocktoberfest in the Nevada desert for a screaming crowd of tens of thousands of fans next week. Bands like Corvus Rising, Queen Anne's Revenge, Maiden Voyage, and Midnight Hunt would be playing as well. This was our break. Our chance to gain international attention.

And Pauletta was fucking with that.

"No, way. They're going to be in the way."

"They're a professional crew who know what they're doing. You won't even know they're there."

I arched an eyebrow.

"Okay, well, not much. Within a few hours, you won't—you'll be so focused on the show that you won't notice them. They'll fade into the background."

"That's highly unlikely." I didn't even try to keep the sarcasm from my voice.

Pauletta's glare intensified.

I moved closer to her. Backstage at the Pacific National Exhibition—the PNE—wasn't the place to be having this argument. We'd done our sound check, but the opening act wasn't due to start for another few minutes. The buzz of the gathering crowd electrified me.

Always had. Always would.

We had a girl band as our opening act here. Five spectacularly talented young women who verged on stardom. The harmonies on their ballads could break even the hardest of hearts, and their vocals on the pure-rock songs blew me away every time. Genesis's Progeny might not have been the best band name in the world—to me, anyway—but they were kicking ass and taking numbers. Basically an amped up Spice Girls or Destiny's Child—a throwback to the nineties.

When I'd barely been born.

Some days I felt every one of my twenty-seven years. Other times, I couldn't believe Axel and I had formed the band ten years ago.

I drew a deep breath. "Okay, well, does it have to be *that* guy?" I continued my pacing, dodging an assistant stage manager while fighting the sense of unreality.

Pauletta knew who I meant. And tilted her head as if in consideration.

Damn. I knew better. She wasn't contemplating. Her mind was made up.

"Thornton Graves is one of the best in the business. Look, Ed, he's only thirty-three. He can relate to you guys."

I glared.

She continued. "And the rags-to-riches story's a great one—and you know it. You mentor kids in dire circumstances because you want them to see there's a path out of poverty."

I winced. Yeah, anything that reminded me of my childhood was a trigger. For Axel as well. We hated the stereotype. Two Black boys from neglectful and abusive families living destitute lives. Scrounging together enough to buy guitars and, thanks to a caring music teacher, finding a way to practice. Eventually, through grit and perseverance, they succeed.

Yeah, kids could look up to that. But most youngsters faced horrific challenges to rise above their circumstances—especially racialized kids, including many Indigenous ones. The most-expensive city in Canada wasn't kind when it came to its poorer citizens.

"Okay...but him? You saw the hatchet job he did on Ezra Michaels."

This time, both of Pauletta's eyebrows shot up. "You're defending that scumbag?"

"No...?" I hedged. The guy'd done deplorable—

"Fifteen women, Ed. He abused fifteen women."

"They should've gone to the police, Paulie." *Damn, don't use your nickname for her.* Pissed her right off. Which might've been why I did it. "He didn't even have the benefit of a trial—just a group of women parading their stories to a reporter." I waved her off. "And I get that many women don't go to the police because they think they won't be believed—which is a whole other thing—but why didn't Graves encourage them to report the crimes? Especially when he knew how many there were? No. Instead, he ambushed Ezra. Ruined his career."

"You think a man who committed that kind of crime deserves a career?"

My mind flashed to Kyesha.

Don't go there. That way only led to danger.

"I don't." I glared. "Of course I don't. Men in the spotlight, and women too, shouldn't get away with shit just because they're famous. But he deserved his day in court, not a trial by social media.".

"You're way too sympathetic toward him, Ed. Doesn't suit you." She patted her hair. "And, anyway, I hear he's getting it."

"What?" I stopped my pacing and faced the most-important woman in my life. In the process, I nearly knocked over a mic stand. "And if he's guilty, which I'm betting he is, then he deserves to have the book thrown at him." Jesus, she thought I'd side with a guy who abused women? Did she not know me?

"You probably didn't hear—the cops charged him this afternoon. With multiple counts of sexual assault and battery. Unless a jury lets him off—which is always a possibility, given his celebrity—he's going down for this." Her eyes narrowed. "So, thanks to Thornton Graves pulling the evidence together and empowering those women, Ezra's getting what he deserves."

"Fine." I spat out the word. "So the guy's a do-gooder who deserves a medal or a..."

"Pulitzer."

"Whatever. Or the Nobel thing." I gave her my glare. Or was that just for science? Being immersed in music for every moment of every day meant my mind was full of chord progressions and concert venues. But I also followed a Canadian news site as well as the local Vancouver news. Axel and I shared a condo in the downtown core—about five miles from where we'd grown up. Probably why we felt compelled to go back so often and volunteer.

Pauletta continued to stare.

Damn woman. She knew my buttons. Knew how to press them. Knew exactly how much pressure she could apply before I'd break. "Our past is off-limits for this documentary thing."

She began to speak.

I held up my hand.

She desisted.

"You want us to bare our souls. Axel's not in the right place for that."

"Ed, he's been clean and sober for eight years."

"And he still struggles, Paulie."

Her shocked expression, with the wide eyes and raised eyebrows, almost made me laugh.

Almost. "Look, he doesn't tell you everything—"

"I'm your manager. I should be the first to know everything."

I could take issue with numerous aspects of that statement.

But I wouldn't. "I take care of him. I'll always take care of him."

"You might not always be there for him, Ed."

I winced inwardly.

"He might choose someone else."

Double wince.

She must've caught something, because her eyes narrowed. "Look, you know I don't care about your sexuality—"

I held up my hand to halt the conversation. Obviously, she understood another of my fears about the documentary crew.

She plowed right on through.

"Personally, I think if you came out as bi, there'd be a positive reaction. Bi-erasure is a thing. You've dated both men and women—"

"I'm not ready to come out yet. Not even to help you."

She pursed her lips. Then, after a moment, "I'm not asking you to. I'm proudly bi. And I don't care who knows about it."

Except she did. Her mother's rejection when she'd brought home her first girlfriend still stung. She'd expected kindness and understanding from her bohemian mother—she'd gotten a slap to the face and a demand she never bring home another *trashy* girl again.

According to Paulie's retelling of the story—usually after a couple of cocktails—her girlfriend wore a blouse buttoned to the neck and black slacks with patent leather pumps. Paulie'd been going through her wild rocker chick phase—wearing a torn T-shirt, ripped jeans, and dirty work boots.

"Your mom was wrong."

Pauletta winced.

I'd met this powerhouse a few years later, when I'd been eighteen and she'd been twenty-four. Pauletta's height impressed me—she had a good three inches over my five-eight. Her no-nonsense approach also spoke to me. She'd just earned a business degree at a local college and was prepared to take over the management of our band. I tried to explain we could barely pay our bills, but she assured me she'd take care of everything. Axel and I were living in a one-bedroom basement suite off Commercial Drive and were willing to try anything.

As part of the deal, she had us upgrading our accommodations—both living and venue-wise—within a few months.

Maybe if Axel and I'd stayed in our dive, we wouldn't have had the space to entertain Kyesha. Maybe—

Fucking stop it.

Most of the time, I could keep memories of the young woman at bay. But this Thornton guy's appearance was dredging up bad memories.

I waved Paulie off, trying to refocus. "People aren't interested in me. It's all about the front man. They want Axel. I just worry about his mental health."

"So, watch out for him." She smiled. "Thornton's mostly going to be shooting during the concert prep and the actual concert. You and Axel will be in each other's pockets."

I blinked.

"You'll be hanging around together," she clarified.

"I got that." I didn't always understand the expressions she used, but I usually managed. Our backgrounds couldn't have been more different. She'd grown up in the prestigious British Properties in West Vancouver with her bank executive Black father and her white mother who championed the destitute, working as a lawyer in the Downtown Eastside of Vancouver.

My old neighborhood.

Pauletta'd attended a private day school.

I'd cobbled together a public-school education while working odd jobs to earn lunch money and, eventually, enough to buy my own guitar.

Two different worlds.

I'd written a song about that.

One of our bestsellers.

"I don't like this, Paulie. I don't trust him."

"You have my word everything's going to work out. He'll do a great doc about you folks, you'll get free publicity, and everything will only get better."

Nothing was ever *free* in this world. Everything had a price. Everyone wanted a piece of us. Every time we thought we might get some peace, something would erupt, and chaos would ensue. I'd been doing this long enough to know things never worked out as intended.

Okay, we'd do this damned documentary.

I just didn't know if we were strong enough to get through it.

Chapter Two

Thornton

Pauletta Magnum's call, letting me know the doc was a go, lit a fire within me.

Finally.

Eight years. I'd needed eight years to build enough cred to finally approach Grindstone about doing a documentary. Eight years of mostly fluff pieces about celebrities. Of me boosting egos so they'd trust me with their *secrets*, and with what, when, and how to reveal them. Most of the time, those were banal, like an ill-advised relationship. Others were more serious—like an abusive parent or an addiction. Those stories were few and far between.

One woman admitted to having an abortion. I'd hesitated to air that part of the interview, but she insisted. She'd been fifteen and in no shape to carry a pregnancy. She didn't regret her decision—and she felt other women needed to know they shouldn't feel shame if they made the same choice. As one of the biggest Hollywood celebrities—and a fan favorite—she had the clout.

Focus.

I snagged my phone and shot off three texts.

Within five minutes, my team all confirmed they'd be in Vancouver within three days. I planned a skeleton crew for this shoot—camera, sound, director, and myself as interviewer and producer. I'd worked with this team on the last three projects, so I had every confidence we'd nail this shoot.

And I intended to nail Ed Markham and Axel Townsend in more ways than one.

Don't get ahead of yourself.

I eyed my family photos, lingering on the picture of myself and my five siblings. My parents very much fit the do-gooder image. I was their only biological child. The other five came from just about every ethnic background one might find in Portland.

Then I glanced over the collection of all the documentaries I'd worked on since graduating from film school at age twenty-one. Fourteen in twelve years. I'd cut my teeth on nature documentaries. Those days felt like my distant past—the simple times.

People were so much more complicated.

I set about packing everything I'd need.

Lydia, our videographer, had all her own equipment. She didn't trust anyone else's, and she didn't trust hers to anyone. *Control freak, anyone?*

Of course, if I'd spent that much on equipment, I'd probably be willing to rip off anyone's fingers who dared touch my stuff.

Likewise, Kato had all his own sound equipment.

While I was leaving to drive up to Vancouver within the hour, Kato and Lydia would drive up together the day after tomorrow.

I wanted them sooner, but Lydia's sister was turning twenty-one. Given the young woman'd battled leukemia as a child, the family celebrated every milestone with gusto.

And Kato, being secretly in love with Lydia, would do whatever she asked.

Whether she knew about his crush—and whether she might ever return that affection—were questions I never uttered aloud.

I almost hoped they never consummated the...relationship. Eventually they'd break up—because that happened with virtually every relationship—and that'd mess with the good thing we had going.

Mickey texted me again that they'd fly out of Toronto tomorrow, and would hit Vancouver in the evening. As our Canadian and resident ball-busting director—it thrilled me they'd be with me soon. I'd done tons of background for the piece, but I wanted their take.

For what I intended to share, anyway.

I finished packing, loaded my hybrid SUV, and hit the road.

Five hours later, I reached the Canadian border and the Peace Arch.

Although I'd prepared with documents and a bunch of other stuff, the Canadian border guard scanned my passport, confirmed I was going to only be working for a week for an American employer, and cautioned me to follow the rules.

Rules I'd read up on when I first approached Pauletta.

I thanked the woman, offered my best smile, and headed into White Rock.

The drive to downtown Vancouver took just over an hour since I'd hit rush hour traffic. I crossed yet another bridge—this one the Granville Street Bridge—and found myself surrounded by soaring concrete-and-glass structures. I continued north until my GPS directed me to turn onto Robson Street, and then a left turn into what, at first, appeared to be an alley. But, no, I'd arrived at the entrance to the Hotel BLU Vancouver.

A snappily dressed porter removed my three bags from my SUV.

I handed my keys to a lovely car jockey with bright-blue eyes and a wide smile.

She handed me a ticket in return and had whisked away my vehicle before I could blink.

The porter indicated I should follow him, which I did.

Registration took mere moments, and I was soon on my way up to the twentieth floor. Although Pauletta'd arranged a pleasant room, I'd upgraded myself to one of the penthouse suites. I hadn't visited Vancouver in years, and I planned to enjoy this visit in style.

Don't forget why you're here.

I tipped the porter with an American twenty. With the exchange, he'd do okay.

He gave me an enormous smile, removed my baggage from the cart, and headed out.

You brought too much stuff.

Possibly. I'd be here a week before we headed to Nevada for the concert prep and the actual concert.

I yanked my phone out of my back pocket and shot Pauletta a text, inviting the entire band out for dinner.

Given how close it was to five o'clock, she surprised me by accepting my offer and saying all band members except Songbird would be there. She suggested a pleasant restaurant, but I wanted more upscale and, countering her suggestion, offered to buy dinner for everyone at The Georgian.

Her response was slower in coming, but eventually she agreed.

Good.

I'd already made the reservation and would've been loath to cancel. So that meant six—Axel, Ed, Pauletta, Meg the drummer, Big Mac the bassist, and myself.

Should be interesting.

Since the dinner was scheduled for seven, I grabbed a shower and watched the Canadian national news as I dressed. Although I'd brought a suit, I opted to go more casual. Or at least casual for me—silk shirt, linen trousers, leather shoes, and my Rolex. The Rolex was a gift from my father when I'd turned eighteen. He'd hoped I'd go into medicine, as he had.

I'd disappointed him by heading to film school.

My mother'd been delighted. She liked the idea of me travelling all over the world instead of staying in our little corner of Portland.

Bonita, the eldest of my five younger adopted siblings, had followed Dad into medicine. Barely twenty-eight, she was finishing her residency in nephrology. Pietro, her younger brother, was in his fourth year of nursing at OHSU Portland. Their mother died from cancer when they'd been six and four, respectively. Their father had stuck around for about eight months before turning the kids over to social services and disappearing forever. My parents took in the siblings as foster children and, three years later, they'd adopted the pair. A good lawyer had been needed since courts were always reticent to sever all parental rights. Still, their father's abandonment was pretty clear.

After them had come...

Nope. Couldn't go there.

Ayala and Abigail had arrived six years later. Premature twins with a myriad of medical problems and a mother who couldn't cope, as she had three other kids at home. After a long meeting with my parents, she agreed to give up custody—temporarily.

Less than a month later, she signed over her rights and took her remaining three kids back to Alabama.

We'd never heard from her again.

I'd been eighteen, and both eager to get out in the world and endlessly fascinated with these two tiny creatures who moved in and took over the house.

Now, at a very healthy fifteen, the twins still ruled the roost.

I yanked up my phone to check Ayala's latest post on Facebook. A selfie of her and her sister. So goddamn close. Attached at the hip. *What will they do if something drives them apart?*

After a long moment, I pulled up the family photo taken eight years ago.

I'd been home from an assignment to the wilds of Kenya.

The twins had just celebrated their seventh birthday and were still in the *I want to wear what she's wearing* phase.

Bonita was in the first year of medical curriculum and Pietro was in the last year of high school.

And our other sister was still a teenager.

I couldn't even say her name.

Such a bright, shining light.

I miss you. I fingered the chain in my pocket—a talisman, and reminder why I was here.

After a moment, I moved to the massive floor-to-ceiling windows. I faced the condo tower next door. As always, I wondered about the people across the way. What travails were they facing? What tragedies would they endure today? What triumphs would make life worthwhile?

My four awards were a testimony to my success—somewhat—but they didn't keep me warm at night.

I need to get laid.

A tempting thought. I'd hooked up quite a few times over the past few years, making use of the efficient hookup app and the fact every city had men looking to slake their needs.

I was only too happy to accommodate them. Being a sturdy six-three with muscles, I didn't worry about winding up in a dangerous situation. I probably should have, but I never did. Part of me was a fatalist—if my time came, I'd accept it.

You haven't resolved your anger.

Well, fair enough. My parents urged me to move on with my life. In fact, I'd stopped trying to talk to them about my pain. They'd moved on. And not in a mean way—more that they had five other children, including myself, to care for.

A laugh escaped me.

I hadn't needed caring for in a very long time.

Or so you tell yourself.

After taking a moment to center myself, I took a deep breath, tied my shoelaces, and headed off into the unknown.

Chapter Three

Ed

I yanked at my collar.

Axel nudged me.

I glared at him.

He grinned.

Yeah, sure, yuck it up. You'll see...this is going to end in disaster.

He'd opted for a gray T-shirt with a dinner jacket and khaki pants. The look should've been weird, but he pulled it off.

Pauletta wore a purple satin blouse with her pantsuit. Meticulous—as always.

Meg and Big Mac'd gone casual with band T-shirts and jeans. At least their boots shone.

Songbird's decision to play piano at her family's church tonight rankled. Yes, great, she was doing the family and religion things.

On the other hand, I could've used her support. Her bullshit meter was as accurate as my own.

Not that Pauletta couldn't spot trouble—but she had a reputation to maintain that would prevent her from speaking up.

Songbird had no such compunctions—she said whatever came into her head, consequences be damned.

I tugged at my tie.

Axel nudged me again.

Regretting having gone full dress mode, I eyed my shiny shoes. This wasn't me. Suit? Pressed linen shirt? Silk tie? Ugh.

"Is that him?" Axel whispered into my ear. Of course, he had to lean over to do it. The guy had six inches on me.

And so did the newcomer.

Our gazes locked.

His amber eyes betrayed his surprise.

Yeah, you expected us to be late. Surprise. We're early. We're always early.

That was Pauletta's doing. From day one, she'd run a tight ship. No slackers on her crew. We were to be respectful of others' time.

Even if that consideration wasn't always returned.

Still, Mr. Tall and Handsome wasn't late. No, he'd arrived about ten minutes early.

We'd just been here four minutes before him.

Before I could speak, Pauletta stepped forward, her hand extended. "Mr. Graves, lovely to meet you."

"Please, it's Thornton." He indicated the group. "Thank you for coming."

I bit back the comment that we didn't have a choice.

Pauletta wouldn't have appreciated my candor.

Big Mac stepped forward. The diminutive man, at five-five, barely reached Graves's shoulder. "I loved your interview with Candi Lewis." He offered his hand. "It's great you want to interview us."

My fingers were dwarfed by Graves's long ones. "Well, I'm glad you're open to the idea."

He cut a glance at me, but looked away before I could tell him what I thought of his niceties.

Meg stepped forward next. Our drummer was the same height as Big Mac, and although she was petite, she was also solid. No one got past her if she didn't want them to. While Big Mac was as white as white could be, Meg's mixed Indigenous heritage gave her skin a warm tan. Her Ojibway name was Megis, but she preferred Meg. She stared at Graves with her obsidian eyes. "You'll do us right?"

Glad to see someone else smells something distinctly foul.

The man's responding smile pinged all kinds of warning buzzers in my head.

Possibly because he again cut a quick glance at me before shaking Meg's hand. "I have no hidden agenda. I want to show you all in the best light."

I caught a twitch in his left eye. What the...?

Axel nudged me not so gently as he stepped forward. "I guess you know who I am."

Thornton's eyes lit. With genuine interest or something fake? I couldn't tell, dammit.

"Axel Townsend." Thornton clasped his hand vigorously. "I'm one of Grindstone's biggest fans."

Did his left eye just twitch again?

"I remember you from back in your early days. You played a concert down in Portland."

Axel grinned. "Yeah, our first one down there, right?" He turned to me. "Nine years ago? We were green."

"Something like that."

I met Graves's gaze. His eyes glittered, and I struggled to name their color. Brandy? Amber? Something related to alcohol, that was for certain. I'd never seen anything like them.

And I'm not getting pulled in by them, so don't bother trying.

"You were at the concert?" He didn't look like a rock-band fan. No, he looked more like smooth jazz or classical.

His smile faltered for just a moment. "A friend. She brought home your album and insisted I listen. I've been obsessed ever since."

My bullshit meter hit eleven.

"Oh, *Immortalized*."

He shook his head. "No, that was what, your third album? That came out six years later. No, I'm talking about *Desperation*."

Sloppy on my part—of course he'd know when each of our albums had released. Still, I had to try to trip him up and show him for the phony he was.

Axel gave me a funny look then subtly nodded.

Being a dickhead was getting me nowhere. I stepped forward. "Ed Markham."

"Edward, right?"

I squeezed his hand extra tight. "Edmund. But only my grandmother called me that. You're not my grandmother." *The Fairie Queen* had been her favorite, and she'd convinced my mother to name me after the fricking sixteenth-century poet. As if life wasn't tough enough for a Black kid in Vancouver.

Graves raised an eyebrow. "Apologies. I'll make certain that doesn't get into the doc."

Which refocused me back to why this meeting was taking place. And, for the record, I fucking hated that I had to look up at him. Bloody blond-haired, amber-eyed, clearly well-endowed, entitled asshole wasn't going to derail me.

Well endowed? What, were you checking out his package?

Yes. Yes, I was. And, in linen slacks, judging a guy's size was pretty difficult. But something told me he had a gigantic cock.

Or maybe just a cocky attitude.

Both?

Axel snagged my hand to tug me aside as the maître d' stepped forward.

"Mr. Graves, I have your table ready." She acknowledged each of us in turn.

Thornton offered his arm to Pauletta.

Oh, for fuck's sake.

She took it with a grin. "A gentleman." She met my gaze.

Bring it on.

Axel offered me his arm.

Meg held hers out for Big Mac.

The man grinned and made a big show of taking it.

I glared at Axel and stubbornly kept my hands to myself. Not that I would've minded touching my best friend. Everyone in the band was handsy in a platonic way. Well, except Pauletta. She considered herself above the general fray.

Axel nudged me over and over as we walked through the dining room to a table in a secluded corner.

"Knock it off. What are you, ten?"

"Maybe." He snickered. "You like him."

I stopped.

He nearly knocked into me.

A server barely avoided hitting both of us with an armful of dirty dishes.

She managed to remove the scowl from her expression and instead pasted on a smile. "Can I help you gentlemen?"

Axel bestowed upon her his megawatt smile.

Her eyes widened. "You're Axel."

Yeah, my buddy didn't even need a last name.

"I am. Why don't you drop by our table later?"

"I couldn't." She cleared her throat. "I'm working."

And likely in such an upscale establishment, fawning over famous guests was discouraged.

"What's your name?"

I caught Pauletta's gaze as she cocked her head.

With a wince, I gave her the *one sec* signal.

She subtly nodded and made a show of selecting a chair.

"Um, Alison."

"One *l* or two?" Axel asked.

"One."

"Great." Another megawatt smile. "Have a good night."

She headed to the back of the restaurant while Axel guided me to the table.

"You've got a notepad, right?"

"Something you can scribble your autograph on? Yes. How do you plan to get it to her?"

"I'll figure it out."

He would. He always did.

Meg sat at one end of the table, across from Big Mac. At first, I'd tried to think of him as Joseph. I'd given up after a good half hour. Big Mac just...fit him. Despite the fact he was neither big nor a Mac.

Pauletta'd grabbed the seat next to Meg, and Axel quickly nabbed the seat across from her.

Leaving Thornton and me at the end of the table—facing each other.

Great.

I offered my widest smile as I sat.

He held his open pose for a beat as he met my gaze. His hesitation assured me that he wasn't fooled for even a moment.

My smile faltered slightly.

He sat.

Pauletta already had the drinks menu open.

Despite the fact Axel and I never imbibed, the rest of the group was free to do so. Most of the time, we coped. I caught Axel's gaze.

After a moment, he gave me a barely perceptible nod.

Yeah, he'd be okay.

I breathed a sigh of relief.

"As I told Pauletta, the dinner's on me. As a thank you." Thornton held open his arms, casually draping a hand on the back of Axel's chair.

I stiffened.

Axel grinned. "That's so generous of you." He glanced at Pauletta.

She nodded.

He opened his menu.

Meg and Big Mac also added their appreciation.

The words sat, unspoken, on my tongue.

Pauletta kicked me under the table.

I winced.

Thornton tilted his head.

"Yes, very kind of you. I hope we can repay your generosity." I carefully repeated a variation of the word Axel'd picked.

The interloper nodded.

Nope. I hadn't fooled him. Not for a moment.

Our server appeared.

Pauletta ordered a Hemingway daiquiri, Meg opted for a craft beer, Big Mac chose a Cosmo, and Axel asked for sparkling water.

My mouth salivated over the thought of a rum and coke. I offered the server a smile. "Ginger ale, please."

She grinned. "Of course." She pivoted to Thornton.

He held my gaze. "Same here. I love having Canada Dry when I come to Canada."

"Oh, you're American."

As she continued to smile, I noted her nametag read *Tracey*. Her light makeup didn't hide the lines. I couldn't imagine working a service job well into my fifties.

And what do you envision you'll be doing in your fifties?

Hopefully enjoying still being alive, was the standard response.

Thornton said something about being from Portland.

I was only half-paying attention as Axel tried to get my attention. What...? Oh, notepad. I dug one out of my jacket pocket along with a Sharpie.

By the time Tracey and Thornton were done with their little chat, Axel handed Tracey a folded piece of paper.

She quirked an eyebrow.

"Oh, I knew Alison from school. She asked me to give her that." He pointed to the paper. "It's private."

If Tracey questioned this little interaction, she showed no signs of it. "I'll give it to her right away. And I'll get those drinks shortly." She headed off.

Axel made a big show of returning my Sharpie and notebook.

I quirked an eyebrow.

He grinned unrepentantly.

Aw, shit.

Was I going to have to run interference again, or had he been a good boy and just offered his autograph without including his phone number? After eight years of me nagging him, he'd gotten pretty good at resisting.

Well, better than before.

We could've afforded our own places by now, but I insisted we keep the condo together. Our bedrooms were at opposite ends, and that granted some privacy, but basically Axel'd have to sneak someone in for me not to know. Or go to their place—which I actively discouraged. As much as I didn't want groupies coming into our home, having him staying out all night without me being able to track him would be much worse. He'd asked for my help in staying sober, and I was doing my best.

"I'm eyeing the sirloin."

My stomach churned. Of course Pauletta was.

"Oh, that sounds lovely." Meg pointed. "Although the lamb shoulder sounds delicious as well."

Great. More burned flesh.

Axel grinned. "They have lots of salad options, Ed."

I glared.

He winked impishly.

"I'm thinking the shrimp linguini." Big Mac closed the menu. "In white wine sauce."

So, although I could've asked them to hold the shrimp, holding the wine in a wine sauce wasn't likely to go over well.

Thornton eyed me.

I squinted at the menu. Normally, I looked up the menu on my phone before we got to a restaurant so I could have everything selected ahead of time.

Pauletta's call had come in the middle of a rehearsal. I'd insisted we finish the set before showering and heading over to the restaurant.

And since I'd driven us, I hadn't had time to check the phone while we travelled over.

"Do you use reading glasses?"

My gaze shot to Thornton's.

Axel snickered. "He refuses to see the optometrist because yeah, he needs reading glasses. If I wasn't sure he could read street signs, I'd worry he might need distance glasses as well."

My cheeks heated. "Well, better that than smelling like a locker room."

Axel's inability to smell his own funk was a constant source of amusement.

Pauletta closed her menu with a bit more force than necessary.

I winced.

Axel did as well.

Technically, I wasn't certain who was being reprimanded—because we were both being assholes. In front of a guest. A guest who could spread our secrets into the wide world.

Not a good look.

Axel mouthed *sorry*.

I nodded—he'd understand I was accepting his apology and offering my own.

"Their eggplant parmesan is vegan." Pauletta snagged my menu from my unresisting hands.

Thornton tilted his head. "Vegan?"

I wilted. "No." I swallowed hard. "I'm not that disciplined. I still do eggs and dairy."

"Ah, well good for you. I might consider giving up meat, but you'll have to pry my cheese from my cold, dead hands." He offered a smile. "I think I'll have that as well." He pivoted to Axel. "And you?"

"Northern Pacific halibut with a side of lobster tail."

Great. Fish smell.

Tracey reappeared with our drinks.

I sipped my ginger ale as everyone ordered.

Thornton indicated I should go before him.

I asked for the eggplant parmesan.

He added his request.

Tracey took our menus and headed toward the kitchen.

I met Thornton's gaze.

Somehow I felt like I was the one in the frying pan, not Axel's halibut.

Chapter Four

Thornton

P rickly.

Arrogant.

Sexy as fuck.

I'd expected Axel to be the toughest nut to crack—but he was proving to be easily swayed. By the time we finished our food, I had several solid anecdotes I could get him to recount for the documentary.

Ed's glare intensified with every smile Axel bestowed upon me. I'd bet if the man could've kicked his good friend, he totally would've done it.

And they were friends. Although everyone in the band got along, clearly Axel and Ed shared a special bond. Oh, and Big Mac had the biggest crush on Meg, and the woman obviously had no clue. Kind of adorable. Matchmaking wasn't in my job description. *But it'd make a great story if you can get them to see each other in a romantic light.* Yeah, but what if Meg didn't reciprocate, and the band fell apart?

Would that be so bad? For those two, it might just be. If I ruined things for Axel and Ed, I had no problem with that.

Pauletta discreetly yawned.

"Do you folks want to take this to a lounge?" I held up my hands. "My treat. And I'm certain they've got plenty of ginger ale and sparkling water."

"Sounds great—"

"We have an early practice."

Axel pursed his lips after Ed cut him off.

Pauletta didn't hide the next yawn.

Didn't bands start late morning and work late into the night?

"We're morning people." Meg placed her napkin on the table. "And although I really appreciate the offer, I need to call it a night. My dog's been at doggie daycare all day, and she'll be missing me."

Big Mac perked up. "How is Wren?"

Wren?

Meg perked up as well. "She's doing great. I'm worried about leaving her for the concert in Black Rock, but she'll survive." She fidgeted with her napkin. "It's Kevin's turn with her."

Big Mac nearly growled. "That fucker doesn't deserve time with her."

"He bought her for me—"

"Right. As a gift for you." Big Mac enunciated every word. "He doesn't even like the dog—he keeps up the custody agreement to put the screws to you."

Meg's outrage flashed, but quickly, she deflated.

Ah, so not angry at Big Mac. Good to know.

"I don't see why we can't take her with us." Big Mac stuck out his chin.

Pauletta shifted.

Meg beat her to it, responding to his comment. "It'll never work. We can't leave her on the bus alone for hours at a time. That'd be cruel. No, as horrible as Kevin is, she enjoys spending time with him."

Big Mac grunted.

"And on that note, I need to be going." Meg met my gaze. "Thanks so much."

"My pleasure. I'll see you tomorrow at practice."

Big Mac rose as well. "We can share a cab."

"We live in opposite directions."

"I still want to make certain you're safe."

The offer to pay for the cab was on the tip of my tongue when Meg rose.

"That'd be nice...Big. Thank you."

Had she been about to call him Joseph?

Curious minds.

Perhaps something existed between the two of them.

"We need to be going as well." Ed met Axel's gaze.

"I want to go to a lounge." Axel crossed his arms.

"Early morning practice." Ed snickered. "Some of us are not so much morning people, eh?"

Axel glared.

Ed tried to hide the smile—but didn't manage very well.

"I'm heading over to The Lords's and Ladies' Club. If anyone wants to join me, you're welcome." I gestured to everyone. "Tonight was awesome. I enjoyed getting to know the people behind Grindstone."

At a noise, I glanced at Ed.

He winced.

Pauletta beamed.

I'd lay even money she'd just kicked him in the shin. Or pinched his thigh—given her arm was below the tablecloth.

"Yes." Ed cleared his throat. "Awesome."

Pauletta rose and turned to Meg and Big Mac. "I'll see you out." She nodded to me. "Thank you."

I nodded in acknowledgement.

Axel popped up. "I have to piss."

Ed groaned, but his friend was already following the rest of the party toward the door.

He veered at the last moment and headed toward the restrooms.

After a hesitation, Ed caught my gaze. He leaned forward.

I resisted the urge to mimic his gesture.

"Look, you've been generous tonight. I don't know you. I don't know if you have a big budget and this is a business write-off or if you come from money."

The contempt of the money idea dripped, unmistakably tainting the evening.

Before I could respond, he continued, "I'll always be protective of my band."

"Yes, I got that." I held his gaze. Those deep-brown eyes mesmerized in a way that disturbed me. His dark skin glowed in the low light of the restaurant, and the jacket did little to cover his muscles. His rigorous workout routine had hit legendary status, while Axel's penchant for burgers and fries was also well known. I worried Axel might be bulimic—given how slender he was—but I'd read he had a fabulous metabolism. *Will he still have that in his later years?* And why was I thinking about Axel while Ed sat in front of me? "A nightcap at the lounge is hardly a cause for concern. I can deliver him home, if that makes you feel better." I'd chosen that lounge specifically because it was located just a few blocks from their condo.

Ed pursed his lips. "Sobriety is critical—for both of us."

"I won't order him a bourbon, if that's what you're worried about." I held up my hands. "I respect your choice not to drink." I glanced at the other empty glasses that'd held booze. "But you're able to be around others who drink."

He growled. "This isn't a lounge where booze is the point of the place, and they'll never pressure us. They'll do the opposite—"

"As will I—"

"I don't trust you."

Ah. Now we're getting to the crux of the argument. "You can trust me."

He rose jerkily. "I don't trust anyone." He caught sight of Axel returning. "Thank you, but we won't be joining you."

Before I could argue, he made his way across the room.

A discussion—clearly a heated argument—ensued between the two men. Finally, after more than a minute, Axel looked over, caught my gaze, shrugged, waved, and then headed out with Ed guiding him by the elbow.

I stared at their retreating gorgeous asses until they left my sight.

Well, Axel's ass. Ed's was mostly covered by his suit jacket.

But I'd seen pictures. I'd pored over photographs of the two of them. The other band members as well, for certain, but especially these two.

Well, mostly Ed. I hadn't been wrong—Axel was the way to get to Ed. The way to hurt Ed. And, in the end, that was my goal.

You'd do well to remember that.

My sole focus was Grindstone. Once I took them down, I'd be free to pursue other passion projects.

If I'm not too toxic.

Nah, I wouldn't be. The world would thank me for exposing Axel and Ed as the hypocrites they were.

I paid the bill, leaving a generous tip, and then left the restaurant. Doing the calculations in my head, I figured I was only about six blocks from my hotel. Tonight was the perfect night for a stroll, so I headed that way.

Chapter Five

Ed

Axel prowled the condo.

I sat with my acoustic guitar on my lap and strummed a few chords from a Beatles song I loved.

He glared.

I hummed.

Our bedtime had long come and gone. The witching hour had set in.

Still, he wouldn't settle.

"I don't understand what your problem is with him."

Axel's words caught me off-guard as he'd been stalking for over fifteen minutes. He did this frequently—prowled like a caged animal. While I'd hop on the treadmill, he preferred a less efficient way to exercise. Plus, if he actually got on the treadmill then he wouldn't be able to glare at me. Again, something he did frequently.

Possibly I should've grown tired of this pacing, but I considered the…annoyance…the price of friendship. Honestly, I could do without the notoriety. The money and music were amazing. The rest? I'd be fine if the publicity disappeared.

What about the fans?

Ugh. Yeah. I liked many of them. And we needed fans to buy our records and see our concerts so we could maintain our lifestyle.

The lifestyle always on the verge of being jeopardized if I didn't keep Axel on the straight and narrow.

"I don't have a problem with him." I'd considered playing totally ignorant, but that would've pissed Axel off even more than he already was. "He bought us dinner. I thanked him." I hummed.

"And left a fifty under your plate."

My gaze shot to his.

"That a *fuck you?*"

I shifted, trying for a more comfortable position. "She deserved a fucking generous tip."

"You thought he'd shortchange her?"

Strumming, I tried to ignore the implicit accusation in his question.

He snapped his fingers.

Annoyance ricocheted through me. I shot my gaze to him. "I don't know him well enough to know how generous of a tipper he is. But I saw those prices. I mean, I doubt Tracey can afford to eat in that restaurant. I left chump change."

"I doubt she'll see it that way." Axel dropped onto the couch next to me. "What is it about him?"

Speaking of doubts…they assailed me. *What if he's right? What if Graves isn't a threat?*

Could I afford to trust?

Nope. I really couldn't.

"I'm sure he's a perfectly nice guy."

Axel snorted.

"But you saw what he did to Ezra Michaels."

"Some big football star who abused women? He deserved to pay for that. And the cops arrested him. So that means Thornton did a good thing."

"Maybe if our pasts were clean, and we were virginal, then this might work out." I continued to strum the guitar. "We're not choirboys, Axel."

I didn't need to see his face to see the pain etched there. And since witnessing it might break me, I studiously tried out a new melody that'd been floating around in my mind.

"That was eight years ago, Ed. We've changed. We're not the people we were before. Well, you weren't as much as a fuckup as I was—"

"Don't kid yourself, Axel. We were both fuckups." Some days, I wasn't convinced we'd made that much progress. We didn't drink. We didn't party. Much. But we also didn't act like true grown-ups. At twenty-seven, many people were already parents. Neither of us had dated seriously in eight years. I winced. Okay, even longer for me. Like...ever.

And wasn't that a sobering thought? I'd had hundreds of hookups, but no genuine relationships.

Axel hadn't dated anyone seriously since Kyesha.

Her lovely face flashed before me. Dark skin, pert nose, and dull, dark eyes. I tried to remember the fresh-faced girl who'd first shown up at our Portland concert and who'd followed us back to Canada. Whenever I tried, though, my last image of her superimposed over the sunny one. I hated remembering her.

Yet she'd been on my mind constantly since Pauletta'd informed me that documentary filmmaker Thornton Graves was going to shoot a film about Grindstone.

I softened my tone. "But we straightened up, and we've done some great things since. Like volunteering—"

"You drag me out."

"And once I do, people see you care."

He *did* care—he just felt he couldn't let himself. That if he connected with someone for more than a casual relationship, it'd end in disaster. He did okay with the kids we spent time with, but he never had more than casual affairs with the women passing through his life.

"It's just a show."

Arguing this point would be fruitless, so I patted his thigh. "Did you get Alison's number?"

He shook his head. "She seemed nice but...maybe a little young?"

I'd pegged her as only a couple years younger than us. Did he mean naïve?

"I'm certain you'll meet someone in Nevada."

"To hookup with?" He snagged my guitar and strummed a discordant chord.

I winced. "Yeah, okay, fair enough."

He handed me back the guitar. "I'm going to jerk off." He rose.

"I'm not sure I needed to know that, Axel."

He shrugged. "Keepin' it real. You're way too prudish." He loped off to his bedroom, leaving me along with my thoughts.

Not always a nice place to be. I rose, put the guitar in the case, took my empty water glass to the kitchen, and put it in the dishwasher. I eyed the calendar on the fridge. Five days before we hopped on our tour bus and headed south. Five days with Thornton, plus... He wouldn't be on the bus, would he? Not enough room.

AXE TO GRIND 37

Except the bus had six bunks, and Pauletta always flew, since she suffered from severe motion sickness if she wasn't driving. Well, that or being around five rockers for hours on end made her nauseous. Could go either way.

Why did Thornton keep getting under my skin? What was it about *him* in particular? I'd dealt with plenty of reporters over the last ten years. Well, mostly in the last three years. Our third studio album had sold really well, and we'd ridden that wave pretty high—opening for some big names on a couple of concert tours. Last night's concert had been our first major headlining gig in Vancouver.

Pauletta's insistence we practice this morning was more proof of how important Rocktoberfest was for us. Yes, we were a newbie band. But we'd nabbed a spot on the main stage. And yeah, we were playing amongst the first on opening day—but that slot was a good one. We could warm the crowd up for some of the bigger bands, like Warrior Black and Embrace the Fear.

I flipped off the light in the kitchen and headed for my bathroom. I'd showered after practice, so I didn't really need one. Except I needed to relax, and showering was the quickest way to get me into a state of bliss.

Plus, if Axel was rubbing one out, I could as well.

I hung up my jacket and pants carefully while tossing my shirt into the laundry hamper. My perfectly made bed awaited me. We had a lovely woman, Gratzia, who came in twice a week to take care of stuff for us.

Axel sometimes talked about getting a big house and maybe having live-in staff.

After I pointed to our bank balance and savings, he'd wander on to the next idea. We had this place paid for, and we had decent savings, but we weren't close to top tier yet. We still didn't have a consistent income. That being said, we had a couple of big endorsements coming up for carefully cultivated companies with products or services we believed in. The five of us had sworn we'd never become sellouts—but if we made a few extra dollars to put into our personal coffers, that wasn't a bad thing.

Pauletta kept us on the straight and narrow.

If only we'd listened earlier.

Maybe...

Nope, couldn't go down that road. That way lay recriminations and pain.

I hopped into the shower and wet my hair, using the clear, fragrance-free shampoo designed for locs. Then I soaped my body and tried to think of anything sexy. *Like Thorton Graves?*

Fucking hell.

Yeah, deep-amber eyes, blond, slightly floppy hair that fell over his right eye sometimes when he spoke animatedly, and a sexy body. And, yeah, I liked guys who towered above me.

You don't know if he's even gay.

I palmed my cock. *Who gives a shit?* Imagining his hands roaming all over my body wasn't a hardship. Envisioning me sucking him off into a blissful orgasm came easily. Fucking him into oblivion finished the picture nicely.

I came hard.

And sighed.

Most big guys didn't like being topped by someone a good eight inches shorter. Yet those were the guys I found sexiest and wanted to pin down and fuck.

I wasn't too picky, though. I'd fuck a smaller guy. And, if I was desperate enough, I'd allow a guy to fuck me. That didn't happen often, though. I understood the appeal—had enjoyed prostate play—but that wasn't my jam. Now, if I could just find a way to get Thornton and his nice ass out of my mind, I'd be doing good.

Chapter Six

Thornton

I hadn't slept well the night before, but after eating my continental breakfast at the hotel, I hopped into my SUV and headed to the rehearsal space Grindstone used. The converted warehouse in the heart of Strathcona didn't appear all that impressive when I pulled up, but from the moment I stepped inside, I knew the owners had done a ton of work.

Concert posters adorned the walls. I assumed they came from bands who'd worked in the warehouse, which had several rehearsal spaces as well as two recording studios.

A bubbly, older gentleman with a nametag proclaiming he was *Mark* greeted me. His graying hair and deeply grooved face seemed incongruous with his infectious smile and the fact he nearly bounced out of his seat.

"You're Thornton Graves!"

I heard the exclamation mark. "I am. I believe I'm early—"

"Axel, Ed, Meg, and Pauletta are already in." He pointed to a long corridor. "Last door on the left."

I wondered if I needed a pass, but clearly, he sat there all day and vetted everyone.

What happens when he needs to take a piss?

Maybe they had someone who'd come out and relieve him or maybe he locked the doors to the outside. Maybe their procedures were none of my damn business.

A distinct possibility.

I headed to the end of the hallway and stood at the door, with my hand poised over the knob.

Before I could summon my courage, the door flew open and Ed stood before me.

For reasons I couldn't explain, I didn't like that I towered over him. Well just over half-a-foot wasn't towering, per se, but our height difference was noticeable. Also, he appeared more delicate. His muscles were on full display in that tank top, yet he looked slight. At least in comparison to me.

Ed glared. "Are you coming in or not? You're in my way, and I have to piss."

Not wanting to cause a problem, I quickly stepped aside, letting him pass.

He mumbled something unintelligible as he pushed past me.

I entered the cavernous space to find Pauletta sitting at a table typing furiously on her laptop, Axel standing in a corner with earbuds in, and Meg examining her drum set.

Before I could inquire, Songbird and Big Mac barrelled in. Both carried trays laden with Tim Hortons coffee cups. Big Mac also carried a box of what I suspected were Timbits. Only one of the best Canadian treats ever—little donut holes in various flavors. Maple walnut was my fav, but—if offered—I wouldn't be picky. I'd meant to pick up a coffee, but hadn't gotten that far. I'd figured I might have something delivered for everyone, another gesture to get on their good side.

Apparently delivery came unbidden.

Pauletta, Axel, Meg, and a returning Ed all swarmed like locusts.

I stood back and watched in amusement.

Songbird held out an extra-large coffee for me. "I didn't know if you drank coffee. The studio has a kettle and various teas." She smiled sweetly. "They also have a coffee machine."

I tilted my head.

"None of us can figure out how to make a decent cup." Meg held a precious Timbit in her hand. "Seriously. Six adults who can't master the machine."

Ed grunted as he popped a chocolate Timbit into his mouth.

Big Mac offered me the box. I selected blindly as I didn't want to seem picky. I pulled out another chocolate.

Ed narrowed his eyes.

Shit. Were the chocolate only for him? I offered it up.

He grunted again, shook his head, and took his black coffee off to a corner where his guitar rested on a stand.

As I added a bit of milk and two sugars to my coffee, I noticed Songbird dunking her tea a couple of times before dropping the bag into the garbage.

Axel added a drop of milk and then a packet of artificial sweetener. Meg grabbed her black coffee, while Big Mac added multiple milk and sugar packets to his.

So...more like a latté. A bit over the top, but each to their own.

"Normally Timmies will doctor the coffees for us, but we weren't certain what you wanted." Songbird eyed me. "You're a double-double."

I arched an eyebrow.

"Two milk and two sugars."

Glancing at my discarded containers, I nodded.

"Okay, good to know. We do a run after lunch as well."

Meg grunted in Songbird's direction.

"Well, the rest of us caffeinate. Unless we have a show, Meg can't. She opts for caffeine-free."

I almost mock-shuddered, but caught myself. "That's very sensible."

She saluted me and headed back to her drum set.

"Well, I'll buy this afternoon." I held up my coffee. "Least I can do."

Songbird watched me intently.

I held her gaze. Not sure what she saw—or what she thought she saw—but I wasn't going to yield on this.

After a long moment, she nodded. "You'll do." Then she wandered over to her keyboard. She set down her coffee and began playing, but without sound.

In fact, to my surprise, no one played their instruments for the first few minutes. Everyone appeared to be in a meditative trance as they looked at their stuff.

Except Pauletta. She'd nabbed her black coffee and was back at her laptop, typing furiously.

Ed pulled out his phone.

Had it vibrated?

He scrolled a bit, then put it back in his back pocket. "You guys ready?"

Everyone except Pauletta nodded, and they gathered in a circle. Axel gave a note, then they began an a cappella version of…"Row, Row, Row Your Boat".

I couldn't have been more stunned. I also cursed myself for not having brought even a small camera. Having my phone to record wouldn't do much—and I hadn't obtained their permission to film, so that wouldn't work.

Their harmonies as they made their way through the simple song were amazing. My sisters used to love that song, but I hadn't heard it in years. Ayala, I was certain, would get the biggest kick out of this.

Have to ask for next time.

Ed caught my gaze.

I held it.

Something passed between the two of us. Not friendly...but not hostile. Clearly he was trying to convey a message but, as with most of his actions, I wasn't certain what. Something about him had me always on edge.

Do I do the same to him?

If so, I'd have to watch myself. I didn't need him to be wary of me. Lull him until I brought out the big guns.

They transitioned into... "Scarborough Fair"? I couldn't fathom why they opted for a Simon and Garfunkel song, but they sang that as well. They moved on to "God Only Knows". I was still puzzling over that when they moved to the keyboard and transitioned to "My Immortal".

That nearly broke me. It'd been one of my sister's favorite songs. She loved her rock'n'roll, but she also loved her ballads.

I blinked rapidly. Repeatedly.

Ed caught my gaze. He cocked his head.

After a moment, I shook mine. *Get a fucking grip.*

To my relief, when the song ended, they moved into a rendition of "Bohemian Rhapsody".

I nearly laughed.

All the songs had layered lyrics and strong harmonies, so they made sense. Funny, I understood the band sang—that's what bands did—but I hadn't spent a lot of time thinking about their vocal talents. As I quickly replayed all their songs in my mind, I picked out the ones with trickier vocals. And, I reflected, most of them had more than just Axel singing.

Their anthem, the ballad "Immortalized", came from their third album with the same name. That song had rocketed them to the next tier, and was likely the reason they'd been invited to Rocktoberfest. Likely they'd either play it first or last.

One intrepid music critic thought the song was about a particular death. They'd couldn't figure out who might've died.

I had my suspicions. Although I could be wrong. Ed's mother passed that year. He'd spoken highly of her—how she'd supported the family on a minimum-wage job—but I'd read ambivalence in his answers. Like he knew he was supposed to say nice things about his mother, but that he couldn't quite manage to do it with a straight face.

Axel never talked about his family, and I wasn't certain Songbird, Meg, or Big Mac'd ever been asked. As I wanted to get a full picture of the group, I'd need to make inquiries of everyone. I'd caught a profile of Pauletta in a local Vancouver business magazine featuring successful women of color. Great profile, and she'd delivered a solid interview.

She'd talked about all the mentoring she did—acknowledging she'd come from a privileged background, and that she felt she needed to pay it forward.

I hadn't found any substantial articles about Songbird, Meg, or Big Mac. Whether they'd chosen to stay out of the limelight or because no one'd asked, I wasn't sure.

The various members sipped a bit of their drinks as they discussed, in hushed tones, their practice list. I caught just enough words to have some idea what they planned for the day. Spotting a comfortable-looking chair in the corner, I settled into it, pulled out my phone, and began making notes about what I'd witnessed. I had no frame of reference. Did all bands do those vocal acrobatic warmups?

As I typed the Evanescence song title, my heart took a knock. My sister'd always had a flair for the dramatic. She'd be the one holding up a lighter in the audience. Holding up the flashlight on one's phone hadn't really become a thing until after she passed. I still didn't understand people's obsession with taking photos of the band while they were way in the back and the photo could be of anyone. And, it obviously annoyed people behind them.

You're an old fossil.

Yep. I was. And I didn't care.

My mother always claimed I was an old soul. I hadn't argued. I figured my parents providing me with five younger siblings—all with varying degrees of physical ailments or trauma of some kind—had forced me to grow up. To be protective. To be a worrywart.

My father insisted that was his role.

Consciously, I might've agreed. In my heart, though, I'd felt the weight of responsibility.

I eyed Ed as he strummed a few chords on his electric guitar.

As if he sensed my gaze on him, he glanced up.

Something passed between us. Yes, the hostility was there. But also an awareness that'd been missing last night.

I'd read somewhere that Ed was bi. Or that was the rumor. He hadn't been photographed with a male date—ever.

Axel favored leggy women—of every color and size. His preference appeared to be taller women, but the paps had spotted him with a wide variety. And never the same woman twice. Obviously he felt women were expendable. Someone to be disposed of.

That knowledge hurt—but also reinforced my impression of him. Solidified the information I'd ascertained in my years-long research project.

The band ran through an entire set. Whether for my benefit or because that'd been the plan, I wasn't certain. I spotted two new songs. Great choice to be introducing them at Rocktoberfest—they'd have an audience of a few fans who knew them and a ton of people who'd had no exposure. They ended their set with "Immortalized", and the silence after the last chord reverberated through the room.

Feeling compelled to acknowledge the performance I'd just witnessed, I clapped enthusiastically.

Meg rose from her drums, took a bow, then grabbed her water bottle and guzzled half of it.

Songbird eyed me, then, after what felt like an eternal moment, smiled.

Big Mac pulled his damp T-shirt from his body.

Axel bent at the waist and stretched his fingers down to his toes.

Ed, after putting his guitar on the stand, finally met my gaze. He was, in the end, the one who headed my way.

When he stood before me, I scented the man-sweat wafting off him. Not the disgusting version—just the *I've just done an honest day's labor* version. He grabbed the hem of his tank top and wiped his brow.

I got a tantalizing view of his washboard abs.

He dropped the fabric and gazed up at me.

I swallowed.

He cocked his head.

An electric charge passed between the two of us.

He narrowed his eyes. "I heard you offered Candi Lewis sexual favors for the interview she gave you."

Fuck. "That was a rumor put out by a rival of mine. She'd initially agreed to speak to him, but...he's a bit of a sleaze. She figured that out quickly, and when I approached, she was only too happy to sit down with me." I cleared my throat. "And since I'm gay, that wouldn't have been very successful."

"Some guys can manage."

I flashed to all the closeted guys who married women because of societal expectations. A few might be bi, but many were completely on the one side of the Kinsey scale.

As was I.

"I'm gay. One hundred percent. Women are perfectly lovely creatures, but I have yet to be attracted to any of them."

"So what *is* your type—" Ed grinned like he knew he was out of line.

I had the sudden impulse to shake him up. "Slightly shorter than me. Slightly more muscular than me. Longer hair that I can grab and tug on while we're fucking."

He swallowed visibly. "And?"

"Skin color, ethnicity, and religion don't mean anything. And yes, I've dated a few guys. Less than many, more than some. I'm...discerning. I won't invite just anyone to my bed."

"And how big is that bed?"

"Enough for two healthy, clean, and enthusiastic men."

His cool had returned. He cocked his head. "As well as yourself?"

I nearly choked. "I've never done a threesome."

"Too bad, they can be fun." He winked, turned, then sauntered away.

Man, I'm screwed.

Chapter Seven

Ed

Well, that went better than expected.

Maybe because I had such low expectations?

That's a distinct possibility.

I'd wondered last night about Thornton's sexuality. He could've fallen anywhere on the spectrum. That being said, I compared the gazes he'd given Pauletta versus the ones he'd given Axel.

Oh, and the ones he'd shot my way.

And this morning he'd barely showed any interest in Songbird. Well, not of the sexual kind. He'd been interested with her as a potential person to grill about Axel, but I hadn't spotted a flicker of awareness.

Objectively, Songbird was smoking hot. So was Meg. Both women had significant followings. And Pauletta garnered plenty of attention wherever she went.

He'd just gazed blandly at them all.

Slightly shorter than me. Slightly more muscular than me. Longer hair that I can grab and tug on while we're fucking.

He'd met my gaze directly when he'd said those words. If he hadn't meant them for me, then...I'd eat my shoe.

I glanced down at my boots.

They'd be fucking difficult to eat.

So, better to keep my observations to myself.

Although...if I could attract his attention, then maybe he'd back off Axel. If I could keep him occupied, he wouldn't have time to do the deep research I feared so much. If I could tease him and keep him in a constant state of arousal, he might miss what was visible just beneath the surface.

Axel and I didn't drink—but we weren't just sober because of a problem with alcohol. Our problems ran much deeper.

"You like him."

I glanced up from my water guzzling to find Songbird in front of me. "He's here to dig up the past. Sometimes the past needs to stay buried."

She narrowed her eyes. She knew. All our bandmates did. They needed to understand why all mind-altering substances were banned from all of our events. And since, to some degree, they all enjoyed healthy lifestyles, they didn't mind.

Pauletta grabbed a cigarette or two a week, but she was the only one, and Axel harassed her constantly about it. For such a smart woman, she could do dumb shit.

"So, what, you're going to blow him to distract him?"

I spewed water all over the floor at Songbird's comment. I glared at her as I wiped the dribble off my chin.

My glare never had an effect on her. She shrugged, then wandered away.

"Gross, man." Axel approached. "Pauletta's thinking pizza for lunch. She wants the whole-wheat crap."

"That crap keeps you healthy."

"Yeah, and she wants chicken instead of pepperoni or beef." He eyed me. "And veggie for you, of course."

"Of course." I held in my smirk—barely.

"Oh, she's inviting Thornton. You can make googly eyes at him."

I elbowed Axel in the gut.

He *oofed*.

I took a small amount of satisfaction from that. "I gotta piss."

"TMI, buddy." Axel headed over to the recorder Pauletta'd set up and was likely going to listen to "AI" again.

The song was our response to the recent phenomenon of assholes using artificial intelligence to mimic singers' voices and to create new songs. Or, in one case, someone had created a song with Axel covering a Weekn'd song. We'd had to issue a denial that it'd been the band. The culprit had pulled the song down, but not before thousands of people'd heard it and then clamored for one Canadian singer to cover another Canadian singer—without their permission.

Some fans just didn't understand copyright or why we might be proprietary of Axel's voice. We couldn't stop the imitations, but we could fight when his voice was used for commercial purposes.

Jesus.

We'd written our frustration into a song—a song we'd launch at Rocktoberfest.

Part of me wanted to ask Thornton what he thought of it, and part of me pretended I didn't give a shit.

Keep telling yourself that.

I headed into the bathroom.

And found Thornton pissing at a urinal.

If my bladder hadn't been making demands, I would've turned around and left. As it was, we had a gender-neutral bathroom where I could duck into a stall, but—

He caught sight of me and…I couldn't chicken out.

Reliving myself meant exposing myself in a way I didn't appreciate, but desperation could make a man do many things. As I pissed, he shook himself off, tucked himself back in—and I did *not* try to check out his size—then he meandered over to the sink and took his fucking time washing his hands.

I finished and had no choice but to zip myself back in and make my way over to the sink.

As he fingered his hair, I couldn't help but be drawn to the blond locks. Or the way it flopped over his right eye in just that perfect coif.

Probably spends a fortune on haircuts.

I didn't. More than I wanted, but less than Pauletta would've had me do if I'd bowed to her wishes.

Thornton met my gaze in the mirror, and my breath caught. That amber color almost defied description.

You could write a song about them.

I tried to silence the voice in my mind even as lyrics danced in my head.

He cocked his head.

Damn—caught staring.

I shut off the tap and wiped my damp hands on my jeans rather than use either a paper towel or the air dryer. That noise, for reasons I couldn't explain, drove me nuts.

Thornton grabbed a single paper towel. He wiped his hands, then tossed it into the garbage can.

He advanced toward me.

I held my ground. Then, as he entered my personal space, I glanced up at him.

He blocked my exit. "You're hiding something."

My gut churned. He was fishing, right? He didn't *actually* know. He couldn't. We'd been so careful. "Look, I have to get back to rehearsal—"

"I'm going to figure it out, Ed."

"I thought you were here to document the band's journey to Rocktoberfest." Him revealing his true intention meant I could go to Paulie and call the whole thing off.

Except I didn't want to. I wanted him around. And I hated admitting that to myself. "I need to go."

And still, he didn't move.

I tried to push past him.

Stubborn bastard wouldn't yield.

Unhappy at being forced to look up, my gaze clashed with his.

The lust I'd held at bay for almost twenty-four hours crashed hard. I grabbed his neck and dragged him down for a kiss. I forced his lips to mine, then demanded entrance.

So much for consent.

He was a big guy. He could pull away. Instead, he opened his mouth and welcomed my invading tongue.

I plundered. I demanded. I took no prisoners. I wrapped my arms around his waist, cupped his ass, and dragged him closer.

He snagged the back of my neck and angled so his tongue could reach the recesses of my mouth.

The fact Big Mac or Axel—or any other person using the building—could wander in at any moment barely registered.

I was ready to drag him into the nearest stall and to fuck him senseless.

Three things stopped me. First, I didn't want to risk getting caught. Second...pizza. And third—perhaps the most critical piece of the puzzle—was that I didn't know his preferences. Guys? Obviously. Top, bottom, or vers? No clue.

He pulled back, scraping his cheek against mine. "You're so fucking sexy."

Okay, a guy always liked to hear that. Women too, I suspected. Although most of the time it was just a line.

What are you doing? He's the enemy.

Perhaps. But if I kept him occupied with sex, he might give up on his crusade to uncover our secrets.

Thornton dropped his gaze to my mouth. "Come to my hotel tonight?"

I reared back.

He winced. "Too forward?"

I gulped. "Not this close to the tour starting. I have too much to do." *And I still don't trust you.*

"Come to my hotel, and we can get to know each other. I'm sure you can spare an hour or two."

Is he bullshitting me? I didn't know him well enough to tell.

"Not tonight." I went up on my toes and pressed a kiss to his cheek. "But we'll see." I exited the bathroom. And nearly ran back to the rehearsal studio.

We'll see? What the actual fuck?

Axel eyed me when I came back into the room. My darker skin afforded me *some* ability to hide my blushes, and my hair was always a mess after we'd run a set. Still, the way he tracked me with his gaze assured me that I hadn't fooled him.

Thornton sauntered in about a minute later—looking all casual and easy-breezy.

Fortunately, the erection that'd pressed against my hip had disappeared.

My cock had plumped, but hadn't hit semi, and I'd walked away at precisely the correct moment. A bit more of that...handsy stuff...and I'd have been even more willing to find the nearest stall or private room.

Big Mac entered the room, carrying four boxes of large pizzas.

Like locusts, we all descended.

All except Thornton, whose attention remained fixed on me.

I scrambled for distance. "I'm taking a slice out to Mark." Anything to escape the room that felt devoid of oxygen.

"Already gave him two." Big Mac grinned. "And he was ever so grateful. Even though I gave him veggie."

"Fucker." Said without malice. So my escape had been foiled. I'd thought to take him a slice—of pepperoni—and maybe hang with him.

Meg and Big Mac grabbed multiple slices of pepperoni and placed them on plates.

Songbird and Pauletta placed their Greek-with-chicken on plates.

Axel nabbed three slices of the meat lover's, dropped them onto his plate, and headed over to the center of the room where he plopped down on the floor.

I gazed at Thornton. "Preference?"

"How about I take a slice of meat lover's—"

"They're small slices—"

"And a Greek, and a veggie? That way I'm not taking too many of any one flavor. Unless you plan to eat the remaining six slices of veggie." He indicated the rest of the room. "Or unless anyone else wants to share—"

Four heads shook vigorously to indicate zero interest in my healthy choice.

Thornton chuckled.

The sound went right to my belly and caused butterflies to flutter.

I handed Thornton a plate, grabbed one for myself, then dropped three pieces of veggie onto mine. Even with Mark getting two and our interloper taking one, I'd still have two left—likely more than I needed. But man, Pauletta'd splurged for the deep dish with extra cheese. My salivary glands worked overtime as I dropped onto the floor next to Axel.

He nudged me.

Studiously ignoring him, I picked up the first piece and took a huge bite.

Thornton pointed to a spot directly across from us.

Before I could react, Axel indicated the man was welcome to join us.

As he sat, I glared at Axel.

He offered me his trademark grin. The one that showed his dimples. The one that had women—and men—swooning repeatedly.

Pauletta snapped her fingers.

Like Pavlov's dogs, all band members' heads whipped to attention.

She grinned. "I landed the photographer I wanted to do our new promo material. We're having a shoot tomorrow at seven down at the docks."

Axel raised his hand. "You mean, like the port of Vancouver?"

"Yep. I've got the Port Authority's authorization—but we've only got a window of an hour."

Meg moaned. Of all of us, she was the least morning person. Axel ran a close second.

Thornton raised his hand.

Pauletta nodded.

"My crew are arriving late tonight. Would it be okay if we tag along? Even just the camerawoman?"

"Of course."

"But not while we're getting our makeup done," I interjected. "Only after we're made up." This was more for some of the other members of the band who didn't look their best after having just rolled out of bed.

Axel nudged me. "Vanity run amok."

I glared. "I'm doing that for your benefit. You ever look in the mirror at five a.m.? Which is the time we'll need to get up."

He winced. "That's a little excessive—"

Pauletta shook her head. "No, Ed's right. I've organized a makeup tent—and security. We'll be at the foot of Clarke Drive. I'll text everyone the coordinates."

Big Mac clapped his hands excitedly, covertly glanced over at Meg, then turned back to Pauletta. "New promo pics? Cool. What's it been, a year?"

"Nearly two." Songbird eyed me. "You okay with this?"

"Why wouldn't I be?" But I knew exactly what she was referring to. I loathed having my photo taken. Of the five of us, I was the most likely to hide in the back.

"He'll be fine." Pauletta glared.

I took a big bite of pizza.

And hoped for rain.

Chapter Eight

Thornton

Since Lydia and Kato had arrived late the night before, my normally cheerful videographer was grumpy this morning.

Kato, smart man, gave her a wide berth at the breakfast buffet. And, no doubt went right back to bed after Lydia and I headed down to the docks.

Mickey's flight had been delayed, and they were due to arrive this morning. We'd planned a confab for this afternoon. Luckily they weren't needed for the morning's opportunity.

Lydia and I parked in a designated spot and made our way over to the makeup tent.

The sun had yet to appear.

A gorgeous woman with generous curves and funky blue-and-purple hair worked on Axel while a scrawny guy worked on Ed. Big Mac, Songbird, and Meg huddled in the corner, clutching their coffees.

Pauletta was nowhere to be seen.

I held up the box of Timbits.

Ravenous wolves after a long winter wouldn't have moved so quickly.

Meg secured hers and then grabbed ones for Axel and Ed.

Songbird popped hers into her mouth and then used napkins to provide ones to each of the makeup artists.

The woman with the funky hair accepted hers with enthusiasm.

The scrawny guy winced and held up his hand to decline.

Songbird held it out. When no one else snagged it, she grinned, saluted me, and popped it into her mouth.

I couldn't help returning the grin. "Everyone, this is Lydia. She's our videographer." I gazed around to gauge reactions.

The musicians waved with varying degrees on enthusiasm. Big Mac showed the most, while Ed was, unsurprisingly, the least happy.

I'd sent a long email to my team last night after I'd gotten home from yesterday's rehearsal, giving them the lay of the land. I wanted everyone on the same page as we headed into this perilous journey. Each new doc had unique challenges. This one, clearly, hinged on getting Axel, and to a certain extent Ed, to open up.

Lydia pushed her mop of red curls from her face and glanced up at me with her big, green, bloodshot eyes.

I winced, realizing just how tired she must be. Then gave her a nod.

She picked up the small camera she'd brought and fiddled a bit before heading over to makeup area.

Axel grinned and waved.

Ed couldn't even manage a smile.

And that pretty much summed up the next half hour.

Axel was playful with both Lydia and the still-photography crew. He even tried to flirt, but Lydia gently shut him down.

Songbird and Meg patiently tolerated the intrusive nature of both us filming as well as the professional photographers getting initial shots in the filtered light of the tent.

Big Mac hammed it up and tried to drag the women into some of his antics—with varying degrees of success.

Pauletta finally appeared just as an employee from the docks guided us to the approved photo location.

Huge shipping containers, massive cranes, and tractor trailer trucks proved unique backdrops—a nod to Axel and Ed's blue-collar backgrounds, I assumed. I made a note to check out the other three band members to get a read on where they'd all come from. I winced at realizing I'd been so focused on the leads that I hadn't done much work. In my defense, Pauletta's green light had come at the last minute. I shot off a text to Mickey asking them to do some research before our meeting this afternoon.

The sun crested the horizon at the perfect moment, leading to some amazing footage. The still photographer actually smiled several times—something I assumed the woman didn't do often, having a distinct frown line in her brow.

Lydia gave me the thumbs-up twice as she insinuated herself into the shoot as if she were part of the main crew instead of an interloper. That ability to become a chameleon was the woman's talent.

And I loved her for it.

We broke up a couple of hours after we'd all congregated. Pauletta ordered everyone to go home and pack. They had one more practice session tomorrow, then they'd load into the tour bus and head out.

As Lydia put her equipment away, I caught up with Pauletta.

She held up her hand before I could speak. "We've got a bunk reserved for you on the bus. If you want to—with the band's express permission—do a bit of informal shooting, that's fine. We've got a concert at a dive bar in Utah to try out the new material, and then we're heading to Black Rock. Any questions?"

"Absolutely none. Mickey, Kato, and Lydia are going to follow in the SUV. If they can hunker down for a few hours along the drive, that'd be great."

"We're spending the night in Utah. We're only taking one driver, so we're limited by the number of hours we can travel each day. Vera's done all our tours, and she's a skilful driver."

"I appreciate you accommodating us."

"I'll book rooms for your crew in Utah. How many rooms?"

"Two would be great."

She nodded, making a note on her phone. "You've got something arranged for the desert?"

"Yeah, we've rented a camper."

"Well, glad to see your people are organized."

I'd done the legwork, but I wasn't going to toot my own horn. Let her believe we worked together as a team—because we did. I just happened to be anal about plans and never left anything to chance. We'd considered renting a camper to drive from Canada, but those logistics proved too difficult. Better to snag something in Reno to drive out to the desert. It'd be a tight fit for the team, but we'd endured much-worse conditions. In fact, this'd be downright decadent compared to the camping trip we took with one of Ezra Michaels' victims who would only speak to us in her *happy place*. We didn't complain that it was in the middle of a forest—but we came away with plenty of bug bites and, poor Mickey, a case of poison ivy.

As I bid everyone goodbye, Ed glanced from me to Lydia and back.

I couldn't interpret that look. I considered extending the invitation to my room again—totally platonically—but the opportunity didn't present itself. Plus, his refusal had been clear. I needed to respect that.

And you have three days in a tour bus before you even get to Nevada, and three once you're there.

And, if I hadn't worn out my welcome, another few days as we came back to Canada.

The band had dates in LA and Portland. All smaller venues. Would success at Rocktoberfest translate into standing-room-only crowds in those venues? Or, at least, more-enthusiastic fans? Interesting to see.

For dinner, my crew joined me in my luxurious suite, and we chowed down on gourmet meals.

"You know—" Mickey wiped their mouth with their cloth napkin. "—we're damn lucky to have you."

I arched an eyebrow.

Kato grinned, and Lydia suppressed a laugh in her napkin.

"Yeah, yeah, yuk it up." I eyed the crew. "I should make you sleep in Kato's van instead of the nice camper I've arranged."

"Better than a tent." Lydia toasted me with her wineglass. "I don't want to see what Kato'd use for a mattress this time."

Kato colored. "I'd get something new for you."

Mickey snorted.

I pointed to my phone. "I've sent everyone the agenda. Tomorrow's going to be a busy day."

Lydia nodded. "I wish we had more time in the studio so they could get used to us. And it sucks I can't be on the bus." She turned her attention to me. "I've got a mini for you."

"Glad you trust me with it."

Her blinking, blank expression assured me that she didn't. Likely she was only lending me the equipment because of heavy insurance.

Mickey scrolled through their phone. "And Pauletta's sent me the confirmation of two rooms." They eyed me. "Who exactly is sharing?"

I grinned unrepentantly. "I leave that between the three of you to figure out."

"I'll see if I can get a third room," Mickey muttered.

"Oh, Lydia and I'll share." Kato popped a shrimp in his mouth. "Keeping costs low." He winced as Lydia smacked his chest. "Hey."

Lydia glared. "Don't talk with your mouth full. Jesus, what are you, ten?"

He scratched his unshaven cheek. "No." He cut me a glance. "Sorry. I forgot."

I snickered. I didn't give a shit if he spoke with his mouth full in this crowd. I appreciated if he didn't do it while we worked, though. Looking uncouth to the interviewees didn't leave the impression of professionalism we strove for.

"Are we filming in Utah?" Kato asked.

"Yes, we're filming the concert. I'd love if we could get a shot from the back of the hall and a simultaneous one from onstage."

Lydia turned to Mickey. "You think you can manage the handheld at the back? If the band's okay with it, I can shoot them onstage as well as getting some crowd shots from their vantage point."

"Don't see why not." Mickey didn't love camerawork, but they were damn competent at it. They speared an asparagus spear. "Anything else?"

We all shook our heads.

"Good. We'll check out of the hotel in the morning. I'm not thrilled about leaving our suitcases in the car at the studio—"

"They've got CCTV and a security guard." I'd thought Mark was the extent of security, but apparently the building had a roaming guard who patrolled the entire complex. Some bigger bands also recorded there and, once in a while, some fans caught wind and showed up.

"That's great." Lydia pushed her plate away. "Delicious food, but a little heavy. I think I need a walk."

"I'll come." Kato shoved the last of his scalloped potatoes in his mouth.

Lydia held up her hand. "You finish your food. I'll be fine."

"But…Vancouver's not safe…" He mumbled through potatoes.

This time, Mickey kicked him in the shin.

He placed a hand over his mouth.

"The sun hasn't set, and Vancouver's a very safe city." Lydia rose. "I want to do some mood shots of the city."

"Well, you shouldn't be out with expensive equipment—" At least Kato still held his hand over his mouth.

I held back the gag. I had a superior gag reflex, and anyone eating and talking with their mouths open might trigger me.

Lydia snapped. "I want to be alone for a bit. You've been with me every second for the past two days. We're about to spend a week and a half together in the same van. I need a break." She cut Mickey a glance. "No offense."

Mickey grinned. "None taken. Go. I'll hold down the fort."

With that, Lydia left.

Kato grunted.

I handed him the dessert menu.

At least some things in my world were a constant.

Chapter Nine

Ed

I liked Thornton's crew.

Lydia had a bawdy sense of humor.

Kato talked with his mouth full.

Mickey carried a poise and calm. They were also perfectly charming, yet clearly in charge of the crew.

Even Thornton deferred to them.

Hadn't seen that coming—I thought everyone deferred to him.

Kind of like how the band, after expressing their various opinions, would always defer to Pauletta. I could only think of a handful of times when we hadn't done it her way.

And given we were on our way to Rocktoberfest, clearly we'd been right to give her that deference.

We dressed in backup costumes, then ran through the full set with Pauletta, Thornton, and Mickey watching, while Lydia filmed us and Kato did sound shit. We didn't have fancy decorations or sets or anything like that. We chose to be purists—all about the music. We had a small, two-person road crew driving down in their own van who'd take care of gear and stuff, but we did almost everything ourselves—the way we preferred it.

By the end of the last song, we all managed to take bows while soaked in sweat and clearly exhausted.

Well, I was. I'd slept poorly the last three nights.

Since Thornton'd shown up.

Right, like you're blaming him.

Well, he's the one invading my dreams.

And that's his fault?

I'd decided he was the cause of the insomnia, and I intended to give him a wide berth.

On the tour bus.

Yeah, I was laughing at myself over that concept as well.

Still, Mr. Sexy with Smoking Eyes gave us a standing ovation. The first to stand, in fact.

Mickey leapt up as well, offering their support.

Pauletta'd risen after that—clearly not as impressed. She met my gaze.

Shit.

She'd caught me missing the chord progression in "Calling for Help".

Fuck.

I'd hoped the vocals covered the mistake, but the woman's sharpness knew no limits.

As Lydia filmed Axel stripping off his shirt and making a big show of wiping his face, Pauletta beckoned me aside.

After ensuring we didn't have any prying eyes or ears, I met her gaze. "I'm sorry, Paulie. My bad."

"What the hell's wrong with you, Ed? You're the most reliable one. You've never missed that song in a full rehearsal."

"And I won't miss it on concert night either."

She arched an eyebrow. "You'd better not."

I held back the nasty comment I wanted to make.

She was right.

She was always right.

Defending myself felt like a good idea, but I noticed both Mickey and Thornton had turned their attention to us. Subtle, but clear nonetheless. So I patted Pauletta on the shoulder, offered a weak smile, and headed to the shower room carrying a stack of clean clothes.

Twenty minutes later, I emerged. A good shower always refreshed and, after giving Axel and Big Mac a thumbs-up, I returned to the studio.

Our hired crew—Jenny and Mikhail—stacked equipment and organized everything we'd need for the various concerts.

I'd once offered to help Jenny carry something.

She'd given me a glare for the ages. Once, for fun, we'd bench-pressed weights. She beat me—by a lot.

Mikhail later confided she'd gone easy on me because, one, she worried about my ego, and two, she worried about how she'd be perceived. For all her strength and muscles, Jenny liked her curves. Her body. Which was, frankly, smokin' hot. And since Mikhail felt the same way, they had a good thing going.

Now, if we could just settle the sexual tension between Big Mac and Meg once and for all. Well, more like tension on his part and cluelessness on hers.

Within an hour, we were packed up and ready to go. We were leaving just before rush hour was set to begin in Vancouver. We'd hit the US border in about an hour, then we planned to push as far as

Yakima, Washington. We'd bunk down there, then make the drive to Park City in the late afternoon.

I alternated between pumped and exhausted as I settled onto the bench seat near the front of the bus.

Meg wanted to crash, but she'd just have to get up at the border. The woman could easily nap half the day then put down a solid ten at night.

I might've been envious.

Thornton stowed his go-bag in his bunk and returned to sit across from me.

Axel sat next to me, laid his head on my shoulder, and pretended to sleep.

Songbird sat next to Big Mac as they discussed a potential drum solo for a song we were still working on. Wouldn't be ready for Nevada, but maybe after that. Maybe an album. If we got a deal.

Meg put on her headphones and closed her eyes.

After gazing out over the group, Thornton grinned. "Quite a crew you have."

"And Pauletta's heading to the airport first thing in the morning. There's a direct flight from Vancouver to Salt Lake City."

"Nice work if you can get it."

I waved him off. "After dealing with her motion sickness often enough, we decided we didn't mind the added expense. She's so damn good at her job..." I trailed off, thinking of the various scrapes she'd help us get out of.

Thornton arched an eyebrow.

"I'm thirsty." I tried to dislodge Axel.

Our guest rose. "What can I grab you?"

"A flavored water—doesn't matter which flavor. And grab yourself something as well."

He did, nabbing a root beer.

When he handed me the bottle of water, he made certain our fingers brushed.

Or at least that's the impression I got.

Axel squeezed my thigh under the table.

Fucking traitor.

Thornton and I spent the entire trip to the border discussing some of the differences between Portland and Vancouver.

The cities were close in population size. Had significant drug and other substance-abuse problems. Way more homeless people than could be managed. Vancouver was highly racialized, with Indigenous peoples making up a portion of the minorities in the city. Canada's history with these peoples was horrible—from colonization to residential schools to the Indian Act through to the deplorable conditions many people on reserves faced.

The entire situation depressed me...but I spent a lot of time thinking about it. Not just because of Meg's heritage, but because I'd grown up with kids in our school who came from that background. I hadn't had the ability to comprehend all the barriers they faced. As a Black kid, I encountered many of the same, but in the end, I always felt I hadn't been empathetic enough.

But I didn't tell Thornton any of these things. I confirmed that our song "We Need To Do Better" was a rallying cry for all groups that faced discrimination. And yes, that meant LGBTQ as well.

Thornton winked.

My cock stirred.

Fucking traitor.

Whether that thought was directed at the gorgeous man across from me or at my dick, I wasn't certain. And didn't have to engage with that reflection since we'd arrived at the border.

A cheerful agent, a thorough search, and we were on our way.

Vera's smooth driving got us onto the I-5 heading south to Seattle.

Big Mac and Songbird started a card game. They invited us to join, but I kept eyeing Thornton.

Axel grabbed a bag of ketchup potato chips and ate ten before offering some to the rest of us.

Big Mac grabbed a handful, Songbird passed—as did I—while Thornton took one.

He eyed it for a while.

I grinned. "Never tried it?"

He shook his head.

"Well, you're missing out on what is, apparently, a quintessentially Canadian experience." I frowned. "No ketchup chips in the States?"

He shrugged. "We have everything, so likely, somewhere. I've never encountered them." He took a tentative bite.

Axel shoved in another five.

I eyed the bag. Could I...? We were stopping for dinner in Seattle, but that was nearly two hours from now. I snagged a chip, broke it in half, and tossed both pieces in my mouth.

Thornton took another nibble.

Axel snorted. "Man, just eat it already."

After a moment, Thornton put the rest of the chip in his mouth. He chewed pensively.

Or at least that was how I interpreted the furrow in his brow.

And you're not going to think how sexy that makes him. Like how he'd furrow that way while you drilled into him...

My cock stirred.

Every time I glanced his way, I saw possibilities.

Bending him over the table.

Fucking him in a bunk and somehow not banging my head.

Leading him into our tiny shower and thrusting into him as he clung to the glass wall.

So many possibilities.

And all involved us being alone. Because, as permissive as my bandmates were, they'd draw the line at sex on the bus. We had unspoken rules. Other bands weren't likely nearly as picky, but we wanted to maintain the glue that held us together.

Songbird shouted in triumph.

Big Mac tossed his cards down. Then he looked at Meg who'd grabbed a notebook and pencil and was sketching furiously while still listening to whatever music she'd selected.

She never showed her drawings to anyone, and she never shared her playlist. She played everything close to the vest.

I imagined Pachelbel's Canon or Kenny G or something else just as improbable. I'd considered asking her about Wren before we left, but mentioning her dog in the context of leaving always made her sad. I said a brief prayer that her asshat ex was caring for the dog.

And considered yet again the logistics of bringing a dog on tour.

Nope, too much chaos.

Which made me think of babies. Both Meg and Songbird were in their prime, fertility-wise. And that was way more information than I needed to know, but I liked to plan for all contingencies.

I'd fight anything that might break up the band. Taking a break would be fine, but the idea of replacing someone made my stomach churn.

Axel offered me another chip.

I waved him off. I just didn't feel like it.

Thornton held out his hand.

Axel grinned as he held the bag in the man's direction.

Said man took a number of chips and slowly nibbled on them.

I cocked my head.

"Getting used to the taste. I'm not certain I'd drive six hours north just to get some—"

"You send me waffle cookies from Trader Joe's, and I'll send you ketchup chips." Axel tossed another chip into his mouth, looking quite proud at himself for suggesting the swap.

Thornton tilted his head, and his blond hair flopped over his right eye. "You know, I just might do that." He ate another chip and grinned.

I continued to sip my flavored water.

Once Axel finished eating—and wiped his fingers—he grabbed his phone and started playing.

Thornton gestured.

"Word game," I replied to his unasked question.

He nodded, betraying no emotion.

I wanted to ask if he thought we were all dumb fucks. But that was the classism speaking. And racism. I had a nasty habit of dumping all rich white pricks in a basket and applying some pretty broad ideas to them. My bias.

And I wasn't proud of that.

"What do you do in your spare time?" Thornton broadly indicated the bus. "You must have a fair amount of time to kill."

Instantly defensive, I fought to keep myself calm. "I do a few games on my phone as well. Mostly…" I indicated Meg. "She draws, I write."

"Write?"

"Music. Sometimes poetry and shit like that."

"I'd love to see it."

"Nah." I waved him off. "It's not fit for human consumption."

"Have you ever shared it with anyone?"

I considered. "I've shared some songs. But that's it."

"Then how do you know the poetry isn't *fit for human consumption*?"

The answer died on my tongue. Truthfully, I'd never considered showing anyone else. Hell, I couldn't even come up with a good idea why I'd told this virtual stranger one of my most private secrets.

"I just know. I'm going to go crash." Without another word, I headed to my bunk. I only intended to scroll on my phone, but within five minutes, I was down for the count.

Chapter Ten

Thornton

"I'm not doing it." Axel stood with his hands on his hips.

"Well, there's no way I'm doing it." Meg yawned. She appeared amazingly well rested.

"I did it last time." Songbird moved toward the front of the stopped bus.

"Yeah, but he likes you the most." Big Mac gently snagged her arm, halting her forward motion.

"You mean he's least likely to bitch at me if I do it?"

The other three bandmates beamed as if she'd just won a contest.

She scowled.

"I can do it."

All four pivoted to me.

The driver, Vera, poked her head around the divider.

"Ed's asleep," Axel supplied.

She held up her hands, backed away, and headed out of the bus.

"Smart woman," Meg murmured.

I cleared my throat. "Perhaps we could just grab some food for him—"

"The 5 Points Café is his favorite diner." Songbird scratched her elbow. "He also needs to wake up now or he'll sleep through, wake up at three, and be cranky for the rest of the day tomorrow."

Meg yawned. "Yeah."

Big Mac guffawed. "Uh, you'd sleep twenty-four hours a day if you could."

"Nothing wrong with that. Look, I'm starving. Newbie offered. Let's leave him to it." She grabbed Axel's hand and dragged him to the front of the bus.

Songbird offered her arm to a slightly stunned Big Mac. She gave me a soft, if rueful, smile, as they headed out as well.

I ran through all my options and found none particularly appealing. If the band was to be believed—and I had no reason not to—Ed despised being woken but he needed to get up. Like, right now. We needed to be back on the road at a decent hour if we were to hit Yakima, get the necessary sleep, and then head back on to Park City.

None of which was technically my responsibility. I'd stayed up for days at a time while watching horny walruses. And I'd once fought off a territorial and angry bull moose.

One rock star? How hard could this possibly be?

Girding my loins, I headed to Ed's bunk.

He lay under a thin blanket, facing me, and snoring lightly. As always, his beauty stole my breath. His was a quiet attractiveness. While Axel oozed sex appeal, Ed was the quiet one. The one that needed to be watched carefully.

An adorable, if slightly worn, teddy bear sat in the back corner of the bunk.

Oh, the stories you could tell.

I crouched so our faces were at the same level. Slowly, I caressed his cheek.

After a moment, he swatted my hand away.

Uncertain if he was conscious or not, I stubbornly repeated the gesture.

He grunted.

Ah, progress.

"Ed, dear, you need to wake up."

He growled. "Did you just call me your fucking *dear*?" He still wouldn't open his eyes.

"Well, sure. I mean, I like to be affectionate with all the guys I've made out with. Babe. Darling." Total bullshit line. I'd never called anyone *dear, sweetheart, babe,* or *darling,* in my life. I couldn't explain or justify odd protectiveness for the man—but it overwhelmed.

His eyes popped open, but they immediately narrowed. They glittered dark brown in the crappy light. "Seriously? Guys let you call them *darling*?"

I wasn't certain he could've put more derision in that word. Unrepentantly, I grinned. "Yep."

"Huh." He continued to scrutinize me.

Hold your ground. Don't back down.

"You're lying. I can't prove you're lying, but I know you are. And I intend to prove it."

"Well, you'd have to track down every guy I've ever been with—"

"And how many is that?"

I pretended to consider.

He punched my arm.

"Okay, okay. Not as many as you might think."

"I can think of a pretty big number. Pretty guy like you—"

"You think I'm pretty?"

"I think I'm still groggy and can't be held responsible for anything I say."

"Guy's I've kissed let me call them anything."

"I don't remember your kiss being all that."

"Maybe you need another sample." Suddenly reckless, I pushed myself up, careful not to hit my head, and leaned over him so I could press a kiss to his lips.

Instantly, he opened up. He grabbed the back of my neck and pulled me into the kiss.

And, in return, I instantly hardened. *Take. Take me. Let me give myself to you.*

I didn't understand where the compulsion came from, but I wanted this man more than I'd ever wanted anyone before. I'd had plenty of other hot guys who turned me on. One-night stands. Two-week affairs. Once, I'd managed three months. I could barely remember that guy's name as I let Ed dominate the kiss. Would he dominate me? I needed to find out.

Finally, though, he nipped my upper lip and dropped his hand from my neck.

After a second, I pulled back.

And hit my head. "Fuck."

He chuckled. "Yeah, you get used to it. Where are we?"

"The 5 Point Diner?"

"The 5 Points Café," he corrected. Then he pushed me back so he could rise. "I need to piss."

"Wash your hands after and we'll go together."

He screwed up his face. "What kind of guys have you been around?"

"After a week in the wilderness, some guys need a reminder."

"Do you prefer nature or civilization?" He didn't wait for an answer, instead heading into the bathroom and closing the door.

Well, shit. *Please let him not remember the question when he comes out.* Because the truthful answer was complicated. Something I shared with no one. Certainly something I didn't want to blurt out to *this* guy. He and Axel were the reason I'd left nature photography. Telling him that would open Pandora's box...and I wasn't ready for that yet.

Fortunately, when he emerged, he headed straight for the front of the bus—leaving me to follow or risk getting left behind.

He shut the bus door, did something to obviously secure it, then we hoofed across the parking lot to the street and, eventually, the diner.

Café.

Well, the place really reminded me more of the stereotypical American diner. We had the Grits'N'Gravy in Portland, but this place felt a bit more Americana. Like you'd expect to find on an interstate in the middle of nowhere.

The write-up in the menu made me chuckle as it made no apologies for the clientele, loud music, or blasphemous patrons.

I loved it.

And clearly Ed did as well as he appeared to soak up the ambiance.

Jenny, Mikhail, and Vera joined the six of us, and we made a rowdy bunch—totally in keeping with the place. Meals varied from burgers to Philly cheesesteak, salads, steaks, fish—Axel's choice, big surprise—and pancakes. Ed nabbed those with a huge grin.

I opted for a black-bean burger.

Ed raised an eyebrow.

I shrugged. Vegetarian food wouldn't be the death of me, and I liked guacamole.

In the end, the choice turned out to be really good. And virtually all the food disappeared.

As we chose desserts to share, Axel headed for the loo. On his way back, he had two enthusiastic young women following him.

Ed yanked a notebook and sharpie from his back pocket.

Axel grinned, signed two autographs, and the women took off.

As Axel slid back in, Ed left.

I tried not to track him—mostly because I didn't want the others seeing me ogling his ass—and he disappeared.

"He's paying," Songbird told me. "Pauletta trusted him with the company credit card."

"Damn."

She grinned. "Yeah, I heard about you comping the meal at The Georgian. I'm sorry I missed it."

"You were...?"

"Playing piano at my parents' church. They have a lovely older woman who does it, but sometimes she appreciates the break. So I go whenever I'm in town and available."

"That's kind of you."

"Keeps me connected to my roots." She gestured to the table. "We all believe in different things to varying degrees. Except Ed." She nodded as he returned. "Well, higher powers, just not God."

Ed placed his hands on the table. "We're settled and should be going."

Without a single word of complaint, the remaining eight of us left the table. Various people visited the washrooms while the rest of us trooped back to the bus.

Within a few minutes, Vera had us heading south for a bit before we headed eastward—deeper into Washington State.

I'd grown up very West Coast Democrat. Even my parents, conservative though they might be, embraced the life of those in a solid-blue city. People in red America fascinated me, but I hadn't spent much time in those places. My interviews with celebrities tended to be split between New York and Los Angeles. I hadn't done much in fly-over country.

Bonita wanted me to change that. My sister was adamant that chasing celebrities and uncovering secrets of the privileged wasn't what I was meant to be doing.

As I eyed Grindstone, I wondered if she might have a point.

Nail them. Then move on.

Axel and Ed gazed at something on one of their phones and had matching grins. They'd done such a great job escaping grinding poverty and moving up to successful musicians.

When I brought them down, what would that mean for their loyal fans? For all the young kids who looked up to them and thought *maybe one day that could be me*? Or maybe those legions of supporters would look at what they'd done and learn from their behavior. Decide they didn't want to follow the path of their idols.

I didn't have a good answer for my dilemma. Because the more I got to know all the band members, the more I realized I wasn't just going to destroy Axel and Ed. Songbird, Big Mac, Meg, Pauletta, and all the other people who relied on the band for their employment would be screwed as well.

That idea didn't sit well with me.

But neither did letting those two get away with what they'd done.

Chapter Eleven

Ed

I plopped down on the couch and scratched my stomach. My sleep pants rode low on my hips, and I probably should've put on a T-shirt—given how my nipples pebbled in the cool air—but I couldn't be bothered.

"Hey."

Glancing up, I caught Thornton's gaze as he wandered into the living area. He wore jeans, a Henley, and no socks.

"Your feet'll get cold." We kept the bus at a reasonable temperature, but the floor was always super cold.

He blinked several times, held up his hand, disappeared for a few moments, then returned with a pair of socks. He sat across from me and put them on.

My blood heated. I wasn't really a foot-fetish guy, but Thornton's had me rethinking that assertion. Strong, sexy, and big.

Kind of like the man.

He caught my gaze and grinned wryly. "I don't always pay attention to the mundane."

"Head in the clouds?"

"Something like that." He halted, gave me a once-over, and grinned. "So, casual's okay?"

"Well, Songbird wears her sports bra and track shorts while Big Mac's been known to wander around in his boxer briefs. Scrawny white ass."

"They show his ass?"

I waved him off. "No, but the guy never goes out in the sun, so you know it's lily white." Truthfully, I didn't want to be talking about Big Mac's ass. "You go out in the sun?"

Thornton gazed at his hands. "Not purposely. I burn easily."

"What activities do you do inside?" *Please say fuck. I want to hear you say fuck.*

He eyed me. "I enjoy pickup basketball with a group of friends from college."

I snickered.

He arched an eyebrow.

"Tall." I offered this as a way of explanation for my response.

"Several of my friends are your height or shorter. And being tall doesn't make me a good player. I don't practice, so often I'm the lowest scorer on the team. But I'm good at stealing the ball and passing it to people who can score."

Okay, hadn't expected that. "So you're a real team player? Not in it for the glory?"

"I couldn't do what I do without a solid team behind me. All four of us will be working tomorrow night to capture the concert."

A reminder, if I needed one, of why he was really here. Certainly not to fulfill any of my sexual fantasies. *Pull down his jeans and underwear, bend him over the table—*

"What about you, Ed? What activities do you do?"

I flexed my arm. "Weights. Treadmill. Sometimes I run along the seawall in downtown Vancouver—to Stanley Park and back."

"I'd love to shoot you with that backdrop."

My stomach dropped. "I, uh—"

"But we can talk about that later." He rose, wandered over to the fridge, and grabbed an orange juice. He held it up.

I shook my head. "I'm trying to find the energy to make coffee."

Immediately, he located the coffee machine. He showed me a pod.

I nodded. I loathed the things for their environmental impact, adding plastic to the environment even if they could be recycled, but we'd be at the diner within an hour, so it didn't make sense to make a full pot.

Within a few moments, he had the coffee brewing for me. He returned to his seat, shook his OJ, popped the lid, and drank deeply.

Watching him swallow made more dirty images come to my mind. Like him—swallowing my cum.

He finished the bottle and sighed.

My cock stirred.

He tossed the bottle into the recycling container under the sink and moved to make my coffee. "Black, right?"

I snickered.

Grunting, he held up the mug.

Right. "Yes, I take my coffee black. Excellent memory." I almost asked him if he remembered how the rest of the band took their drinks, but I didn't want to shatter the illusion that he'd been laser-focused on me. Probably me and Axel. Which made sense—for the story anyway.

We founded the band. Axel might be the front man, but I often accompanied him. Because, as much as I loved him, I didn't trust him not to fuck up.

As soon as Thornton had handed me the mug and retaken his seat, stirrings came from farther down. Murmurs also reached me, but nothing distinct.

"Should I make another few cups? Or put on the kettle for Songbird?"

Ah, so he was observant.

"No. I need to get dressed, and we'll head over to the diner. Vera's going to want to get on the road as soon as we can. We've got a long day ahead."

True to my word, within an hour, we were on the road to Park City.

Since we were hanging out in the bus lounge, Thornton coaxed us into doing some a cappella songs for him to record on his phone.

I didn't see the point, since the recording's quality wouldn't be up to broadcast standards, but he made some bullshit excuse that Axel bought. The next thing I knew, we'd gathered around his phone, and were singing several of our warmup songs and a couple from our last album.

Axel coaxed me into grabbing my guitar, and those songs carried us through to Boise.

We grabbed fast food and were back on the road as soon as Vera'd rested up.

As we resumed the journey, Meg grabbed her notebook again, put in her earphones, and disconnected.

Axel, Songbird, and Big Mac began a game of cards. Soon, Axel'd convinced Thornton to join.

I declined the invitation, but watched the game closely as I doodled in my notebook. Words bounced in my mind, and I couldn't figure out if they were the beginnings of a poem or the lyrics of a new song.

The sun had long since set by the time we pulled up to the hotel in Park City.

A perfectly coiffed and completely refreshed Pauletta greeted us at the entrance. We had the option to stay in the hotel or to continue crashing on the bus. Despite knowing how much money we were about to spend, we all opted for rooms. Sharing, of course. Much to several bandmates' annoyance.

"We could've chosen a cheap motel," Axel griped as he settled in our room.

Big Mac made a beeline for the shower.

"We're only here one night. We do the concert tomorrow night, and then Vera's going to drive us to Nevada." I eyed him. "You weren't thinking of hooking up, were you?"

He grunted.

I hid a grin. "Sorry to burst your bubble."

"There's always backstage."

"TMI, man. I'm so not going there with you."

He waved to me as he headed out of the room.

Truthfully, he didn't hookup that way often. If he had a choice, he'd choose a woman who wasn't enamored with being a groupie, someone away from the venue who maybe didn't even know who he was.

If I had my choice, I'd chose someone who saw life beyond the music. Man or woman—I didn't mind. I often sought out people objectively smarter than myself, or at least way better educated. I told myself they weren't slumming and that I gave them...stuff to think about?

Pauletta'd kick my ass if she saw me putting myself down. A college education might not mean what it used to, but I still prized what I didn't have. I'd taken a few entry-level courses through a local college, but I couldn't find something that piqued my interest. I didn't know what I wanted beyond music. Maybe something to do with languages? Literature? Communications? Or maybe something to do with music? Aside from high school, I didn't have any formal training. Mr. Threadgold had been amazing as a teacher, and even better as a mentor, but he'd been limited in what he could give us.

Axel and I learned intuitively. We learned by doing. And our music was developing maturity—or so I told myself. Some reviewers had recently noted our transition from the hard, banging rock into something more. We varied our songs—mixing ballads with anthems, and providing the audience more variety.

From what I'd observed—through concerts, reviews, and album sales—fans were enjoying the transition.

Big Mac emerged from the bathroom with a billow of steam following him. He wore sleep pants, an old band T-shirt, and had a toothbrush stuck in his mouth.

"We haven't had dinner yet." I picked up the room-service menu.

He pulled the toothbrush out of his mouth like he didn't quite understand what he was doing. "Yuck." Apparently the thought of mint and whatever he was about to order didn't sit well.

"What did you want to eat?"

"They've got burgers, right?"

"Yes."

He scrunched up his nose. "What're you going to eat?"

"A quinoa salad."

He made a gagging noise.

The laughter bubbled up from me before I could stop it. I'd encouraged the team to try quinoa a few years ago. Well, coerced might've been a better word. Or blackmailed. Regardless, my forcing them to try it hadn't gone over well.

Meg'd been the only one to have it again—about once a year.

Pauletta, Big Mac, Songbird, and Axel still brought up the incident as more proof that vegetarians were crazy.

Big Mac returned from the bathroom, having deposited his toothbrush, snagged a warm cola from his bag, and guzzled.

I nearly gagged.

Still, he grabbed the menu. "I'm seeing if they have those truffle fries."

"Seriously?" I wasn't a fan.

"All right." He clapped his hands. "You want a ginger ale, a quinoa salad and..."

"A piece of chocolate cake."

"Well, that's a great idea. The cake, not the salad," he quickly added—lest there be any confusion.

Before I could answer, he'd placed the call.

I grabbed my nightwear and headed into the bathroom.

Pauletta'd given us a decently late call time tomorrow—so going out tonight would've been possible—but I didn't feel like trying to find a place, or a person, in Utah.

Axel is...

Well, I wasn't positive what he was up to. He might just be wandering around the city. I'd seen him on his phone earlier, and he hadn't shared, but that didn't mean he'd arranged a hookup.

Or maybe it did.

As I emerged from the bathroom, a knock sounded at the door.

Big Mac opened it, then grinned. "Oh, hi."

I stepped forward so I could see who'd tripped him up.

Thornton.

Big Mac beckoned him in, and he carried a plate and a glass to the small table. He offered a sheepish smile. "I hope you don't mind."

"We don't." Big Mac barely had the door closed before another knock sounded. This time, room service delivered our tray of food.

I signed the tip while Big Mac organized the food on the table. I nearly groaned as he lifted the final lid. "You bought the entire cake?"

"Well, you knew I'd likely have more than one piece. One for you and Axel. I thought maybe we could invite the ladies." He indicated Thornton with his plate. "And he called while you were in the shower and asked if he could join us..." He squinted. "That was okay, right? I mean—"

"It's fine. No worries." I plopped down in the chair to dig into my salad.

The smell of charbroiled burgers teased my nose. Infrequently, I'd have a hankering for meat. Most of the time I'd wait a moment, and it'd pass.

Axel returned halfway through the meal carrying a bucket of fried chicken.

I might've snagged a few of his fries and, tempted as I was, chosen ketchup over gravy. I didn't grab the second handful I craved. I found I had more energy and performed better when I avoided fried foods. Cake was fine, fries didn't sit as well.

The conversation was inconsequential, and I didn't follow half of it. I kept stealing covert glances at Thornton.

Does he feel this? This pull? This need to explore? To dive in?

After we finished the chocolate cake, we organized the dishes.

"You know, I've got two queen-sized beds in my room." Thornton grinned wickedly. "If one of you crashed with me—"

Axel said, "Ed would love to—"

Just as Big Mac leapt up and gave Thornton a big hug. "Oh, you're the best. Let me grab my stuff."

"But—" Axel, again.

"You snore," Big Mac shot back, even as he stuffed everything into his suitcase and was at the door before I could blink. We teased each other, but three to a room meant saving cash.

Thornton caught my gaze.

I stood, transfixed under his stare.

"Another time," he mouthed. He turned, offered Big Mac a huge smile, and led the way from the room.

Cockblocked.

Chapter Twelve

Thornton

Big Mac was a nice guy. He also talked nonstop. When he was awake, when he was in the bathroom, when he was asleep...

Yeah, the guy talked in his sleep. And farted a couple of times as well, but he was under the blankets, so I was mostly saved from that... Whatever.

At least Ed had known the invitation was extended because I wanted him in my bed. Well, in my room.

No, in my bed. I could admit that much.

I palmed my cock and willed it into submission. My morning wood was particularly...hard this morning.

After about five minutes, I slid out of bed and headed to the bathroom. I stripped and stepped into the hot spray. This time, I didn't stop the images from coming. Ed stepping into the shower with me. Ed going to his knees and blowing me. Ed grasping my balls and giving them a rough squeeze.

Me grasping his hair to hold him in place. Me turning the tables and blowing him. Me lying on the bed and him fucking me into the mattress. I didn't care how—I just wanted him to overpower me and take what I was more than willing to give.

I encircled my hard cock.

Yeah, I could visualize all those things. Of all my senses, my vision was most acute. And it translated into the most vivid images. I imagined, for Ed, his prime sense would be aural. Well, and oral.

The slow strokes increased in franticness as I increased the pace—chasing the orgasm I'd needed since the moment I'd awakened.

Hell, since the moment I laid eyes on Ed.

Or, if I was brutally honest, the first time my sister'd shown me a poster.

And that should've shut down the attraction. It didn't. Instead, rage blended with desire and combined into one of the most intense orgasms of my life. Ropes of cum spurted from my cock and mixed with the hot spray.

I gasped for breath. Despite having turned on the bathroom fan, I worried Big Mac might hear me. That he might figure out what I was doing. And why.

Ridiculous.

Possibly.

Probably.

But I didn't need him knowing my deepest, darkest secrets.

I didn't need Ed knowing them either.

Scrubbing myself down took little time, and I washed my hair with the dandruff shampoo I'd brought. Bane of my existence. Still, this good stuff worked, and I didn't have flakes.

I shut off the water, shook myself out like a dog, and exited the shower. Being considerate, I only used one towel to dry myself off.

Shaving took a decent amount of time as I was still an old-fashioned razor guy. I'd yet to find an electric shaver I liked. One place where having money hadn't helped.

He's not impressed with your money.

True. But he seemed impressed with my body—so I'd use that to my full advantage. Not because of this stupid attraction I felt, but strategically. Wanting Ed was convenient, hell, it was useful. If I could keep him distracted, I might be able to get closer to Axel. Both men knew the truth—of that I had no doubt. And, of the two men, I'd decided Axel was more likely to be tricked into revealing the secrets they held.

Axel was impetuous. A little reckless. Even, at times, a little flighty. He was the opposite of Ed in so many ways. Not just physically—although those differences were stark. Axel's tall and lanky frame contrasted with Ed's shorter and more compact look. I'd describe Axel as lithe while Ed...

I sought to find the right word in my mind. He just seemed more...solid.

If I had a type, he'd be it. Good thing I could keep attraction and emotions separate.

After finishing up my shave, I stowed my kit. I added a touch of gel to my hair, then crept silently into the room.

I needn't have bothered.

Big Mac lay on his back, an arm thrown over his eyes, and he snored as if sawing logs.

Smiling to myself, I grabbed my jeans and a T-shirt that might've been a little tight, and dressed. Part of me wanted to do some exercise, and the rest of me wanted to do more research. I grabbed my phone and headed down to the restaurant.

At this early hour, I only spotted a few people in business suits. One bleary looking family sat in a corner and—

Ed sat at a back table—hunched over and scrolling on his phone.

As a server approached me, I requested coffee with cream and sugar, then I waved toward Ed's table.

She nodded and disappeared.

I wandered over to Ed's table and, uninvited, sat across from him.

Whatever response I expected, his offering me a cheeky grin wasn't it.

He turned his phone to me. "Last minute change-up at Rocktoberfest."

I scrolled the article about a band dropping out because—

"Jesus."

"I know, right?"

"Isn't this, like, urban legend or something?"

He shuddered. "Nope. I have a friend who works in the emergency department at St. Paul's hospital." He cleared his throat. "You wouldn't believe what people try to, uh, insert—"

I held up my hand. "I don't need that mental image at six-thirty in the morning." Seriously. And how had word gotten out? If I'd been caught...well, I wouldn't have let anyone know. I'd have claimed strep throat and not put anything else near my—

Nope. Just couldn't go there.

"What mental image would you like at six-thirty in the morning?" Ed blinked adorably.

The server arrived with my coffee and a menu.

I offered my most endearing smile. "Do you have Eggs Benedict?"

She nodded.

"With hash browns and a side of bacon?"

She nodded. "You want OJ?"

"No thank you, just keep the coffee coming." I grinned.

After she held my gaze and returned my smile, she pivoted to Ed.

"Uh, I'll have Eggs Benedict but no ham." He scratched his nose. "A fruit salad and an extra side of brown toast."

The server—Angelique, according to her nametag—nodded. "No problem."

She took off, and I pivoted to Ed. "Are you a purist? You won't eat anything that has touched meat?"

He snickered. "You wanted my ham?"

"Gladly."

"Oh." He laid his phone down. "I wanted to come to your room last night."

I snickered. "Well, you would've been more interesting than Big Mac's company."

Ed laughed. "Snoring and farting."

"Uh...is there a right way to answer that?"

"Just keeping it real." He sipped his coffee. "We could probably afford another room—or any number of us could've stayed in the bus—but we appreciate being able to stretch out."

"Tight budget?"

He indicated my phone with his chin.

"Off the record," I promised. Although I didn't promise not to use the info if it helped my quest.

"Yeah. We have a tour sponsor. A family trust that pays for the bus rental, van rental, as well as hotel rooms, and Pauletta's flight."

I cocked my head.

"Yeah, her family's trust. There's some kind of write-off that I don't understand. Pauletta's father wants his daughter travelling in comfort."

"So the motion sickness is a pretense?"

"Oh no, it's real. She turns green and pukes. But she might be more inclined to take pills if not for the ability to travel in comfort."

"She seems great."

The corners of Ed's lips turned up. "Paulie's the best thing that ever happened to me and Axel. We wouldn't be where we are without her. It's not just all Daddy's money. He only sponsors the big stuff. We might've had some success on our own, but Pauletta gets us to the next level. We've been indie so far, but we're hoping to secure a record contract. Rocktoberfest is our chance to do just that. Pauletta's ready to fight tooth and nail—if we get approached."

"I heard one of the bands last year signed a big contract."

"Yeah, it happens. But..." He tapped his nose. "We have to put on the performance of a lifetime."

"And you don't think you can?"

"Oh, we can. We're at the top of our game." He eyed my phone. "Unless someone distracts us."

"I would never—"

"Yeah, you totally would—especially if it got you a juicy story."

He sat back as Angelique delivered our food.

We murmured our thanks, and she withdrew.

I poked at my eggs, wondering if he planned to continue.

To my surprise, he grabbed the bottle of hot sauce and doused his hash browns. "You're out for a *gotcha* moment. You want to catch us doing or saying something that's worthy of a great reveal on television." He pierced the hash browns with his fork. "Am I wrong?"

I pressed my hand to my left eye. Damn, I was about to get a headache. "You're wrong. I see a lot of promise in your band, and you're heading to one of the biggest festivals in North America. Why wouldn't I want to document the meteoric rise?"

"Meteoric?" He pointed his fork at me. "Ten years in the making."

I shrugged. "Okay, sure. Rags to riches, then."

He sniggered.

"Well, how would you showcase it?"

"I wouldn't." His expression sobered. "I don't think we're worthy of the attention."

"Bullshit." I poked my egg again, trying to figure out the best way to eat it. "Everyone wants to be special. To get attention. You're in a rock band, for crying out loud. You need every opportunity possible to get your name and your songs into every possible television, computer, and phone."

"Not everyone wants to be special." He cut his egg. "I've known some introverts who are just happy to watch the world go by."

"You're an introvert?" Had we had this conversation?

He eyed me. "Yeah. But I also want Grindstone to be the best band it can—so that means stepping out of my comfort zone. That means supporting Axel, Pauletta, and the others in every way I can." He met my gaze. "I'm protective of my own." He put a forkful of egg into his mouth.

"So you've said." I tried to focus. "And that role suits you. You're all young. You're all single, which fans like..."

I waited for him to correct me.

When he didn't, I continued. "And you're looking for exposure, right? I can give you that."

"At what cost?" He swallowed, then set his mesmerizing dark-brown eyes on me.

"You act like you're guilty of something. Like you have something to hide—"

"I don't."

Inside, I did a little dance. That denial had come way too quickly. Still, I held up my hands. "Then you don't have anything to worry about."

His eyes narrowed.

Yeah, he didn't believe me. He still didn't trust me. *Smart man.*

Turn this around. "We hoped to get some footage of you folks eating dinner tonight before the show. Just...you know...doing normal shit."

He eyed me. "With our mouths full?"

"Only Big Mac talks with his mouth full."

Ed snorted. "Word. So watch that, okay?"

Tacit agreement. I'd take it. "Sure." I wanted to ask what they might discuss, but Pauletta grabbed an empty chair.

Whatever chance I might've had to initiate a more-intimate conversation ended. Still, I had more to work with than before. *Some guilt there. An introvert. Protective.*

Chalking that up as a win, I continued to eat my breakfast.

Chapter Thirteen

Ed

Rehearsal went well. Jenny and Mikhail, having just arrived, did an awesome job setting up all our equipment and, to my relief, Pauletta'd nabbed us a great venue. Axel wanted bigger, but I'd pushed for more intimate. I wanted to get a genuine sense of the crowd's reaction. We were trying out our new songs tonight, and I needed to know they'd go over well before properly debuting them at Rocktoberfest.

Which was coming up on us hard.

Nerves were setting in with everyone—even Pauletta.

We tried to put all that aside as we headed into a little diner tucked away in a corner of Park City that obviously didn't see a lot of traffic.

Our group took up most of the back, and despite my best efforts, I wound up sitting next to Thornton.

I'd hoped he wouldn't want to be in the shot as Lydia panned her camera around the group, but I missed the mark on that one.

He coaxed us into telling him some of our crazier stories.

This made me slightly queasy, but no one went for the gross stuff. And the truly personal didn't get touched either. So I supposed I should've been happy.

I wasn't. I was nervous. I was stressed.

Of all of us, I was the one most likely to suffer from anxiety—and the one least likely to speak up about it.

Axel stilled my tapping foot with a hand to my thigh.

Thornton noticed. I caught him quirking an eyebrow.

Does he think there's something between Axel and me?

No, I didn't think so. He appeared to merely be recognizing the power of friendship—of knowing someone for over twenty years.

Before I realized how much time had passed, Pauletta clapped her hands.

We all sat up.

She grinned. "Thornton's generously picked up the tab. We need to get over to the venue."

I caught the flash of surprise on Lydia's face before she hid it. Ha. Just as I'd suspected—Thornton throwing around his money with us wasn't his normal modus operandi. But perhaps he'd done it before and she hadn't realized? To butter up interviewees?

But buying meals for an upstart band?

Hard to say.

Meg looped her arm in mine as we left the diner. "You need to at least pretend to be enjoying yourself, my friend. You don't want all the footage to be of you scowling at the generous man." She halted, turned me toward her, and met my gaze.

Seeing as we were almost the same height, I couldn't glare down at her.

She met my gaze and held it. "Look—the more he pays for, the less we have to rely on Pauletta's dad." She held up her hand. "And I get that it's a tax write-off for him. Or something."

Yeah, we'd never quite gotten clarity on that.

"My point is we can take the profits from the concerts and put it back into the business. That's what we all want, right? To be more successful? The more money we can pour into tours and studio time—the more likely we are to get closer to that goal." She poked me in the chest. "Don't fuck this up, Ed. You know very well that people who've never heard of us will buy the album when they see the documentary. Thornton's docs get huge distribution. This is a tremendous opportunity. You glaring at him all the time isn't going to help."

Axel thumped me on the back as he passed by. "Let's get going. Too much seriousness."

He wasn't wrong.

Meg went pressed a kiss to my cheek. "Whatever you're afraid of—you need to get over it. Your mind is the enemy, Ed. Not Thornton."

She wasn't wrong either.

We'd scored a local band to open for us. That part still felt surreal, as we'd been opening for people just earlier this year. Nabbing a spot in Rocktoberfest had elevated us in the music world—and we planned to take full advantage.

Nailed it.

They delivered a solid performance and got the audience amped up so we got a fantastic welcome. We headed right into "Desperation" which nearly blew out the speakers. Meg's drum solo earned extra cheers, and as we transitioned into "Day's Pay for a Day's Labor", some of my stress released. We were in our element. This was our happy place.

Axel was just plain on fire.

I caught him hamming it up for Lydia's camera a few times. I also spotted Mickey with another camera at the back of the venue. Hopefully they'd both snag some good footage.

When Lydia pivoted to me, I chanced a glance to see Thornton in the wings.

His gaze met mine.

You've got it, he seemed to say.

I performed one of the best guitar solos I'd ever done.

The audience went nuts.

We transitioned into "Immortalized", and the audience hushed. This was the song we were best known for, and people recognized it as a solemn ballad.

If only they knew...

As always, I avoided looking at Axel.

Every time I performed this song, it tore into my heart. And, just as critically, it helped heal the gaping hole in my soul.

The last note held before the crowd erupted in raucous applause.

Yep, nailed it again.

We transitioned into "AI", and I sensed the shift in the crowd as they got more of the rock beat they expected of us.

Then, to mix it up, we went back to a ballad with "Calling for Help". Songbird's backup vocals felt especially strong tonight, and I eased off a bit on a couple of harmonies so she could shine through.

We dove into another ballad, "Sunrise".

This one was all Axel.

A wave of confusion washed over the crowd as it took them a moment to understand they were listening to a new song.

I'd worked hard to make the lyrics as crisp as possible—given this was new material and, I thought, an important topic.

Songbird's fingers flew across her keyboard as she sank into the song which, ironically, she'd been the most vocally opposed to. Convincing her had taken a bit of work—but that never daunted me. If I believed in a song, I'd push until everyone agreed with me...or until everyone vetoed me.

Almost never happened. I had a good sense what audiences wanted. Sometimes my songs didn't follow traditional beats, but I always managed to get the crowd to see the genius of the music. Plus, although I considered myself innovative—both with lyrics and with rhythm—it'd all been done before.

We finished the song, and the crowd lost their proverbial shit.

Finally, we rocked it out with the familiar and known "We Need to do Better".

Axel waved to the crowd.

Big Mac thumped me on the back.

Songbird and Meg exchanged a thumbs-up.

I caught Pauletta and Thornton leaning toward each other and whispering. I barely had a chance to wonder what that was about when Axel held up his hands.

The crowd stilled.

"Y'all want more?"

They roared.

We'd prepared for this. No encores at Rocktoberfest, but in this place we could do a couple. We gave them several numbers from our first three albums and, frankly, the crowd lapped it up.

As we finished the ultimate song, "Two Different Worlds", Axel nabbed a towel, wiped himself down, and threw it into the audience.

My inner clean freak fought the nausea. Someone would keep that forever. Someone would have Axel's DNA.

I was never so careless.

Pauletta gave us the signal to shut it down.

We did one final bow, then headed offstage. Just as most of us had vanished behind the curtain, Axel tore off his tank top and threw that into the crowd as well.

Ha. Bet he'd be cold on the way back to the bus.

He plastered himself to my back, mixing his sweat with mine.

Ugh. I'd be cold as well.

Jenny had towels for all of us. She offered me a "great show" as she handed me one.

"You think so?"

"Of course it was." We both pivoted at Thornton's deep voice.

Jenny scurried off to give away other towels.

Chickenshit.

I faced Thornton, wiped my brow, and gazed up at him. "I wasn't sure they were onboard with "Sunrise"."

His brow knit. "I didn't get that sense from backstage. They loved it. They loved everything." His amber eyes sparkled. "You fucking rocked it. Do that again, and you'll be the talk of Rocktoberfest."

My gut clenched at the mention of the show. The raison d'être for us.

"Hey." Pauletta presented herself between the two of us. "There's a quick meet and greet with some select fans, after you've showered, and then you're getting on the bus. Vera's rested up and ready to drive to Reno. It's just over seven hours."

"I'm still not sure why we have to get there so early. We're arriving Tuesday and don't perform until Friday night."

She tapped my chest. "Networking. Getting to know people. Knowing the lay of the land so you look like you belong." She frowned. "We talked about this." She indicated Thornton. "And we want time to get some good footage."

How could I have forgotten?

I glanced over at Thornton.

He offered a subtle smile. And an arching of an eyebrow. As if to prompt me into saying something intelligent.

Yeah, good luck with that.

"Sure, Paulie, that's great."

She huffed.

Thornton grinned.

I headed to the shower.

Twenty minutes later I was in a crowded room with way more people than I liked.

Axel sat in the middle of the room in the middle of the couch amid a throng of adoring fans. Mostly women—but I spotted a couple of dudes in the mix.

Pauletta pressed a can of ginger ale in my hand. "Go mingle."

Songbird stood to one side, chatting with the opening act.

Meg signed some guy's T-shirt while Big Mac glared.

Thornton and Lydia stood off to one side. She had her camera with her and was doing a slow sweep of the room. He met my gaze. After a moment, he gestured to a quiet corner.

I'd made it two steps when a petite woman stopped me.

"Uh, hello."

"Will you sign my song sheet?"

She'd brought me up short. "Your song sheet?"

The clearly young woman nodded. "Yes. I'm writing a song. Do you want to see it?"

Part of me wanted to—but the business part of me understood she could later try to claim I stole it. "Do you have any other paper?" I reached for my back pocket and came up with my sharpie and a notepad. "What's your name?"

The owlish brown eyes blinked. "You don't want to see?"

I pointed to Thornton. "I have to speak to him. I'm so sorry. What's your name?"

"Meadow."

"Oh, that's a lovely name."

"I'm named after some character in a television show about gangsters."

That brought me up short as I had no idea which show she was referring to. I signed my name with a flourish, handed her the paper, and made my escape.

Chapter Fourteen

Thornton

I nearly intervened with Ed and the barely legal girl. Well, no alcohol was being served, so age wasn't a factor, but she couldn't have been over eighteen, and Ed was clearly uncomfortable.

Shifting, I was looking for a place to put my drink down when Ed handed the girl a piece of paper from his omnipresent notebook and then darted my way.

Somehow, he still clutched his can of ginger ale. When he stood before me, he nodded.

I read the discomfort.

"Like them older?" I pitched my voice low so no one—not even Lydia—could hear us.

Ed shivered. "Maturity's a big part. And she wanted to me to look at a song she's working on."

"But...?"

"I'm worried she might later accuse me of stealing it. I've met with other musicians, for sure, but always in controlled environments. Pauletta'd birth kittens if I started looking at someone else's music like that."

I snickered, amused by the image of Pauletta birthing anything. Well, undoubtedly she'd be an exceptional mother if she set her mind on it—hell, she kept this crew in line. Still, kittens were definitely an image.

"You're okay now?" With his coloring, judging his state of mind was tougher. My emotions often were written across my cheeks—pale for upset and crimson for anger or embarrassment. Thanks to my parents, I had no chance of hiding anything.

"Yeah, I'm okay." He ran the cold can along his forehead, letting the condensation sink into his skin. A droplet skittered down the side of his face to his cheek, along his jaw, and then it petered off.

I imagined licking it.

Ed caught my expression. "Oh, like that, is it?"

"I haven't been subtle. I want you. You want me."

"I'm not out to the fans."

If he thought that was the biggest impediment to a relationship, then I was winning the battle of wills. "I'm not asking you to come out. We could just, you know, have fun."

He glanced over to where Lydia stood, filming Axel surrounded by about ten young women.

"Do you want to join him?"

"Uh, no. Thanks."

"But you do like women, right?"

He eyed me. "I like everyone. I just..." He sighed. "Paulie's always pushing me to come out as bi. She wants *representation*."

I cocked my head.

"To be a good example."

Ah. I knew nothing of Pauletta's love life. Perhaps I should've done more research. I'd seen her as a means to an end—not a potential pivot point in the story. Still, a successful young Black entrepreneur managing a band on the verge of stardom held some appeal. That she used her daddy's money—even in a business context—read a bit like nepotism. Many young people wouldn't be able to replicate that part of her success. "She thinks if you come out that more people will be comfortable doing so?"

"Who knows? Rare are the times when I can get inside Pauletta's head."

"Do you enjoy dating women?"

His gaze sharpened on me.

"Well, do you enjoy dating men?"

"Yes."

I'd assume he meant to both. "But you think the popularity of the band will be affected if you're seen dating men?"

He pursed his lips.

Yeah, that'd been my impression. "Times are changing, Ed."

After taking a long pull of his drink—which I watched him swallow—he continued to hold my gaze. "We tell kids that they can come out and be accepted. We have celebrities who come out. But are those people really treated equally?"

I didn't repeat my *times are changing* comment. Part of me knew he was right—queer people still faced much higher levels of discrimination. Trans people often found this country an inhospitable space. "How is it in Canada?"

He snickered. "Well, better than you guys—but that's not hard. We have anti-discrimination legislation across the country. Does that mean it doesn't happen? Of course not. Bigots will always find a way to show their bigotry. Add in racism..." He swallowed. "I just don't want to be the one assuring kids everything'll be all right if they just come out."

"Did your mother know?"

"No." His answer left no room for inquiries.

"My parents know."

His dark-brown eyes sharpened.

"I mean, I don't want to make my work about my sexuality, so I'm not blatantly *out*. But my family knows. I've even introduced them to a few guys."

"Really?" His expression screamed *I call bullshit*.

"Well, only Sven and Rod—"

"Sven?" He said the name on a choked laugh.

"Yeah."

"Why do I see a broad-chested blond with ice-blue eyes?"

I almost answered the question with a knee-jerk reaction. I reined myself in. "A failure of imagination, I'm certain. He was a brunet with hazel eyes."

Ed frowned.

"He was Swedish," I conceded.

"You've never taken a guy like me home."

Ah, so that's where he was going. "Rock star? Nope. Computer programmer and a waste-management specialist once."

He cocked his head.

"A garbage collector," I translated.

His eyebrows shot up. "No shit?"

"No shit. I'm not as snobby as you seem to think. I respect a hard day's work. Rod certainly did that all day—although he specialized in compost."

"Gross." Ed pressed a hand to his lips.

"Well, he only came over after he showered." I frowned. "We're getting off topic—"

"I wasn't aware we had a topic."

That brought me up short as I searched my memory for the genesis of this conversation. "Bi erasure?" I had to try.

He grunted.

"So you don't come out. I don't come out. But a little fun in the Nevada sun—"

"Is that even a thing? We're near Death Valley. That's...fucking hot."

"Not that close." I tried to pull up a map of Nevada in my mind. "We're going to be in a mountain range. And you don't do heat?"

He gave me a deadpan look. "I'm from Canada."

"I'm from Portland...what's your point?"

"In Vancouver? We freak out if it goes over thirty degrees."

"In Fahrenheit?"

He growled.

I found that way sexier than I was certain he intended.

"Like, ninety."

"Yeah, okay, but that's pretty hot." Portland got hot sometimes, though we didn't see temperatures like they saw in Nevada, Texas, or even SoCal. I had to keep us on track. "Still, Nevada isn't *that* bad in October. We'll be fine."

"You want me to spend time alone with you."

I nodded.

"That feels...unsafe."

His words caught me off-guard. "Because of the doc?"

"Sure...and other stuff."

"You've been with a guy before."

He rolled his eyes.

"Well, I'm just an average guy. Nobody special. Nothing of note here." *Convince him.*

"Something tells me that's absolute bullshit."

Before I could respond, Pauletta gave Ed a subtle signal.

"Shit."

"What?"

"I haven't mingled. She's going to give me hell."

Glancing around, I didn't spot a single unhappy fan. Axel was still enveloped. Songbird had a cluster of young men surrounding her, and...huh. Big Mac and Meg appeared to be having a heated discussion about something.

I caught Lydia's eye.

She started to move that way.

Pauletta waylaid her.

Ed growled. "Nice try."

I pretended all innocence, holding up my hands defensively.

"Whatever's going on between the two of them, it's exactly that—between the two of them. You don't get carte blanche to upend our lives."

Before I could offer a defense—any defense—he stalked away.

Pauletta clapped to get everyone's attention. She thanked everyone, but said the band needed to go.

A general chorus of moans came up, but the band members each clearly respected her, because they all started to move away.

I snagged another can of soda from the table and followed behind.

Within just a few minutes, we were loaded on the bus.

"Be good." Pauletta met each of our gazes, and I felt a little like a child being scolded. "I'll see you in Reno."

Apparently she was spending another night in the Park City hotel, then flying out first thing in the morning.

I might've been slightly envious. I might also be looking forward to some more alone-time with Ed.

He beat me to the punch, though. He was the first in the can, and then the first to bed in his single bunk.

I sipped my cola as the bus sped into the night, and as each of the other members took their turns and headed to bed.

Only Songbird stayed in her seat.

"You not tired?"

She waved me off, then appeared to reconsider. "Pauletta's got us on this weird kick where we try to get eight hours of sleep starting as early as possible. Most nights that's between eleven and midnight—unless we've got a late show. The last band I played with often stayed up jamming all night. Slept in past noon. Crazy hours. Pauletta doesn't tolerate any of that."

"Does it bother you—being so tied to someone else's idea of a proper schedule?"

"Nah. I like consistency. Just...tonight was such a rush. I did a lot of the harmonies on "Day's Pay for Day's Labor". I wasn't sure how the fans would react to something so different."

"They loved it."

She moved her head in a so-so motion. "Eventually, yeah. But they weren't sure what to make of it at first. We've got to nail every note in Black Rock."

"I'm sure you'll be fine."

"Yeah, I'm sure you're right. I just..." She glanced over to the bunks, as if verifying we were alone. "This is a huge deal. I mean, I can always go back to teaching piano, playing keyboard in my church, and doing rock on the side. For some of these folks? They've got everything riding on this—they're counting on getting a contract."

"You've done okay with indie so far."

"Sure...but mostly due to Pauletta's dad. Ed really wants us to be out from under that gravy train."

I wanted to ask if she thought that was the reason Ed hadn't come out—but that question was way too personal.

And none of your fucking business.

"Which church?"

Songbird grinned and started to open up about her South Korean parents, their immigration to Canada, and the church she attended with them as did her younger brother. Her mother taught at a local university and that had gotten the family visas to come over. They'd loved Vancouver and decided to stay.

I kept her words in mind when she headed off to the washroom, and I jotted a few notes in my phone before following her.

Sleep, though, was a long time coming.

For all I'd spoken to Ed tonight—and that we'd spoken of personal things—I still didn't have a read on the guy. And I hadn't spent a moment alone with Axel today. I fingered the chain in my pants pocket before I tucked the clothes away.

Have to do better tomorrow.

Chapter Fifteen

Ed

The lack of motion assured me we'd arrived at our destination. Well, the destination before the destination. The plan was for a day in Reno before we moved on.

Woohoo. More American capitalism at its finest. I couldn't contain my excitement. With just the right note of sarcasm.

Thornton's American.

What's your point?

You'd like to contain him...

Fucking voice in my head. Yeah, okay, I was interested in him. And he'd all but propositioned me last night. So I could probably say the attraction went both ways.

I tried to draw in a deep breath.

Then promptly remembered we were forty-five hundred feet above sea level. Vancouver was exactly at sea level—which didn't bode well if the polar ice caps melted and the seas rose.

But that was beside the point.

I'd gone up Grouse Mountain, part of the North Shore Mountain Range in North Vancouver, a couple of times when I was younger. That height was somewhere between ground and Reno. Overall, despite the stunning views, I'd pick a place where the air wasn't so thin.

What was the level of Portland?

Despite the demands of my bladder, I checked.

Fifteen feet.

Quite reasonable.

I slid out of bed and was about to hit the head when the door opened and a freshly shaven Thornton emerged.

He spotted me, grinned, and advanced.

I backed up against the wall.

He pressed me against it, pushing his body flush with mine.

I murmured something about *morning breath*.

His wicked grin told me he didn't care. And he gave me every opportunity to escape.

If I'd wanted to.

I didn't.

When his mouth dropped to mine, I snagged the back of his neck, and dragged him closer. I ground my cock against his as he bent to fit our bodies together.

I demanded.

He responded.

I upped the ante by pressing my hand to his denim-covered cock.

He reciprocated with easing a hand in my sleep pants and grabbing my naked ass.

Someone stirred, murmured, then apparently went back to sleep.

I pulled back, meeting his gaze in the near-darkness. "Motel?" We had a couple of hours for sightseeing in Reno before we headed to Black Rock tonight.

He swallowed, then lowered his head so he could nuzzle my neck. "Bring the condoms. I hope you're up for the challenge." With that, he moved away.

Leaving me stunned.

Okay, the bring condoms—and presumably lube—was obvious. But the 'up for the challenge'? Did that mean he'd let me fuck him?

You haven't told him that's your jam...

Well, fair enough. I hadn't been overly aggressive with him and he hadn't been overly aggressive with me—everything'd been mutual.

Are you up for this?

Well, I was going to fucking try, that was for sure. Telling myself I was doing this for the band felt pretty fucking thin. I had an itch to scratch.

I intended to get Thornton to scratch it for me.

On that thought, I showered and got ready for the day. I didn't bother to shave because I'd do it before we met all the important people.

Within fifteen minutes, everyone except Pauletta sat in the bus's front.

"I'm doing the river walk," Meg pronounced.

"Oh, hey, that was on my list too." Big Mac nearly bounced.

Dude, too obvious.

Meg arched an eyebrow. "I'd have thought adult entertainment would've been more your style."

Well, she's got him nailed. Before he discovered feelings for Meg, that would've been his go-to.

"I'm going to the casino." Songbird buffed her nails. "Don't worry—I have a set budget. *If* I lose, I'll quit."

She wouldn't lose, though. More often than not, she doubled her money.

We might play cards with her—but we'd learned early on to never put money on the table.

"Jenny, Mikhail, and Pauletta spent the night in Park City. Pauletta's flying in today, and the other two are driving down." I yawned.

"That's no fun." Axel pouted. "I wanted to take Jenny out to see a show."

"Well, she has tomorrow off while we're schmoozing, so you can check them out today and then recommend something for her for tomorrow." That should keep him busy.

He beamed. "That's a great idea."

Yeah, I'm known for them.

"What are you doing?" Meg eyed me.

"We're going to the Nevada Museum of Art," Thornton said smoothly.

Oh, we are? Is that before or after I fuck you into the mattress in a hotel?

A small part of me liked the idea of staying on the bus and having an illicit sex romp, but logistics and small bunks were a thing.

Meg nodded. "You know, that could be fun—"

"You said we were doing the Riverwalk." Big Mac sounded almost desperate. Like he didn't want to share her with us.

Dude, back off.

"True." She offered him a smile. "Okay, after breakfast we'll head out."

We'd parked close to The Original Mel's diner. En masse, we trooped out and headed into the place.

Coffee abounded as our server—an adorable younger guy—took our orders, ranging from corned beef, hash, and eggs to the hangover to a meat-and-cheese omelette.

I opted for banana hotcakes—as did Thornton. I wondered if he might be doing it to curry favor with me—until he added a side of bacon.

We'd nearly finished our meal when Pauletta breezed in, looking refreshed and stunning in a white sheath dress and high-heeled sandals.

Thornton pressed against me, causing me to move farther into the booth.

Pauletta perched on the space he'd made for her. "Everyone behaving?"

"Yes, ma'am." Big Mac saluted her.

She arched an eyebrow at him.

He flushed. "I always behave. Meg and I are heading to the Riverwalk."

"And the rest of you?"

Songbird pointed to herself. "Casino." Then she pointed to Thornton and myself. "Art museum thingy."

Pauletta's expression of surprise might've been priceless—if it hadn't hurt a bit.

Okay, this wasn't my normal thing—but that didn't mean that I couldn't do something more than hang out at an amusement park or something.

She pivoted to Axel.

He shifted. "I'm a little tired. I thought I'd sleep. Maybe jam a bit. Just...hey."

She'd pressed her hand to his forehead.

He batted her away. "I'm fine."

"You could come to the museum with us," Thornton suggested.

I kicked him under the table for that stupid idea. My cock wanted action—preferably sooner rather than later.

Axel considered.

Aw, fuck.

Wouldn't be the first time he'd unknowingly cockblocked me. He came first. Always. If he needed me, then I dropped everything and did whatever he needed.

Still, Axel considered.

Make a fucking decision. Even as I waited, I tried to calculate the odds of finding a way to bone Thornton once we reached Black Rock.

The odds didn't look good.

"Nah, I appreciate the offer." Axel offered Thornton a wan smile. "I just need some downtime. Alone would be best." He turned to Pauletta. "You have plans?"

"I'm setting myself up in a business center with several tasks. I want to refresh the website and get some social media. You guys take any selfies or other shots?"

Obediently, we all pulled out our phones and shot the new pics to her. Early on, she'd declared all social media would be curated by her. Axel'd fought that the most, saying he wanted his fans to get to know the *real* guy behind the singing persona.

Pauletta'd listed ten celebrities who'd gotten themselves into trouble and the consequences—without batting an eyelash.

We'd agreed to let her do everything for us. Or, more accurately, to vet everything. My presence was minimal. I didn't have a Facebook account. Pauletta handled my Instagram, and no way was I going to shout out my thoughts on anything. I had a journal and, if I really felt passionately about something, I'd compose a song.

"We should be going." Meg nudged Big Mac.

He sat up straighter.

"Let's grab a cab together." She pointed to me. "The Riverwalk isn't far from the museum. We can share on the way back as well."

"Uh—"

Thornton stilled my tapping leg.

"That would be great." His voice was smooth as silk. "My treat, though."

She frowned. "Maybe one way, but we'll do the return trip."

This time, I pressed my hand to Thornton's thigh. "Sounds perfect." I pivoted to Songbird.

Grinning, she waved around us. "Any casino's as good as the next. I'll stay here."

"And I'm using the business center here as well," Pauletta volunteered. "Vera's asleep for the day. I'll coordinate with Jenny and Mikhail when they arrive." She waved around the table. "Covered. So head out and enjoy."

I glanced between her and Thornton—trying to figure out who'd actually paid for the meal. This was getting to be ridiculous. I could afford my own fucking meal.

Neither gave up the game.

As much as I wanted to argue, I was also wanting some action, so I nudged Thornton.

He took the hint and slid out of the booth.

Within moments, the group headed in our different directions.

A minivan taxi waited at the stand, so we nabbed that one.

Thornton and I got in the back.

Meg and Big Mac took the middle bench.

I had my phone out before the driver even pulled away from the curb.

So did Thornton. His brow furrowed as he swiped and typed.

I squinted because, of course, I needed reading glasses. When I enlarged the screen I was looking at, I had to keep moving the website this way and that way and—

"I've secured us a room in a hotel a couple of blocks from the museum." Thornton pitched his voice low.

I held up my phone.

He glanced, snickered, and pushed it back.

I frowned.

After a moment, he leaned over and whispered into my ear. "I'm not taking you to a two-star hotel—even if all we're going to do is shag."

Shag? Seriously? Who talks like that?

Well, apparently the guy I hoped to be nailing in the next twenty minutes.

We hit a snag of traffic as we hit the downtown and I was forced to revise my estimate upwards.

Goddamnit.

Meg pointed out the window and made a comment about the number of casinos.

Big Mac tried to casually put his arm around her shoulder.

She tensed.

He desisted.

Fucking clueless. I loved my bassist, but I saw this coming to a head sooner rather than later. Why couldn't we just go back to the time when he wasn't attracted to her? In fact, upon reflection, I couldn't nail the moment things had changed for him. Maybe when she'd found the courage to dump Kevin? Big Mac wasn't someone who would venture into someone else's territory—so maybe he'd always been attracted to Meg but had bided his time until she became single. Or her becoming single had knocked him upside the head. Either way, this infatuation—clearly not reciprocated—had the chance to take down the entire band if he didn't get his shit together.

I glanced at Thornton.

My infatuation—and my desire to keep Thornton from discovering our secrets—might just be our downfall as well.

Chapter Sixteen

Thornton

As soon as Meg and Big Mac got out of the car, I nuzzled Ed's neck.

"The driver," he whispered.

"I'm certain he's seen much worse." I nibbled.

He sucked in a breath.

"You guys said you're going to the museum?"

"No, the Marriott."

"Sure." The driver pulled back into traffic.

I resumed my nuzzling, even nipping at one point. Not enough to leave a mark—but enough to make sure he was aware how I felt.

He pressed a hand to my crotch.

I moaned.

He tisked. "Patience."

"I don't want to be patient. I want to open your jeans and give you a blow job right now."

"We're here." The cabbie's voice reached us.

Ed pulled back.

I pulled my wallet out of my back pocket.

Within moments, I'd paid the driver—and given him a hefty tip—and was headed into the hotel. I wasn't worried about privacy here. Grindstone had a decent following, but Ed didn't have a recognition factor in Nevada that concerned me. And I wasn't taking him to a dive. He deserved, at the very least, a nice bed with pristine linens.

The woman at the check-in desk didn't stutter over the fact we didn't have luggage. In fact, she didn't hesitate to hand over the discreet paper bag I'd requested.

Ed flushed when he spotted it.

His coloring barely changed—but I'd known him long enough to spot the reddening of the tips of his ears.

I would've taken his hand to guide him to the elevator, but his body screamed *hands off*.

As I noticed several women ogling him, I fought the urge to put my hand at the small of his back.

Yes, ladies, he's gorgeous.

He's also mine.

We got into the elevator and, as the door closed and we were finally alone, I let out a long breath.

"Yeah."

"If there weren't cameras—"

"Yeah." He inched his hand over to mine. He grabbed and then squeezed.

"We haven't talked logistics—"

"You. Naked. On the bed. The rest is just fluff."

Fluff? Okay, that was one way to put it.

The elevator dinged, and Ed all but dragged me out and down the hall.

My hand shook as I swiped the card.

He pushed the door open, yanked me inside, closed the door, then slammed me up against it. He grabbed my button-down shirt and tried to yank it over my head. At the same time, he tried to toe off his sneakers.

I put up the hand not holding the paper bag. "You do you, I do me, and we meet in the middle." I opened the bag, extracted the bottle of lube, and made a show of removing the safety seal.

He growled. Then he snagged the bag, grabbed the box of condoms, and proceeded to tear the cardboard as he sought the precious item we both wanted badly. In triumph, he held it up.

I toed off my loafers and reached for my buttons.

Within a minute, we were both naked with our clothes strewn along the floor leading to the king-sized bed.

Ed pulled back the comforter and sheet while I removed the two extra pillows.

Seriously, how many pillows did someone need? Even as a couple, the sheer number felt excessive.

Even as I had the thought, my soon-to-be fuck partner crawled onto the bed. The stark contrast of his dark skin against the white sheets provided a delicious contrast. What I really noticed, though, was his perky cock protruding from the nest of black, wiry pubic hair.

The chub matched my growing erection.

I palmed my cock. "How do you want to do this?"

He cocked his head. "Well, I'd like to fuck you into oblivion." He pushed down on the mattress with a bit of force.

It barely moved.

"I think we're good."

"Yeah, I'd say so." I stroked myself a couple of times. "I'm totally onboard for that plan."

His gaze flickered away before returning to me. "Being topped by a smaller guy?"

Ah. "Frankly, the size of the guy doesn't matter. Most people assume because I'm bigger that I prefer to do the fucking. And I'll do it. But I prefer to receive, if you know what I mean."

"I do." He ran his hand across his forehead. "Just like people see I'm smaller and assume—"

Moving quickly, I hopped onto the bed. "I stay as far away from assumptions as I possibly can."

"Yet you have a set opinion of me. Of Axel."

Shit. Fuck. Damn. I'd forgotten. For the past two hours—since rubbing myself against Ed on the bus—nothing had been in my mind except getting him naked as quickly as possible. I hesitated.

"Fuck, I didn't mean it." He pushed up toward me so my mouth hovered just above his. "Let me fuck you. We'll deal with everything else later."

As I silently asked for my sister's forgiveness, I pressed my lips to his.

We'd kissed before. Yet this felt like the first time—like something special was passing between the two of us. Understanding? Compassion?

I wasn't certain.

He wrapped his arms around my neck and coaxed me to lie down on top of him. He opened his thighs so I could settle between them, and our cocks brushed.

Mine jerked at the contact.

Our tongues tangled as I pressed him down. Everywhere our skin touched, I felt tingles. Every time one of us shifted, little sparks ignited within me. I kept trying to tell myself this was just a fuck—much like all the ones who'd come before—but my body didn't believe me. This man, at this moment, was the center of my universe.

He drew a lazy hand up my side, then down my flank, and over to my ass cheek. He squeezed.

I moaned.

"Yeah." He pulled back, looking up at me with fathomless eyes. "You sure you're ready?"

"Bring it on." The anticipation of this moment hit me like a sledge hammer. I'd thought him attractive when I'd seen videos and stills—but nothing compared to him in the flesh. Since the moment I'd laid eyes on him in The Georgian a week ago, I'd craved him in a way I couldn't understand, and wasn't going to try to unpack.

He nudged me so I rolled off. As he reached for the bottle of lube, I settled in the center of the bed. Was this it? Was he just going to prep and then fuck me? That thought left a little hollow feeling in my chest. I wanted more. Needed more. Maybe not pretty words—how ridiculous to want that from a man I'd vowed to destroy... Except this Ed wasn't the one I'd imagined finding and filming, the callous, cold-hearted bastard I would pull down to applause and satisfaction. This Ed was protective and kind, anxious and, despite the closeness of his bandmates, somehow solitary. This Ed had crept inside my defenses and made me want things I'd never wanted from some any other man—some kind of assurance I meant something to him. That this was more than mutual slaking of need. Of getting our rocks off and moving on.

Wait. This can't be more than that—one time.

That truth hit hard and painfully. Pushing away the desire for more, I gazed up at him—hoping he didn't see the longing in me.

He stilled with the bottle in his hand. Slowly, he put it back down on the bed. He maneuvered himself so he settled between my spread thighs.

My cock, rock hard, lay curled toward my belly.

As he brought his mouth to it, a drop of precum leaked.

He lapped it up. Then, he met my gaze.

I nodded.

He swirled his tongue around the crown of my cock before pulling me into his mouth.

My world spun. As much as I loved being fucked—and I definitely did—I also loved being given head.

And reciprocating was high on my list as well.

He speared my slit, then sucked me deeper, continuing to swirl his tongue.

Oh my God. Just feel. All the rest can get sorted later. I need to ride this pleasure because I wasn't certain it would ever be repeated. That we could be together after I did what I needed to do. That I wouldn't hate myself. *This is just a strategy. So enjoy it.*

My balls tightened. I grasped his cheeks to encourage his ministrations. I wanted to reciprocate in some way, but he felt so far away from me. Within my grasp and yet beyond it as well.

As he kept up a steady pace of bobbing on my cock, he raked his teeth up and down my length.

"I'm coming." Fair warning in case he wanted to pull off.

Apparently he didn't, as he doubled down and sucked harder.

I came.

Hard.

He continued to milk me through the mind-blowing orgasm.

A sated feeling started to sink in, but I fought it. I might've come, but I still wanted him in me—wanted that connection that only came with fucking.

After a long moment, he pulled off me.

My softening dick lay limp.

He crawled up me and, without warning, thrust his tongue into my mouth.

Although startled, I welcomed the invasion. The taste of myself on him was just that special illicit connection I so desperately craved.

His cock lay, insistent, against my hip.

I bucked up against him.

He ground down against me.

"Please, Ed." I met his gaze as he pulled back. "I need this."

Where I expected him to make a smart remark—or ask me how long it'd actually been—he nodded and nuzzled my neck.

I ran my hands up and down his smooth back as he nipped and sucked his way down my body—neck, collarbone, sternum, belly, and even lower. My cock didn't perk, but it gave a vague stirring.

He met my gaze and grinned.

Then, to my relief, he reached for the lube.

I spread my thighs for him, giving him as much access as I could.

He sheathed his erect cock, tossed the wrapper over the side of the bed, then slathered his fingers with lube.

Again, he sought my permission before intimacy.

I nodded frantically, then nearly sighed as he slid one finger inside me. I loved this feeling—this connection—but I shared it with few people. Oh, there'd been guys...but not like this. Yet the feeling of guilt nagged. *Will I forgive myself later? For giving in to this temptation?*

His gaze caressed me as he slid in a second finger.

I revelled in the burn.

Brow furrowed in concentration, he twisted and scissored his fingers—opening me up.

Then he hit my prostate and pleasure zinged through me.

He grinned. "Oh, yeah."

"Yeah." I grinned right back. Probably looked like a loon, but I didn't give a shit.

After a moment, he withdrew his fingers.

I whimpered.

He slathered lube on his cock, then quickly slid between my thighs.

Our gazes locked.

"You okay like this?"

"You think I'm going to roll over? Hell no. I want to see your eyes when you fuck me into the mattress." I opened my thighs as wide as I could.

With the slyest of grins, he lined himself up.

I breathed.

He pushed in.

Having done this many times, I knew what to expect. The burn as I stretched. The shifting to find just the right spot. The pressure of having someone in me. The strength in the joining of flesh.

Today, though, I sensed another layer. Intimacy. Connection. In another place and time, Ed might be my lover in truth, someone I could welcome deeper than just into my body. It hurt to force myself away from that potential. To cover the hurt, I focused on the physical, pulling my legs wider and groaning like a porn star.

As he seated himself, I grasped his muscled biceps and held on tight.

He cocked an eyebrow.

I nodded.

He pulled out. Then pressed back in.

I rose to meet him.

From there, the rhythm he set was both steady and demanding. He pushed me higher and higher, eliciting grunts from me as he drove into me.

The urge to close my eyes overwhelmed, but I fought it because I needed to hold the connection between our locked gazes. Every nuance of his pleasure and pain displayed openly on his face.

He held nothing back.

So neither did I.

My cock perked up.

"Jack yourself. Do it." He gave the order through gritted teeth.

Happy to oblige, I grasped my shaft and tugged. Hard. Where I expected to need time to come to full alert again, because refractory periods were a thing, his unerring nailing of my prostate on every thrust had me hardening with speed.

"Please." He blinked.

I raised my left hand to wipe the sweat from his brow as I continued to work myself to a frenzy. Silly man thought I needed to come before him. "Just come, Ed. It's okay."

Despite his frazzled state, my words appeared to penetrate. He thrust twice more quickly, then held himself still.

As he released into me, I continued the frantic tugs to my cock. Soon enough, I joined him and tipped over the edge into blessed and unobliterated bliss.

Chapter Seventeen

Ed

A ringing phone drew me out of my orgasm-fueled haze. "What the fuck...?"

"That's you." Thornton chuckled beneath me.

The movement caused me to shift and—yuck—our bellies stuck together with cum.

Normally, after I climaxed, I'd withdraw, dispose of the condom, clean up myself and my partner, and be on my way.

After fucking Thornton so thoroughly? Even the thought of moving had overwhelmed. I'd collapsed onto him, sliding out with a pop, and losing any ounce of energy left.

He'd wrapped his arms around me and we'd lain together like that.

At one point, I'd registered the chill. I had not, however, found the energy to move.

"I have to get that?" My mind was still fuzzy.

"You know I can't answer that. I'm not a mind reader. Does that ringtone belong to a particular person?"

At Thornton's words, an idea solidified. "Fuck. Yes. Big Mac." I slowly disentangled myself, wincing at the pulled skin.

The phone ceased.

I sagged in relief.

The ringing began anew.

"Fuck." I nearly tripped on the pile of sheets as I wended my way along the trail of discarded clothes until I located my jeans. I pulled my phone out and swiped. "What?"

Okay, I might've snapped that.

Silence.

I checked the display. *Big Mac*. "Dude, what is it?"

"Did I catch you at a bad time? Like are you in a quiet part of the museum and—"

"What's going on? We're supposed to meet up in—" I squinted at my phone display. "Like, hours from now."

"I need your help."

"Why are you whispering?"

"Because Meg's talking to some kid about, I dunno, like ducks or some shit."

Which did nothing to explain either why he'd called or why he was whispering.

"Spit it out."

"Things aren't going well."

Which told me precisely nothing. "What are you talking about?"

"Well, it's awkward and shit. It never used to be like this."

Your own damn fault for wanting to change things.

But I'd never say that to him. "How can I help?"

He breathed a long sigh of relief. "We swung by the Wild River Grille. They've had a cancellation for this afternoon. The table will be ready in twenty minutes. That's, like, a ten-minute walk from where you are."

I couldn't orient myself and had no idea where the restaurant actually was. "We're in the middle of a tour—"

"But you'll come, right? Man, I need help." He sighed. "And, like, there's a spinach artichoke flatbread thing. That's vegetarian right?"

No missing the *sounds gross to me*.

Movement from the bed caught my eye.

I turned to find Thornton rising.

He pointed to the bathroom.

I nodded.

He walked with a distinctive jiggle.

I sighed. "Yeah, give us thirty."

"Awesome, you're the best." He cut the connection.

Thornton stuck his head out from the bathroom. "I've got the shower running. I can keep my hands to myself, if that helps."

"I appreciate it. Give me two." I managed to sort out the used condom and wrapper, as well as somewhat organizing our clothes.

Fuck my life.

Still, we cleaned off, trying our best not to get our hair wet—lucky none of Thornton's cum had flown up and in that direction. That'd happened to me in the past and getting that shit out of my hair was a pain.

I might've taken a moment to wash his crack and he might've brushed my cock, but we kept it serious and fifteen minutes later, we were dry, dressed, and ready to head out. I glanced longingly at the opened bottle of lube.

"Neither of us has a pocket it'll fit into." Thornton patted my shoulder. "The cleaning crew will get a kick out of it."

Not being certain about that, I took a moment to toss it in the garbage pail with the used condom. I tied off the plastic bag. Terrible for the environment, but at least I didn't feel quite so badly about someone seeing it. "We'll drop the key card off at the desk?"

Thornton nuzzled my neck. "We won't have time to come back. But we'll figure something out, okay?"

My mind flashed to the tour bus, my bandmates, and Pauletta. I sighed. "I don't see that happening."

He pressed up against me. "I can be very creative."

I tipped my chin up so our gazes met. "But this is just a fling, right?"

His eyes widened comically.

I grinned, poked him in the gut, then opened the door. "After you."

He sputtered a bit while we walked to the elevator. Finally, he managed, "I wasn't thinking that far ahead—"

"Just wanted to get your rocks off, eh?"

"How very Canadian of you."

Since I wasn't certain if he meant the *rocks* comment or the *eh*, I let it go. I would've snagged his hand in the elevator, but an older couple were already in it when it arrived.

Thornton stood stiffly.

I debated whether or not I could tease him. The elevator arrived at the ground floor before I found my courage.

Thornton returned the key card to the front desk, and I searched the restaurant online.

"It's an eight-minute walk," I informed Thornton when he came to stand beside me.

"We can make it in six."

I glanced at the time on my phone. "Which will get us there right on time."

"Let's just hope they don't notice we're coming from the wrong direction."

"Shit."

"Indeed." Thornton offered me a smile. "We'll say we got turned around."

"Okay, fair."

As we stepped out in the fresh, mountain air, I cursed not having brought sunglasses as the early afternoon sun beat down upon us.

Thornton squinted as well. Still, he indicated the way.

We headed off.

And didn't talk.

What was there to say?

I enjoyed that, did you?

When can we try for a repeat?

Have you always been a bottom?

Curiosity drove all those questions, but the last one the most. I wanted to know more about him. Needed to know. Like, how often did he hook up with guys? If he wasn't out but wasn't in, what did that mean to him?

Mostly, I just wanted to understand why I wanted to drag him back to the hotel and do that over and over and over. One taste wasn't enough—would never be enough. I'd known that, even as we'd stepped over the threshold to the room. But I'd believed if we could fuck ourselves into exhaustion today, then the need might be slaked.

Missed the mark on that one.

As we approached the restaurant, I didn't spot either Meg or Big Mac. I was about to check my phone when it buzzed with a message from Big Mac telling me they were already at a table. I halted and faced Thornton.

He also stopped, but cocked his head.

"Do we look like we just fucked?"

I'd checked to make sure no one was within hearing distance.

Thornton considered. "Well, as long as I don't have a goofy grin on my face, we should be okay." He tapped my nose. "Hopefully they'll be too wrapped up in each other to notice us."

That turned out to be a hope in vain.

My ass had barely touched the seat when Meg eyed me.

"Why's your hair wet?"

"It's not—"

"I can see the tendrils that you always get after a shower."

"We stepped through a mist," Thornton offered. "Ed forgot."

Big Mac snorted.

I glared.

His eyes widened.

Yeah, yuck it up, fuckwit.

His cheeks darkened.

"How was the exhibit?" Meg slanted her gaze to Thornton.

"Enlightening."

"Oh, really, which was your favorite part?"

"So spinach artichoke flatbread." I picked up the menu and perused it. The cheese plate looked interesting, but I was—unsurprisingly—famished.

"Sorry." Big Mac winced. "They have more vegetarian options for dinner, but we were hungry and didn't want to wait and—"

I held up my hand. "It's fine. Really. We were almost done with the tour." I cursed myself for not having at least searched the museum to see which exhibits they had.

"And I'm famished, so the timing's perfect." Thornton nabbed his menu. "Did the server make a recommendation? Oh, the tuna melt sounds delicious."

Great. Fishy smell. My nose was way too accurate and my gut way too sensitive to certain smells. I never complained, but fish in particular could put me off my food.

Thornton paused, then eyed me. "The brie and pear sandwich looks good. That's vegetarian, right?"

Meg laughed. "I think so. Big Mac's paying, so I'm having the steak sandwich."

The most expensive item on the menu.

I eyed her.

She appeared...annoyed. She had color in her high cheekbones and her jaw was set.

At first, I thought she was mad at me for something, but her glares at Big Mac assured me more was going on.

Shit.

We could not afford complications. We were on the verge of our biggest break ever—I didn't need these two squabbling.

The server appeared. Since Big Mac knew me well, I ordered the flatbread. Thornton chose the sandwich he'd suggested, Meg ordered the steak, and Big Mac selected a BLTA. Oh, and we all ordered different flavors of lemonade because that, apparently, was a thing. Good thing I loved lemonade.

Once the server left, Meg turned on Big Mac. "You could've gotten a BLT anywhere. You said here was special, and you didn't even pick something...unusual."

He flashed a desperate look at me.

You're on your own, buddy.

Thornton grazed my thigh under the table with his knuckles.

My cock stirred.

Our lemonades arrived.

Personally, I enjoyed the drink occasionally—as a treat—but I wouldn't go out of my way to order it.

Meg and Thornton sipped theirs.

Big Mac guzzled his.

My gag reflex nearly activated as I envisioned drinking all that sourness at one time.

"How was the Riverwalk?" Thornton dragged his hand through the condensation on his glass as he ran his foot up and down my shin.

Good to know he can do two things at once. How I intended to put that particular talent to work, I wasn't sure. Hell, I was creative. I'd figure something out. *Planning for more, are you?*

Yep. Yep, I was. Even if all I got was stolen kisses and a bit of frotting, I intended to take full advantage of the next week.

"The Riverwalk was fine." Meg turned to Big Mac. "Why are you acting all weird? What the fuck is wrong with you?" Before she gave him a chance to answer, she stood. "I'm going to the ladies' room." In a heartbeat, she left.

Big Mac sagged in obvious relief.

"What the fuck, buddy?" I stared at him. "This was *your* idea. The Riverwalk and, apparently, sending out the bat signal."

"Did you two really...?" He waved a spoon between Thornton and myself.

Thornton cleared his throat.

"None of your fucking business." I continued to glare.

"Well, yeah, but I didn't mean—"

"What you meant is no longer relevant. The question is what the fuck are you going to do now?"

Chapter Eighteen

Thornton

I would've paid just about any amount of money to be anywhere else in the world at that particular moment.

Ed radiated tension.

Big Mac radiated misery.

And oops, Meg was on her way back to the table.

"Zip it," I shushed the other two. Then I offered my most-sincere smile.

Meg eyed me warily before, after a moment, smiling back. Reserved and wary, but a smile nonetheless. She sat.

I sipped my drink.

Big Mac groused.

"What?" Ed's voice cut sharply.

"I said I wish I could have a drink."

Ed held his hands out wide. "No one's stopping you. You're always free to have a drink."

Since both Big Mac and Meg'd had drinks at The Georgian, his reticence here confounded me.

He waved the suggestion off.

Before any of us could respond, the server returned with our food.

As if by accord, we dug into our food and didn't speak.

The vibe at the table continued to be…weird.

What I couldn't figure out was how Meg felt about Big Mac.

She was a self-possessed woman who didn't tend to show much emotion.

With Pauletta, I could easily sense which way the wind was blowing.

Songbird was enigmatic. But more as a person than how she related to others. She laid the cards on the table and let the chips fall where they may.

Meg, though, hid a lot. Not with the music…just within herself.

I wanted to delve more, but Ed's phone vibrated.

He gave us all a sheepish look as he pulled his phone out of his back pocket. "Paulie says Songbird's tired of winning. Jenny and Mikhail have arrived. She's proposing we leave sooner than planned."

"I'm fine with that." Meg indicated the phone with her chin. "Tell her we're all here together and eating."

"Sure." Ed tapped out a message—likely to that effect—and, within a moment, his phone buzzed again. "She said we're to meet the bus in an hour." He eyed the table. "I think that's more than enough time."

We'd all pretty much demolished our meals.

"They have a flourless chocolate torte." Meg glanced at all of us. "We should order one and take it for everyone."

"Will that be enough? Should we get a second?" I eyed Big Mac. "I'm happy to pay."

"I can pay." He glared.

Ah. Pride.

"I didn't say you couldn't."

At that moment, the server arrived. As she cleared the plates, Meg requested two chocolate tortes.

Ed cut me a look that I struggled to interpret.

I went for a change of subject. "You guys must be so excited—you'll be in Black Rock by tonight."

"Yeah, excited." Meg again looked at Big Mac. "What is up with you?"

"Uh—"

"Your film crew is already up there?" Ed turned to me. "I've lost track."

He hadn't. Of that, I was certain.

"Yes. They went straight from Reno to Black Rock. They're doing background work, getting us set up…stuff like that."

"I don't know if this is such a good idea." Big Mac rose. "I'm going to go pay. I'll see you out front."

He left so abruptly, he nearly knocked into the server with the two boxes with our cakes.

She righted herself as he apologized and then fled.

Meg accepted the boxes from the clearly flustered server.

We all thanked her, and she moved on.

Meg turned back to Ed. "What's with him? He's been getting progressively weirder for months. I can't figure out what's changed. Is there something I don't know? I might not be the most perceptive person in the world, but this shit's getting ridiculous. I'm frustrated."

Of that, I had no doubt. But how she could be so blind to something that I, as an outsider, had picked up on almost immediately, left me confused.

"He's worried about Rocktoberfest." Ed cleared his throat. "This is an enormous deal—for all of us. Make or break time, you know.

So maybe we should just set aside…whatever this is…and focus on the music."

She held his gaze for a long moment.

Then she turned to me.

I held up my hands as if pleading innocence, all the while feeling uncomfortable. Most of the people at this table held secrets we were withholding from each other. That was never a good thing.

Ed rose, grabbed the boxes, and indicated we should leave.

Meg and I rose, following suit.

We met up with Big Mac just outside the restaurant.

The sun shone brightly even as it moved toward the western horizon. We were getting closer to the winter solstice and further from the fall equinox. I very much saw life in terms of seasons—of time marching on. Or absent people. People like Kyesha and my mother.

Which brought me back to why I stood with these three members of Grindstone on the side of a road in Reno, waiting for the tour bus.

Ed swayed gently against me.

I looked down.

He looked up.

The moment stood still in time. Suddenly, I was back in that hotel room with him fucking me into the mattress. With him looming over me. With the release of sexual tension that we'd carried around for days.

I wanted him even more now—now I'd had a taste and known what true, uninhibited pleasure looked like. *Uninhibited pleasure? Don't get carried away. It was just a fuck. A great one, yeah, but you've had great sex before.* As I searched my memory for the last time I'd had such a good fuck, Vera drove the bus to the side of the road and opened the door.

Meg pushed her way to the front of us—a position we would've all accorded her anyway—and stomped onto the bus.

Big Mac followed, head hung.

I indicated Ed should go next. After all, he had the cakes.

Finally, I mounted the stairs, giving Vera a wide smile.

She grinned back.

"I'll make sure to save a slice of cake for you."

She cocked her head.

"Chocolate torte."

"Oh, a man after my heart."

I pressed a hand to my chest as I moved into the bus.

She shut the door, pulled back into traffic, and we were soon on our way.

As I entered the living area, I found Songbird playing solitaire, Big Mac folded in a chair staring out the window, Ed stowing the cake, and Meg nowhere to be found.

Okay, then.

I settled into one of the seats that afforded me a view of the outside. Reno, with all her casinos, hotels, and many other buildings, passed in a blur. Soon, we hit the city limits, and the landscape changed. Our route vaguely followed a waterway until we left the interstate and headed north.

Ed sat beside me. From where we sat, no one could see when he snagged my hand and squeezed.

I turned my head to meet his gaze.

"I'm sorry." I could barely hear his quiet words above the hum of the bus.

"Why don't you two go make out in the back? It'll give Meg some entertainment." Songbird didn't look up, but continued her game of solitaire.

Ed dropped my hand.

Too late. Too fucking late.

"I don't know what you mean." Ed widened his eyes—obviously in an attempt to look innocent.

Big Mac snickered. "I told her about the wet hair."

I felt color rise in my cheeks. I'd never been embarrassed about my sex life. My parents had always known I was gay. Despite being essentially conservative, they felt I should be more *out*. To be comfortable with myself. They certainly never expected me to hide my sex life from them. I was one of the lucky ones.

Songbird gathered her cards and shuffled them. "The tension between you two was getting unbearable. Only..." She sniffed. "Doesn't seem like it's much better—more like a simmer."

Oh, I was simmering. In so many ways.

"It's not what you think," Ed protested.

"As long as you used condoms, I don't care." She resumed her cards by setting out another game.

Big Mac plopped into the seat across from her. "I want to play as well."

She eyed him. "Oh, I so wish we could play for money—I'd bleed you dry."

"Feeling vampirish?" I tried to discern what exactly was going on, but I struggled with nuances. I'd need to do better if I was going to nail the doc. *I need some objective distance and a handle on these people.*

Of course, after I did the big reveal, odds were the project would never get finished.

"Just deal." Big Mac looked over at Ed and me.

I saw only despair in his dark-brown eyes.

After a long moment, he looked away.

Ed pointed to something out the window.

By the time I looked, though, whatever he'd spotted was gone.

The sun dipped lower still on the horizon.

"What are we going to do?" I whispered the question.

"I have no idea." Ed met my gaze. "But I don't feel any shame. Do I wish we could've been more discreet? Sure. But I can't regret what we did."

And since neither did I, I chose to leave the silence a companionable one.

Eventually, he grasped my hand again. His fingers were callused while mine were smooth.

How can I feel this way while knowing what he did? Is this a betrayal of all I hold sacred?

And, finally, how long was I going to keep lying to myself?

I just didn't have a good answer for that.

Chapter Nineteen

Ed

Electricity zinged through me as Vera pulled our bus into the allotted spot. Several other buses surrounded us, and as I spotted a couple of other band logos, my heart sped up.

This is real.

Knowing we were coming and actually being here were two very different things.

Meg appeared when the bus stopped moving. "I'm going for a walk."

Songbird leapt up. "I'll join you."

Big Mac looked like he was about to speak, but a quick shake of the head from Songbird and he desisted.

The women departed as soon as they could, leaving us four behind.

"Oh, there's my crew." Thornton pointed to three people approaching.

Great.

Still, I plastered on a smile. "Will they want to come in? Shoot some footage?"

"Are you up for an impromptu interview?"

"I'm fucking out of here." Big Mac launched himself from his seat and was out of the bus in a flash.

"Me too." Axel followed, hard on his heels.

Thornton cut me a glance as he rose and ambled to the front. He descended the stairs to greet his crew.

I made a beeline for the bathroom. I didn't just have to piss—I wanted to make sure I looked decent. And I needed a moment to collect myself.

Somehow, over the past day or so, I'd ceased to look at Thornton as the enemy. He'd just become one of the folks on the tour. The one organizing the shoots.

I'd put distance between the interviews and the filming of the concerts.

By doing that, I let my guard down. Perhaps fucking Thornton had been inevitable. Except I'd managed my urges before with other people. Nailing down the reason I was willing to be so vulnerable so I could nail Thornton wasn't so clear to me.

After I pissed, I washed my hands and gave myself a good look in the mirror. I needed another shave, but otherwise I was pretty decent. Or, at least I felt good enough. But I often felt *good enough*. Pauletta tried to convince me that I was exceptional—yet I never made the leap. I could point to each of our bandmates and explain clearly why they were special. But I struggled to do the same with myself.

I exited the bathroom and made my way to the front of the bus.

Thornton sat with his team around the table.

The fading light caught Lydia's fiery-red, curly hair.

I had a soft spot for redheads, but felt no stirring of attraction.

Kato's blue eyes settled on me, and his long blond hair also sparkled in the light.

Nothing.

Finally, Mickey's curly, brown hair framed their face perfectly. They definitely had appealing qualities.

Nada.

I chuckled and pointed to Thornton. "You should grow your hair long and curl it—then you'll fit in with your crew."

Thornton tilted his head. Then, slowly, he looked at each member of his crew and his eyes widened.

Mickey burst out laughing. "Seriously? You never noticed?"

He shook his head. "Nope. I see you for your talents, not your looks."

Lydia blinked. "I don't know if I should be offended or not."

"Not." Thornton was quick to assure.

"Right." Kato fingered one of Lydia's long curls. "I find curls sexy."

She gave him a downright annoyed look.

He dropped her hair.

Ah. Glad to see Meg and Big Mac aren't the only potential train wreck.

Lydia placed her hand on the camera.

I glanced behind me to make certain no stray socks or other detritus littered the bus. All clear. In response to Lydia's unasked question, I offered a weak smile. "Uh, yeah I'm pretty sure we're boring."

"Don't think of it that way." Mickey offered me a smile. "We want to give a sense of who you all are. What your environs are like."

"We rent this tour bus a couple of times a year." I swept my hand around the space. "We're more like the folks at the diner than, you know, real rock stars."

Thornton cocked his head.

I waved away my thoughts. "Sorry. Momentary lapse." *Sell the band. Don't downplay our talent and abilities.*

Lydia didn't move. "We can do this another time."

"No. Might as well get it over with. Do you need me to do a cheesy tour or are you just going to film?"

"I was just planning to film. Maybe you can strum your guitar or work on lyrics or something? Not forced, though. If you never do those things, don't do them at my suggestion."

"Yeah, okay." I pulled down my acoustic guitar from the overhead rack. As I strummed and tuned it, Lydia walked slowly to the back of the bus. To my relief, she didn't film the john. As she made her way back, I ducked my head and started picking out a melody that'd been going around in my head. I sensed her, but chose to continue working away. Soon, I sank into the song. I was a little annoyed that I hadn't also grabbed a pencil and paper to jot notes, but I figured some of this would stay with me. Plus, I could always request a copy of the footage from Thornton.

Right?

I just didn't know. Nothing felt secure. The world kept shifting below my feet and every time I thought I might be on terra firma, something would happen to shake my confidence.

As promised, Lydia wasn't intrusive.

Despite sensing her presence, I kept playing. I loved my acoustic—probably because I'd started on her more than ten years ago. I'd always been very much of the rock'n'roll vintage, but I could appreciate a good pop or folk song. Music across the spectrum appealed to me, and while I focused on rock bands, I had a soft spot in my heart for Canadian folk singers.

Once I'd gone as far as I could with the song, I transitioned into a Gordon Lightfoot ballad I'd always enjoyed. A few bars of that and then I moved on to a Tragically Hip tune. Finally, just to annoy a certain segment of the population, I did Nickelback. An in-joke for Canadians.

"That's quite a medley." Thornton spoke quietly as the reverberation of the last notes carried through the space.

"It's music. I love music."

"Any favorites?"

"Naming them feels like I'm dismissing others. It's like being asked to pick your favorite child."

"Do you have children to pick from?"

My gaze shot to his. *What the fuck is he getting at?* I cleared my throat. "Uh, no kids. That's..." I sought the right words. "The responsibility of being a parent is monumental. I'm not ready. Not sure I'll ever be ready." I patted my guitar. "I'm in love with my music."

"So, no romantic attachments?"

Ah. "No." I caressed the neck of my guitar. "Music is my mistress."

My entire *audience* chuckled.

Thornton winked.

Lydia turned off the camera.

Mickey smiled. "I think we got some great footage."

Their words made me uncomfortable. "This is supposed to be about the band. About Axel."

Thornton waved his hand in a *so-so* motion.

I arched an eyebrow.

Lydia, Mickey, and Kato all slipped out of the bus, giving us backward looks that felt unmistakable.

"They know."

"I didn't tell them, if that's what you're asking."

"But they know," I persisted.

"I don't lie to my people."

"And I do?"

He tilted his head. "We can agree, I think, that any kind of liaison between the two of us would be complicated."

"And it crosses all kinds of lines. Won't your objectivity be compromised?" I narrowed my eyes. "Did you sleep with Candi Lewis?" The actress who'd made the revelation.

His look of hurt had me wanting to retract the words.

Well, almost.

"No, I didn't." Thornton put his hands on his hips. "And she didn't ask me to. That's not how I operate."

I opened my mouth.

He held up his hand to waylay any viable argument I might make.

"Okay, not how I normally operate. Look…" He took a deep breath. "Are we just scratching an itch? We're from two different worlds—"

"Yeah, dirt poor and fucking loaded—"

"Hey."

His sharp rebuke had me taking a mental step back.

"Start down that road and you'll start naming all kinds of differences between us—none of which matter. Well, except for the Canadian/American thing."

I glared. We had bigger differences than that. Still, I understood what he was trying to say.

He must've spotted my acquiescence because he held out his hand. "What…?"

"We're alone in the bus. I think we should take advantage."

"No way. Anyone could come back at any moment."

"So, no blow jobs in the bunks?"

"Uh, no."

"I can see you wavering."

After sliding out so I could stand, I advanced toward him. With a boldness I didn't necessarily feel, I grabbed his package.

He bucked into my hand.

"I'm not risking this. I respect my team too much. You should feel the same way." I squeezed.

He hardened.

"But you can go jerk off while you think of me. I'm going for a walk." With one last squeeze, I leaned in for a kiss.

He grabbed my cheeks and pulled me up while his mouth descended on mine.

The frantic kiss overwhelmed my senses even as I wrapped my arm around his waist and dragged him closer.

We ground our cocks together.

His breathing hitched.

I pulled back, offered a cheeky grin, and sauntered down to the front of the bus.

"Sadist."

"You bet." I grinned at his mild insult. In fact, I considered it a compliment. I was big on edging my partners—and he was clearly game for anything. *But to what end?* We were playing with fire. This couldn't end well. We'd go our separate ways and, what, have the memories for comfort on a cold night? That sounded pretty shitty to me.

I descended the stairs of the bus and out into early evening air. I caught sight of several buses of bands whose eagerness likely matched ours. As I spotted the main stage, I marveled at the size of the venue.

We'd never played anything close to this size.

Knowing how big the venue would be—and actually seeing it in person—were two very different things. Vancouver didn't have anything like this. I had dreams of playing Rogers Arena or BC Place. But they were just that—dreams. My wildest fantasies were of opening for a great band. Still, in the back of my mind, I wondered what it'd be like to be the headliner for a show.

Fanciful.

I was allowed to dream...right?

Pauletta kept our heads out of the clouds—we focused on the next step. Reached for what we could accomplish. Celebrated the small and big victories.

My mind flashed back to the day she arrived at the rehearsal hall to announce we'd been accepted into Rocktoberfest. Last year, several bands had dropped out before the show. We'd hoped the same thing might happen this year.

We needn't have worried. Based on our demo, we nailed a spot in the lineup when the organizers announced it.

That day, Pauletta had Axel and me quit our day jobs. Songbird, Big Mac, and Meg all cut back on their side hustles.

I really didn't want to know how much this adventure was costing her father. Our album sales gave us a small income, but his generosity paid for the lead-up to this tour. If we didn't break out here, I'd be back to driving deliveries, Axel would be back to his telemarketing job—because he could talk anyone into anything—and we'd be back to trying to reach a wider audience.

We have to nail this contract.

Any contract.

Failure was simply not an option.

Humming one of my favorite of our songs, *Day's Pay for a Day's Labor,* I meandered down to where technicians set up equipment.

"Hey."

I turned.

Pauletta approached.

"Everything okay with your rental car?"

She nodded.

"And you're checked into Bruno's?"

She nodded.

"And...?"

"I'm grateful not to be staying on the tour bus."

I grinned. "That bad?"

She shook her head. "It's civilization—as close as I can get to you without actually being out here. I don't mind the half-hour drive to Gerlach."

I adored Pauletta, but she was very much a city girl. I didn't question how much she was paying for an actual motel room during one of the busiest weekends of the year.

"How's everyone else doing?" She gazed around, as if trying to spot our people.

"Well..." I toed the ground.

"Spill."

"Things are shit between Meg and Big Mac." I held up my hand to waylay the questions. "Songbird's happy. Well, you know."

"Right."

"Axel's thrilled to be here."

"And you?"

I flashed to the very hard and very horny man I'd left on the tour bus. "Thornton and his crew filmed some shots of me strumming my acoustic and working on a new song."

"Anything promising?"

"I haven't seen the footage."

"I mean with the song."

A snort escaped. "Your mind is always on business."

"You know it. Even with the new songs we're introducing—and the ones we rejected—we still don't have enough for an entire new album. I want us to be able to move quickly if we nail a contract. The more potential songs we have, the better off we'll be."

I hemmed. "You seem awfully sure we're going to get something."

"Many bands do, Ed." She waved her hand. "Several signed contracts here last year...or at least the groundwork was laid for future contracts. Add the prestige of the documentary, and I really think you guys have a legit shot."

Wanting to believe her and actually letting myself believe her were two very different things.

She slid her arm around my shoulders and directed me toward the stage. "One day, this'll all be yours."

I wanted to believe her.

Chapter Twenty

Thornton

My team was set up in the camper van they'd rented in Reno. Mickey, with their omnipresent grin, offered a tour. "Height of luxury."

About a tenth the size of the tour bus and without running water, but I wouldn't argue.

"They wouldn't spring for anything more...utilitarian?" I glanced around. "Where's the bathroom?"

"We shower and shit with the masses."

I shuddered.

They bopped me on the shoulder. "Didn't you used to live rough? When you did nature photography?"

"Well, sure. But living rough didn't mean sharing a bathroom with sixty thousand other people. I'm sure if you wanted to use the band's—"

They held up their hands. "There's already been enough boundaries crossed." They cocked their head. "You're looking a little peaked."

"It's the altitude. I thought Reno was bad." Somehow, during our bedroom escapades, altitude hadn't been an issue. Again, though, I might've felt like I couldn't get enough oxygen in bed with Ed, but it wasn't the altitude "We're lower here than Reno."

As if that helped.

"But still way above what I'm accustomed to."

They cocked their head. "Have you thought about what you're going to do after this assignment?"

I frowned. "What do you mean?"

They tapped my chest. "Well, usually you're in the process of lining up the next gig. This one only has a few more days, right?"

"Eight or nine, yeah." Panic clutched my chest. Not at the thought that I hadn't lined up the next project—although that was pretty crappy of me—but that we were moving inexorably closer to the big reveal, and I still hadn't spoken to Axel alone. "Post production will take weeks, Mickey. Maybe months."

"You know I'm doing some rough editing on the fly. I always do. Post isn't going to be nearly as complicated as you think."

Oh, they had no idea the shitshow I was about to drop in their lap. Guilt gnawed at me, but not enough to dissuade me from my mission. "Right, well we might be able to land another band while we're here."

"Or maybe there's a celebrity ready to reveal some huge secret." They tapped my chest again. "I know you've been trying to convince that country singer to talk about that relationship everyone knew about that ended so catastrophically."

"Yeah." I had been. Getting her side of the story—and then hopefully the guy's response—had been a priority. Before I landed the

Grindstone gig. Knowing this would likely be my last celebrity doc had me hesitating to reach out and try to build connections with other people.

Are you going to wind up filming horny zebras?

I didn't know. My family had enough money for me to live off of for years. And I could always pick up gigs here and there to supplement the money.

Would you be happy just lazing about? And what about the rest of the crew?

I couldn't answer either question. So I squeezed Mickey's arm. "Have a great night. The band has arranged an early rehearsal. Nerves, I think."

"Or they're hoping to be scouted."

"I doubt the execs are here this early." The grounds were still mostly empty. By tomorrow night, though, things would have picked up. "We need to do the interviews as well. Were you thinking in the tour bus or—"

"Sure, for one or two. I like the idea of you walking while you talk, you're good at that. Maybe with Axel? And then sitting outside. On a rock or something. That'd work with Ed."

They were right—about all of it. Of course they were. That's why they were a fantastic director. "I also want an interview with Pauletta herself. I'm pretty sure she'll go for it."

Mickey winked. "Oh, I can make that happen. Now, vamoose."

Following their directions, I exited their camper and headed back to the tour bus.

Is Mickey saying they might...have a thing for Pauletta?

Having never seen Mickey with a romantic or sexual partner, I didn't know how they chose people to be with intimately. I'd always figured none of my business.

Because it's not.

Pauletta? From the photos I'd spotted, she'd been either alone or with a man. Including a football player, a soccer player, a famous chef, and a tech entrepreneur from California. I couldn't discern that any of those helped with Grindstone's career aspirations, so I'd assumed they were chosen because she was attracted to them. Or something like that. Who knew the motivations of people these days?

You want Ed.

Yeah, I really did. Having one taste of him hadn't been enough. And, to my shame, I'd jerked off in the bathroom after he suggested I do so. Fantasizing him fucking me again, of course.

Upon entering the tour bus, I found the lights on. Seeing as night'd set in, that made sense.

Songbird and Meg stopped speaking as I approached.

Ed, scribbling furiously in a notebook, didn't look up.

Axel, scrolling on his phone, did look up. He gave me a perfunctory nod, then went back to his device.

Big Mac's soft snores carried from the back through the deafening silence.

At the tilt of my head, Songbird smiled. "He had six beers. Which is four more than he should. He's down for the count."

"Ah." As my bunk was directly below his, I cursed I hadn't thought to bring earplugs. "I'm going to head to bed."

Ed's head snapped up. He checked his watch. "It's barely nine."

I snickered. "You're the ones who are always up early."

Meg scrubbed at her knuckle. "Pauletta said we can sleep in."

"Ah."

"You got a problem with that?" Ed continued to regard me.

"No. Just hoping to interview each of you tomorrow. Mickey's scouted out a couple of viable locations for solo interviews and I still want to do one with the entire band. Not sure what the right setting for that is."

"I'd have thought you'd have everything planned down to the last detail."

I didn't detect malice in Ed's tone—but he wasn't teasing, either. "I do my best."

He held my gaze.

Then he blinked. A slow, lazy blink.

My cock tried to sit up and take notice.

Jesus, what are you, fifteen?

"Well, you have a good night." Ed quickly glanced at the others.

When he found no one was watching him, he winked.

I swallowed. As I headed toward the back, I tried to think of all the things I needed to do tomorrow as opposed to remembering how Ed's skin had shone in the diffuse light of the hotel room. Or how nice his cut cock was. Or how badly I wanted to give him a blow job. Worshiping said cock.

Which did nothing to curb my growing erection. Around Ed, I did feel like a randy, horny teenager.

After pissing and changing into my nightwear, I headed to my bunk.

Furious, hissing conversation carried to me—coming from the front. Some of the voices were higher while others hit a lower register.

Wonder what that's about. Me? Big Mac? The state of geopolitics?

I could always ask Ed in the morning.

And although I kept that thought in my mind as I plugged in my phone and settled in for the night, I didn't particularly hold on to the thought as my mind replayed the hotel room in Reno over and over again.

Half hard, I finally drifted off.

I woke first and stole a quick shower, then headed to the kitchen to put on the much-needed coffee. Vaguely, I worried the scent might wake the others. With no notion of what time most of them had gone to bed—or what shape Big Mac'd be in this morning—I had a moment's pause, but after that fraction of a second, I put the water in the maker and flipped it on. Coffee was non-negotiable.

Having forgotten my phone, I went back to grab it.

As I pivoted, someone smacked my ass.

I turned.

The hand disappeared back into Ed's bunk.

Well, okay then.

No one else made an immediate appearance, so I headed back to the kitchen. By the time the coffee had brewed, I had a rough outline of what I hoped to accomplish today.

Mickey had forwarded a couple of notes as well, and I integrated them into my document.

I checked the weather forecast, and nothing but sunny skies were predicted. Not a surprise, given we were in a desert, but I shuddered at the daytime high for today. Portland wasn't that much cooler, and it had more rain, but I just didn't want to admit we were well-entrenched into autumn. The long, lazy days of summer were gone.

Sipping my coffee, I again contemplated the future. I couldn't foresee a moment when Ed and I might be alone in the next four days. Even after leaving Black Rock, the time in LA and Portland seemed pretty crammed as well.

Vancouver felt like a million years from now instead of a week.

And when are you going to do the explosive gotcha interview?

A question I didn't have an answer for—could I fit in another fuck before I brought his world crumbling down?

I didn't know.

The fact I was hesitating at all shamed me. Each moment that passed where I wasn't laying the groundwork was a missed opportunity. A second that took me further and further away from my sister.

From my vengeance.

Ed plonked down onto the seat next to me, startling me.

He snagged my jaw and brought his lips to mine.

I sank into the kiss.

Time ceased to have meaning as his tongue lazily explored the recesses of my mouth. As his hand caressed down my front, trailed downward, and landed in my lap, I hardened.

I squirmed.

He grinned.

Then, as quickly as he'd sat down, he popped back up. "You made coffee."

I chuckled sardonically, shelving my horniness. "Seemed the least I could do."

Just as he plopped back down with his cup—only wearing sleep pants—Songbird emerged. She wore jeans and a sweater. She glanced over at Ed's bare, muscular, and sparsely covered chest. "How are you not freezing?"

I said, "I didn't put the kettle on to boil. Sorry."

She cocked her head as she regarded me. "Totally fine. I'm going to steal half a cup of coffee while the tea steeps. Then I'm whipping up eggs, bacon, and toast for everyone."

"Oh." I swallowed. "Can I help?"

A snicker escaped. "This kitchen is not designed for more than one person." She considered. "Well, you can help Axel prepare sandwiches at lunch."

"That's all we trust him to do," Ed muttered.

I suppressed a grin. "I'm happy to help."

"We've got a frozen lasagna and garlic bread for dinner." Songbird opened the fridge and started unloading eggs, bacon, and some vegetables. Then she pulled the bread from the breadbox.

"You guys prepare most of your own meals?"

Songbird considered. "Sometimes. The food trucks are pretty good here, but, personally, I like to control the food. Wouldn't do for us to get food poisoning or something."

Honestly, I hadn't given that much thought. I'd brought a pile of cash and expected to grab something along the way. "I should be contributing to your food."

She pointed a knife at me. "We can afford a few eggs and peppers. I don't know if we'll have enough lasagna to share. You'll have to beg Ed." She pivoted back to cleaning the pepper.

I glanced over at Ed.

"Sure." He winked. "I'm always game to share."

Soon enough, the bus smelled like frying bacon. Whether awakened by that smell or because of the coffee, Meg and Big Mac eventually appeared.

Axel was the last to arrive—timing it perfectly to get the last cup of coffee and the first plate of food.

He endured the good-natured ribbing as he devoured his crispy bacon.

Songbird served me next.

I snagged the bacon, then tried to push my plate toward Ed.

He held out his hand.

Reading something of a warning in his dark eyes, I dug into the food.

As the meal started to wind down, and the last of the bacon was fought over—Meg won—I pulled out my phone.

"Mickey's prepared a tentative shooting schedule. If you let me know what time you're rehearsing, we can put together each of the interviews."

"Each." Big Mac suddenly appeared a little queasy. A little green.

"Dude." Axel nudged him. "This is what we agreed to. Price of fame." He high-fived Meg, who appeared way more interested.

"We've got a couple of minutes on the stage this morning. Not a rehearsal...more just a walkthrough." Ed speared the last pepper. "Then we can follow whatever schedule Mickey has planned."

Songbird raised her hand as if wanting to be called on in third grade. "Oh, can I go first? I like to get shit over with, so I can relax."

"Of course."

Mickey had scheduled Big Mac first and Songbird second. Judging by Big Mac's gripping of his gut, I wondered if he'd make it at all.

In the end, though, the band did their tour of the stage, and I managed to get through interviews with Songbird, Big Mac, Meg, and Axel.

We'd thought to do him last, but Ed pushed him to go ahead.

Which left Ed as my final interview.

Chapter Twenty-One

Ed

I didn't want to be the last interview. I didn't want to be interviewed at all.

Technically, I wasn't last.

Mickey had talked Pauletta into something or other, but they planned that for tomorrow.

Part of me liked that Paulie was included in everything.

Part of me worried just what she might say.

Not that she'd reveal our secrets—I had faith in her. No, more that, at times, she felt even more ambitious than I did. Sometimes I felt she hyped us a bit too much.

The counselor I'd spoken to in therapy had tried to work on my self-esteem. She didn't point out that, as an aspiring rock star, I needed to be more…whatever. She was also tactful enough not to blame my upbringing. How I'd spent as much time as possible making myself as small as possible. Although I knew my lack of height wasn't because of that—I understood genetics—I couldn't help thinking that if I'd stood straighter, if I'd had more confidence, then maybe I might've been taller. Or at least felt less self-conscious.

All this flitted through my mind as I waited for Mickey to work with Lydia and Kato for the perfect shot. Apparently they'd intended to have a walk-and-talk with Songbird, but she found a perching spot she liked, so they rolled with it.

"You mind walking?" Thornton caught my gaze.

"As long as it's on even ground. It'd be pretty shitty if I tripped."

"If you trip, I promise we'll edit it out."

He said the words with absolute seriousness.

I believed him.

"Yeah, okay." I fingered my sunglasses.

"I didn't let Axel wear his."

"Oh, I bet that went over well."

Thornton shrugged impishly. "Mickey can be persuasive."

Thinking about how they'd wrangled an interview with Pauletta, I couldn't argue.

"Okay, no sunglasses."

Lunch had already come and gone.

True to his word, Thornton had helped Axel make ham-and-lettuce sandwiches. He took his with mayo.

I preferred mustard.

While I brushed my teeth, he'd spirited Axel away for their interview.

I'd paced in the bus.

Meg bitched.

I snapped.

Big Mac tried to run interference.

Songbird grabbed both of them, and the three headed out.

The entire time, Pauletta continued to tap away on her laptop as if our angst was of no consequence.

Okay, *my* angst.

I wanted to demand to know how she could be so calm—but remaining calm was Paulie's gift.

And I did well when I remembered that.

I wasn't the hotheaded one—that was Axel. I wasn't the zen one—that was Songbird. I wasn't the oblivious one—that was Meg. I wasn't the funny one—that was Big Mac.

Me? I was the intense one. The one who ran roughshod over the group when Paulie wasn't around to do it. The one who kept us focused. The one who sweated the details.

"You okay?"

Caught off-guard, I gazed up into dark-amber eyes, shaded as Thornton faced away from the sun. In fact, he shaded me as well.

"I'm not going to lie—I'm nervous. This isn't usually my thing. I mean, I love that you're speaking to each of us. Even if you don't use all the footage…I appreciate that you're making each member feel important."

"Because it's usually all about Axel?"

"Well, frankly, yeah. He's the lead singer."

"When you break out, the rest of you will feel an increased scrutiny. More spotlight, if you want."

"I don't want."

"You might not have a say." He grinned. "A reluctant rock star?"

The way he said that made my insides go all liquid. He understood me. He got it. Most people didn't—including the other members of the band. They played a good game at being reticent. But each had returned from their interview with Thornton with huge grins on their faces.

"We're ready." Mickey popped up next to us. "All set?"

Thornton met my gaze.

I nodded.

He turned back to Mickey and gave them a thumbs-up.

Within moments, Lydia and Kato stepped before us.

Mickey made the signal to start.

Thornton flashed me a grin. "So...music..."

"Yeah, pretty much."

We started walking.

After a moment, I filled the void. "I've known Axel since we started kindergarten together. We liked to bang on the drums. Drove Miss Slater nuts."

"But a friendship was cemented."

I chuckled. "You could say that. Even back then, he always wanted to be center stage whenever the class sang. With his voice, teachers naturally gave him bigger and bigger roles."

"And you?"

"The quiet, behind-the-scenes friend. Encouraging. Supporting. Never wanting the spotlight for himself."

"And that worked?"

"It did. We, uh, didn't go to the best school in town. Our administrators made do. We had some really outstanding teachers—and some crappy ones—but we did okay." I glanced down at my worn running shoes. *Should've worn boots*.

"And..."

"And Axel won a singing contest in the fifth grade, and then he coerced me into doing a lip-sync contest in the seventh grade."

"Coerced?" Thornton laughed. "You don't seem like a guy who doesn't do exactly what he wants."

I cut him a glance.

And nearly tripped.

Fuck.

"Looks can be deceiving. I'm very much able to be coerced under the right circumstances."

"That's funny. The rest of the band feel you're the glue that holds everything together."

Again, I looked up at him.

I appreciated he'd put a bit of distance between us so the height difference wasn't quite as obvious. If I'd thought about this, I would've picked something that didn't...emphasize my lack of height.

Get over it.

"Glue, eh?" I scratched my chin, glad I'd shaved.

"Songbird's word."

"She would be the most articulate one." I wanted to add she could also shovel shit. Almost as good as Paulie.

Almost.

"And Big Mac says you make him want to be a better bassist."

"Yeah?"

"Yeah."

"He's got mad skills."

"Meg says you're mush inside."

"She would say that." *Please don't let the camera pick up my heated cheeks.* My darker coloring usually did a good job of hiding blushes. But if the light hit me just right—

"And Axel says you've pulled him out of more than a few scrapes."

My gaze shot to his. Then I looked up toward the camera. Finally, I looked back at Thornton. "Well, twenty-two years is a long time. We grew up together. Haven't all friends rescued each other at some point?" What the fuck had Axel said? He hadn't given me the heads-up as we'd passed on the tour bus, so obviously nothing that worried him.

He needed to worry more.

"Has he ever rescued you?"

Something in Thornton's tone had my ears perking up. "Sure." I continued walking forward, trying to think of an appropriate answer. "I might've been in an ill-advised relationship a couple of years back—"

"How far back?"

"Maybe three years." I didn't appreciate the interruption as I struggled to get back on track. "Sometimes friends see things we don't. They have to walk a fine line between offering unsolicited advice and flat-out saying what needs to be said." I would never disparage Demelza by name—or even give enough details for anyone except the band to figure out who I was talking about.

"Ill-advised?"

"We wanted...different things. I was really focused on the music—still am—and I missed what, in retrospect, were obvious problems. I'd like to think I'm sensitive, but sometimes I miss what's right in front of me."

"Care to elaborate?"

"Not this time." I offered a small smile. "Axel and I had a music teacher in the ninth grade who helped us get old, beat-up guitars. I have to say, I didn't take to it like Axel did."

"And yet you're the lead guitarist in the band."

"Yeah." I ran my hand along the back of my neck. "I still thought the way out of poverty was to study hard and get into college. Or a trade. Or anything that provided a steady income. I never dreamed I could make a living at music."

"But things changed?"

I blew out a quick breath. "Mr. Threadgold said Axel and I had talent. I didn't think he was blowing smoke up our asses—" I winced. "Shit. Probably no swearing, right?" *And you just said shit, which was way worse...* Rock stars swore all the time, but I didn't want my words bleeped if the interview was marketed for younger audiences. The kids I wanted to inspire.

"We can bleep the curse words. I'd prefer you be yourself."

I gazed at Thornton. Again, sincerity shone through. I still didn't trust him. I took a breath and let it out slowly. "Mr. Threadgold gave us extra lessons, and soon, Axel and I started entering talent contests. We even won a couple small ones. Again, with Mr. Treadgold's help, we got electric guitars and an old crappy amp. The rest, as they say, is history."

"Ah." Thornton looked over at me. "I suspect that's the PG version of the story."

"Well, you wouldn't be wrong." I winced. "We started writing songs and playing bars on weekends. We did some rock 'n'roll stuff that we're not proud of."

"Drinking?"

Hesitantly, I nodded.

"Drugs?"

I held his gaze. "Shit I'm not proud of. But we've been clean almost eight years."

"Since you were nineteen? That feels improbable."

"Yeah, I know. But Pauletta, our manager, sat us down and laid down the law. She said we could keep drinking and fooling around and not taking things seriously, or we could become viable musicians with a real band."

"You chose a real band."

I nodded. "Seemed like the better choice. Some of us had alcoholics in our family—"

"You?"

"I didn't say that."

Thornton held up his hands, making me feel silly for my overreaction.

"My mother had...other issues." *God, do I really want to go down this road?* "She had emotional issues that...led to chronic employment problems. I tried to help her, when I started making some money." I let out a breath. "Some people just can't be helped."

"Are you saying—"

"She killed herself a couple of years ago." I looked over Lydia—off toward the stage. "I don't talk about it because I don't want people to feel sorry for me. You know, the guy who never knew his dad and whose mother killed herself."

"I'm sure—"

"But I think some people with mental health issues can be helped. I wrote "Calling for Help" precisely because I wanted people to know...that there were others out there who wanted to be there for them." *Shit*. "I would've done anything I could to help her...but she didn't want it. She wasn't selfish...she was just unwell."

"That's a tough legacy."

I blew out yet another breath. "I've surrounded myself with folks who care about me—and who I care about in return. I don't think I could've done more for my mother—but I never want to feel I left anything on the table with other people I care about."

"That's pretty profound. I got the sense those feelings were returned by your bandmates."

"Yeah, I think so. There's a helpline in Canada that asked if they could use our song. We were happy to agree." And if we ever made it big, we'd give the proceeds from sales of the song to that charity—but we weren't there yet. *We have to land a deal.*

"Ed?"

"Huh?" I blinked. "Sorry." I gestured as if I could explain away my momentary lapse.

"I asked if there was ever anyone else in your life that you wish you could've helped but didn't?"

Kyesha.

Her image flashed in my mind, and her name was on the tip of my tongue. But nothing except pain could come from dredging up her memory. And, undoubtedly, the story would cast both Axel and myself in an unpleasant light.

"I'm sure I've screwed up." I offered a small smile. "But I've had fans write and say how "Calling for Help" encouraged them to reach out. I take those notes to heart."

"But surely there's someone in your past who you might've helped, but failed to do so. Some regret deep within you."

Jesus, does he know? Or is he fishing?

Don't trust him.

"No. There's no one. We've lived pretty normal, boring lives."

Thornton looked like he was about to say more, but then he offered up what I thought of as a measured smile.

"And you're here. Rocktoberfest. Pretty amazing."

With some regret, I let Kyesha go and moved on.

Chapter Twenty-Two

Thornton

Ed's honesty about his mother nearly slayed me.

His unwillingness to admit to the mistake he made with my sister enraged me.

Axel'd been no better.

I'd read in an article from a few years ago that he came from an abusive household. I'd given him every opportunity to open up about that, but he'd dodged, weaved, and made jokes. And he'd been far less forthcoming about the substance-abuse problem. He'd downplayed it, even when I pointed out he didn't drink. He quipped that he didn't even smoke pot—which was a shame since it'd been legal in Canada for almost five years.

Axel kept me on my toes. His effervescence hid his more-serious side, and I just couldn't get him to talk about anything without making a joke. I shouldn't care, but I worried he might come off as inauthentic. As uncaring.

Why do you give a fuck what people think of him?

I shouldn't. In fact, if he came across as someone who didn't take things seriously, then his role in my sister's death would make him seem callous and unfeeling.

All the better to nail him with.

Yes. A nail in his coffin.

And Ed's too.

Except...Ed didn't come across as the uncaring type. He seemed sincere. The praise from all his bandmates—even Axel, who didn't seem to take anything seriously—came across as genuine. I intended to try to drill down on this with Pauletta.

Mickey had prepared a series of questions for me to ask Pauletta.

With the others, I'd let things meander. I'd gone in with a list of questions, but hadn't felt obliged to stick to the script.

With Pauletta, it'd be different.

Meg, Big Mac, and Songbird were all much-newer to the party—picked up well after the period of sobriety had begun.

Pauletta, however, had clearly been part of forcing the guys to sober up.

Or at least that was the impression Ed left me with.

Axel hadn't been clear on any details. Made me wonder how much he actually remembered about that point in his life.

"Thornton."

"Yeah?" I gazed up from the notes I hadn't been reading to meet Mickey's gaze. "What?"

"I asked if you were ready for your interview with Pauletta."

"Uh—"

"Three times." They snapped their fingers in front of my face. "What gives? You've been off since the interview with Markham. I thought you did a good job."

"Ed...yeah..."

They arched an eyebrow. "Oh, like that, is it? Something you want to tell me?"

"No."

"If that's how you want to play it. I wasn't sure about you staying with the band—"

"You saw the footage I shot."

"Didn't say you didn't do a passable job."

"And I used some of what I learned in those interviews. I'll use more when I interview the entire band."

"Tomorrow."

"Right, tomorrow."

They continued to stare.

"Look, you know I have an excellent memory." I pointed to their questions. "I've got this nailed." I winced at the word as I thought about the nail I was planning to put in Ed and Axel's coffins. No need to think that way with Pauletta.

"Right. Whatever. Kato's got the fire going, and Lydia's set up the camera. I wasn't sure about this idea, but I think the firelight bouncing off Pauletta will make her glow."

Glow?

I wouldn't necessarily have chosen that word, but I agreed this would be a different shoot than what we'd done before.

Pauletta's idea.

Mickey and I left the camper and headed over to the fire.

As promised, Lydia and Kato had everything organized.

Even as I had the thought, Pauletta appeared—coming out of the darkness and into the bright firelight. She spotted me and extended her hand.

We shook.

I pointed to Lydia and Kato.

She nodded.

I indicated Mickey.

Pauletta slowly nodded, taking an assessing perusal of my friend that she hadn't offered either Kato or Lydia.

Interesting.

I told her, "We secured a couple of sturdy camp chairs. Otherwise, we can try to drag over a picnic table or something—"

Pauletta held up her hand. "Camp chairs are perfect." She indicated her jeans, chambray shirt, and wool jacket. "Casual, right?"

Which was in stark contrast to the polished appearance she always had. I couldn't discern her reasoning behind this outfit choice, but I figured it'd either make sense to me by the end of the interview or I'd be left scratching my head.

Could go either way.

We sat.

Mickey indicated we were filming and stepped away.

Pauletta tracked them until they nearly vanished. Then she pivoted her attention back to me.

I smiled. "You're the manager for the up-and-coming band, Grindstone."

She grinned back. "I am. I'm hoping they'll be an overnight-ten-years-in-the-making success story."

"And you've been with them almost that entire time."

"I have. It's been quite a ride."

"What attracted you to Axel and Ed?"

She tapped her chin. "I saw them in a dive bar off Commercial Drive in Vancouver. I just…I saw such potential. I'm only a few years older than them. I'd just finished a business program at university and I saw an opportunity. I talked them into letting me take over as their manager. Let's just say the relationship proved mutually beneficial. I helped them get their act together—so to speak—and they gave me carte blanche to build them into the band they are today."

"Impressive." I crossed my legs. "Both Ed and Axel have admitted they were...rough."

After a moment, Pauletta smiled. "They've admitted to enjoying the booze a little too much? Yes, I convinced them sobriety was the way to go. I proved to them that they did their best work while sober. From there, we got them into small venues. We eventually added Big Mac on bass, Meg on drums, and Songbird on keys. When the five are together, they make magic."

"True. But you'd say Axel and Ed are the heart of the band. Without them, there's no Grindstone, right?"

"Sure." She cocked her head. "I suppose if they left, then the other three might look for another lead singer. But that's not going to happen. They've been through so much as a band—trying to make it big."

"And you think Rocktoberfest is the venue for that?"

"Just watch us." She grinned, letting a flash of teeth show. "I think we're on the cusp of something huge."

We continued with a few more questions about her business acumen, her mentoring program, and her general take on the music industry. I tried to circle back to her involvement with Axel and Ed during those early days, but she smoothly shut it down.

Eventually, I wrapped the interview.

When Mickey gave the signal the interview was over, Pauletta and I both managed to get out of the damn camp chairs, which sat way too low to the ground for two tall people.

"Sorry about that." Mickey advanced toward us.

I offered my hand to Pauletta.

She shook.

"Ms. Magnum..." Mickey swallowed.

Pauletta pivoted her attention to my director. "Yes?"

"I wanted to pass a couple of ideas by you. Do you have a moment?" To my surprise, they shook slightly—completely incongruous from the person I knew them to be.

"Of course." Pauletta offered a huge grin. "Looking forward to it."

Mickey held their notepad to their chest like a shield and pointed to a picnic bench. "Maybe now? It's a lovely evening and not too many bugs. Oh, unless you need to drive back to your hotel. I mean, you're probably tired and need to be getting back. This can wait until tomorrow, right? I'm sure—"

Pauletta placed a hand over Mickey's fingers. "Now's perfect."

"Great." They indicated the table.

"I'll grab you something to drink." I turned to Pauletta. "Do you have a preference...?"

"A cola or root beer or whatever you've got."

"One root beer coming up." I moved swiftly, grabbing two root beers from the cooler. I wiped off the condensation, then took them over to the table.

Both offered me a smile, although Mickey's was discernably tighter.

I took my leave, then headed over to the camper.

Lydia and Kato sat next to each other, watching the replay on a small screen.

"And?"

"We're watching the interview with Axel."

"Why?" I would've figured they'd be watching Pauletta—in case anything needed to be reshot. We didn't generally do that, but sometimes things happened.

"He said something..." Lydia tapped her finger. "About the past..." She looked up. "You remember."

"I do." And I did. The little monologue I planned to entrap him with. Had Lydia seen the trap I'd set?

"Something's not sitting right with me." Lydia hit pause.

She and Kato both looked up at me.

I held up my hands. "It's a documentary. I ask questions that lead in whatever direction is necessary."

Please believe me.

"Sure." Kato sipped his diet soda. "Whatever. We trust you."

I sought confirmation from Lydia. But I didn't get it. She continued to gaze at me with her green cat's eyes unblinking.

"Well, I have to head back to the tour bus. We've got the group interview tomorrow, right?"

Lydia blinked. "Just the five of them, right? Well, and you."

"Yes, Pauletta won't be in the shot."

"I still would prefer to have a camera for each person."

"I know you would, Lydia, but this isn't that kind of shoot—isn't that kind of documentary. We're going for an *in the wild* feel for it. The less the audience feels our presence, the better."

"Sure." To me, she didn't sound convinced.

"I should go."

"Yeah, go." Kato waved me off. "We've got this."

"And you'll watch out for Mickey."

"Mickey can handle themself." Lydia met my gaze. "Unless there's something you're not telling us."

"True. They can handle themself. Also true that they have a crush on Pauletta."

"Don't see anything wrong with that." Kato grabbed a bag of generic potato chips and opened it. Spicy Dijon mustard.

"That a Canadian thing?" I pointed to the bag.

"You bet." He grinned. "They have this company that makes the wackiest flavors. Kettle chips too, you know? The thick ones." He popped one into his mouth.

Lydia glared. Then obviously considered. Then must have given up whatever argument she was about to make and grabbed one for herself.

"Hey."

"You can share." She popped it into her mouth and chewed thoughtfully. She took a swig of pop. "That's spicy."

"But good, right?" Kato nudged her.

"Yeah." Lydia studied the bag and, after a moment, grabbed another one. "Good."

I said, "On that note, I'm outta here."

Before they asked me to try a chip.

Or pushed me on what my ulterior motive was.

Chapter Twenty-Three

Ed

Thornton had an ulterior motive.

For the life of me, though, I couldn't figure it out.

I tried querying Axel.

He claimed he had no idea, thought Thornton and his crew were *good people*, and told me to lighten up.

Songbird, Meg, and Big Mac weren't any more helpful.

I would've queried Pauletta, but she hadn't come back after her interview.

Leaving me stumped.

In retrospect, his questions, during our interview, seemed too pointed. Too precise. Like he wanted me to say something specific. And that he'd been disappointed when I hadn't.

Thornton eventually appeared, but I was too wrung out to deal with my emotions at seeing him. Instead, I headed to bed.

In the morning, I didn't feel like waking everyone by making coffee. I dressed in jeans, a Henley, a warm coat, and I headed out.

I didn't make it more than ten feet before I caught sight of a guy leaving his tour bus.

As I watched, the tall man spun back, pulled himself up the first step, and kissed the man on the stairs. The gesture felt as natural as breathing. As if they'd done it a hundred times before.

You're gawking.

Yeah, I was. Possibly because I wanted that kind of uninhibited freedom to show my affection to Thornton. But, not only was the documentary standing in the way, but we were both in the closet. Even if my bandmates had figured out something was going on, I wasn't free to be open with Thornton.

Looking away from the intimate scene, I caught sight of the logo on the bus.

Holy shit. Hellsbane and Blade.

The breakout band from last year's Rocktoberfest.

Which meant that big, bearded guy was Erik Svenson.

I didn't recognize the man he kissed, although between the man's hair and the early shadows, I likely wouldn't have anyway.

Erik stepped down and closed the door of the bus.

He turned and saw me.

I held up my hand. "Sorry."

He grinned. "I don't hide who I am." He glanced over at the bus. "Or who I love." His grin widened. "Well, I have some secrets." He advanced toward me and indicated our bus. "You're from Vancouver, right? I snagged a copy of your latest album when I heard you'd be here."

Well, fuck me. Erik Svenson had heard of us.

"We have all your albums." I tried for a smile. "I really like "Cracks and Mended Places." Oh, and the song you debuted here last year, "Consequences"? Brilliant." My smile broadened. "Any chance I can meet Blade?" Blade was his mysterious singing partner. "Oh, and are you doing the hologram thing again this year? I didn't see it, but a friend was down here and said she'd never seen anything so cool."

Oh my God, shut the fuck up.

Erik indicated the direction of the food. "I'm grabbing a coffee."

"You don't have that on your bus?"

"I do." He considered. "I wanted to give my partner time to do his yoga and meditation. Another coffee never goes amiss."

"Fair enough."

We fell into step together.

"You're playing tomorrow night, right?"

I nearly tripped. "Yeah, we've got an early slot on Friday. You're Sunday?"

"Yep." His grin was infectious. "I have special memories of this place."

"You landed a record contract, right?"

"Not exactly. We walked away from one that had strings we didn't like. But Rocktoberfest broke us out of the pack, and we signed with a better label later."

"That's our dream." I stood beside him as we joined the lineup. "Our manager's amazing."

Erik chuckled. "We didn't even have a manager this time last year. We've come a long way."

"Overnight success ten years in the making?"

He fingered his long, blond hair. "Something like that. You have the same plans?"

"We're debuting a new song that we hope will generate some buzz. Would help if we had a novelty like a hologram."

"Sure, I guess. But if our music sucked, no amount of fancy wizardry would've captured the crowd's attention. Or gotten us the contract." He gave his order to the young woman with the coffee. Then he pointed to a kruller and a donut.

She offered him a soft smile as she prepared his coffee and put the two gooey concoctions into a mini paper box.

I managed to swipe my card before he could.

He glowered.

"I plan to pick your brain. I can afford coffee and a couple of donuts."

He arched an eyebrow.

I grinned. "Table in the shade?"

"Has to be. Even at this hour, I fry red like a lobster.

"A man with a dead-pale complexion,

"Must avoid any solar connection.

"Lying out in the nude

"Would fry parts of that dude

"And cause sunburny pain on erection."

He coughed behind his hand. "Sorry. Limericks just seem to come out of my mouth."

We became fast friends.

An hour and a half later, I returned to the bus.

Big Mac huddled outside.

"What...?"

"Meg said I was pissing her off and to take a hike. But the documentary crew is going to be here soon, so I figured I'd piss off Pauletta if I actually did take a hike." He glanced down at his army boots, jeans, band T-shirt, and thin jean jacket.

"And not really dressed for a hike?"

He glared. "Hiking is not my thing."

"I'm not certain she meant literally anyway. You could've just gone to your bunk."

"They said they were having a girls' meeting."

"Where's Axel?"

"In there with them."

Okay, that made only a sliver of sense to me. Axel could be...more empathetic...to women.

When he wasn't trying to figure out how to get in their pants.

Big Mac pointed to my coffee and raised an eyebrow.

I indicated the tour bus several spots away.

"No shit. Hellsbane and Blade?"

"Yeah, I just spent the last hour shooting the shit with Erik Svenson."

"Aw, shit."

"They're around for the weekend. I think Jase is doing the drum-off competition. And Erik's entering the shred-off for guitars."

Big Mac pouted. "Pauletta wouldn't let us enter. I bet Meg could've beaten Jase."

"I'm not sure I'd let Jase hear that." I said the words in jest. I'd heard nothing but great things about all the members of Hellsbane. Which made me even more curious about their mystery front man, Blade.

Lydia, Kato, and Mickey appeared—popping out from behind another bus. All three wore matching grins.

Well, Mickey's felt...extra wide.

"Lovely morning," they said.

"Hello, Mickey." I stepped forward. "Anything I can help with? That's a lot of equipment."

"We've got it," they assured me. "Is, uh, Pauletta here? We planned to coordinate with her," they quickly added.

A blush stole across their cheeks.

Okay. Interesting.

"The ladies and Axel are all inside." I pounded on the door. Then offered a grin to the gathered crowd. "Oh, where's Thornton?"

"Here." He popped out from the same direction as his crew'd come from, carrying what appeared to be a camera bag as well as a tripod.

The bus door opened, and Pauletta stuck her head out. She set her sights on me. "You didn't have to pound."

"Hey, it might've been Big Mac—"

"Dude, do not throw me under the bus—" Mac pouted.

"Are we interrupting?"

We all pivoted to face Mickey.

Pauletta's breath caught. "No. Sorry, family squabbles. We're, uh, ready. Truly. Yeah, come in."

My manager and friend was verklempt—for the first time in the almost ten years I'd known her.

Lydia led the way, following Pauletta into the bus.

Mickey followed, with Kato on her heels.

Thornton thrust the tripod into my hands, grinned, then followed.

I glanced over at Big Mac.

He shrugged.

We both got on the bus.

The next two hours felt completely surreal.

Mickey and Lydia each took control of a camera.

Kato and Pauletta stood back. Out of the way.

The five of us from the band, with Thornton in the mix, sat around and shot the shit. We meandered through the beginnings of the band. The highs and the lows of being indie. The advantages of being a mixture of ethnicities, cultures, and genders. The refusal to be branded more than necessary. Which led to a discussion of the arbitrariness of categories.

As we laughed, recalling antics, I sank into a feeling of rightness. Meg and Big Mac would continue on with their...relationship. Pauletta might keep making longing eyes at Mickey—who appeared to return the notice. Songbird's solidity would continue to ground the group. Axel and I would continue to compose songs that not only showed our vulnerability but also the range of talent of the group.

Even if we flopped at Rocktoberfest and didn't land a contract, we'd be okay.

I stole a covert glance at Thornton.

Well, mostly okay.

The time he'd spent with us paid off as we opened up to him much faster than we might've if he were a total stranger.

In other words—his tactics worked.

I'd doubted him, but I shouldn't have. *Let this be a warning*.

"What's one thing you can share that your fans don't know?" Thornton leaned back.

Axel sat up straighter. "I'll go first."

Thornton indicated he should continue.

"That sometimes I don't seem to take things seriously." He met my gaze. "I've been diagnosed with ADHD. My brain doesn't necessarily work the same way as everyone else's. I try, but I come across as scatterbrained and unfocused."

"Hey—"

He cut me off. "I want to do better. Being here—" He swept his hand around the space. "—this is the chance of a lifetime, and I need to step up to the plate."

Meg fingered his hair. "We all bring something different to the table. Your vocals? People melt inside when they hear your voice."

"And we're all different." Songbird drew in a deep breath. "I was diagnosed with chronic depression in my late teens. The doctors tried all kinds of things, but only medication works. If I didn't have the antidepressant, I don't know where I'd be. I'm privileged to have wonderful doctors and enough money to pay for the meds." She waved her hand as if to indicate this wasn't a big deal.

My jaw dropped. I'd no idea.

Meg raised her hand.

We pivoted our attention to her.

"Songbird's being brave—so will I."

To my surprise, she met my gaze.

"My mother died of breast cancer when I was really young. And...last year I did some genetic testing." She fidgeted. "Turns out I have an incredibly high risk for cancer. So high that the doctor recommended thinking about a double mastectomy."

I nodded.

"And...I'm thinking about it. Hard. Because between having boobs or living a long time, I really do choose to live a long time."

"Yeah." Axel reached over and squeezed her knee. "Like, we really need you."

We all sort of half-chuckled.

"But that means taking serious time off. First the surgery, then reconstruction, then recovery." She swallowed as she met all of our gazes.

Well, all except Big Mac's.

"I worry you'll think of me differently."

Songbird, who sat next to her, pulled her in for a hug. "Never. You'll always be the best drummer, and friend, ever."

"Yeah, well, that's it."

Big Mac cleared his throat.

We turned our attention to him.

"I don't have anything." He looked toward Meg.

She wouldn't meet his gaze.

"Like, I'm a little goofy." He pointed to Axel. "But not so I want people to notice. I just want to be the best bassist I can. I'm happy to be in the background—as long as I can make music."

"That's fair." For the first time, Thornton drew attention to himself. "This is more than I expected."

"Sorry you asked?" Meg winked. "Wanted to give audiences their money's worth."

Relief flooded me as I realized we were moving on.

"So, Ed, anything to share? Some dark secret hiding in your closet?"

Fucking hell.

Schooling my features, I met Thornton's gaze.

At least he had the decency not to smirk.

I chanced a glance over at Pauletta.

Her expression was a mixture of wariness and anticipation. Her words about coming out rang through my mind.

The loss of fans flashed in my head.

All the kids who might finally felt seen also held a place.

I smiled. "Well, I haven't been living my authentic self." I indicated to my bandmates. "Nothing so big. Although I think Big Mac could've admitted the time he accidentally mooned the crowd in Mission City."

"Hey." His cheeks flared with color. "Hashtag belt fail."

We all laughed.

"Such a lovely, scrawny, white ass." Finally, Meg looked at him.

My breath caught.

Something in her expression said vulnerability.

"The audience seemed to enjoy it." He stuck out his chin.

"There's a video, buried on YouTube," Axel offered.

"Won't stay buried for long," Thornton commented.

We laughed.

Thornton turned his attention back to me.

I cleared my throat. *You can always say no. Consent's a thing.*

But I wouldn't be a chickenshit.

"I'm bisexual."

Thornton's amber eyes flashed with what looked like surprise.

Huh, I wasn't saying what he expected.

Which raised the question of *what* he'd expected.

I didn't have time to dwell on that. "I've always been attracted to both men and women."

"Not to me," Axel quipped.

"Thank Christ, no." I gave an exaggerated wince. "But I've dated women publicly and men privately. I love both—and so it's time for me to say that out loud. Bisexuals get a bad rap because we can't 'make up our minds'." I used air quotes. "The truth is, I enjoy everyone's company. I'd even go as far to say I'm pansexual because I don't believe in the binary of gender."

"That's a controversial position."

"Only to people with closed minds," I challenged. "I'm attracted to the person." I tapped my chest. "To who they are. Not how they identify."

"So we might see you with a man in the future?"

I held Thornton's gaze. "That depends on whether or not the man wants to be seen with me."

Meg hooted. "Oh, honey, who wouldn't want to be with a sexy beast like you?"

Heat flooded my face.

Songbird pecked me on the cheek.

Everyone laughed.

Somehow, I made it through the wrap-up of the interview.

How I managed, though, I was never sure.

Chapter Twenty-Four

Thornton

Well, fuck me sideways.

Hadn't seen that coming.

Like, holy shit.

Here, I'd been hoping he might slip up and say something incriminating about my sister and his role in her death.

Instead, he'd come out.

And basically challenged me to do the same.

My head spun as I helped Lydia secure her equipment. Pauletta and Mickey had encouraged everyone—except Kato, Lydia, and myself—to exit the bus for *a breath of fresh air*.

Kato tried to shoo me out, but I held firm that I was helping with takedown.

The last thing I wanted was to be anywhere near Ed at the moment.

Lydia zipped up the one bag. "So, that was pretty intense."

Kato snickered. "You think? I can't imagine casually discussing having body parts removed—"

I elbowed him in the ribs.

"What? I'm saying it in an admiring way. You can get cancer of the—" He leaned in conspiratorially. "—of the balls."

"It's called testicular cancer." Lydia expertly collapsed the tripod. "Jesus, you can be so juvenile."

"Uh, right." Kato blushed.

"I think the word you're looking for is brave." Lydia thrust the tripod into my waiting hands. "We got everything?"

Looking around, I couldn't spot anything missing. "I think so."

"You going to collect your stuff and join us?"

My eyes widened. "You expect me to give up this luxury to what...sleep on an air mattress?"

"It's a comfortable mattress." Kato winked. "We'd be sharing."

"Great." I winced. "Unless Pauletta or one of the others asks me to leave, I'm staying. Just because we got *the* interview, doesn't mean more won't happen. I still have the small handheld camera. I might ask if I can get more footage of them goofing off. Or having a serious conversation. Plus, Ed writes poetry and Meg draws. I'm hoping to get a look at those notebooks."

"Love poems?" Kato smirked. "Hoping to find a way into his heart?"

"Fuck off."

Lydia poked my chest. "Keep this up, and we'll have to put a disclosure on the video. You'll be out—whether you want to be or not."

"I didn't—"

"Fuck, Thornton, I'd have to be blind to miss the way you look at him." Her deep-green eyes shone. "I've always taken my job seriously."

"I know."

"I do this for a living."

"I know."

"So do Kato and Mickey."

"I know."

"Then why are you fucking with the job? Is he worth it? Or is he just a piece of ass? Because I'm pretty sure you could find someone else in this sea of tens of thousands of people to scratch that itch."

Her words hit me.

Hard.

She was right. I was jeopardizing everything. Not just the documentary—and the three people whose careers were riding on it—but also of ever holding Axel and Ed accountable for my sister's death.

"We're filming rehearsal tonight, right? Do we have permission to film other bands, for background?"

"Mickey's working on that. I know they got one of them to agree—as long as we promise not to air any footage until after the weekend."

"That's good of them."

"They've also got a line on two other bands as well. Fingers crossed. I'm hoping someone will be interested in us handing over some of the stuff we don't use—promo material, that kind of thing."

"Sounds good."

"Thornton."

"Yes?" I'd been looking out the window at the gathered group, but my head snapped up at her calling my name.

"Is he worth it?" Her incisive eyes bore into me.

"Does it matter? We go our separate ways in a week."

"Then don't blow everything over something that can't go anywhere." She grabbed her camera bag and hauled it over her shoulder. "We're good."

"Yeah...good..."

Kato grinned. "Man, you've got it bad."

Yes. Yes, I did.

When we exited the bus, Lydia unsubtly nudged me toward our camper. Having no way to get out of the job—short of dumping everything on Mickey—I was stuck tromping back with the gear.

I'd tried to catch Ed's gaze, but hadn't managed. Aside from being scheduled to shoot the rehearsal in a couple of hours, I couldn't come up with a single excuse to head back to the tour bus—especially given that Mickey appeared and wanted to review all the footage from this morning.

We huddled around the laptop and watched.

Lydia'd done a masterful job of catching each person as they gave their revelation.

We also needed to review the other angles, but I was quick to admit today was some of our best work.

"Too soon to open a bottle of bubbly, but damn..." Mickey sat back and put their arms behind their head.

Kato grinned. "Seeing Pauletta later?"

Mickey sat up straighter. "To coordinate filming rehearsal."

"You two sat out talking for an awful long time last night." Kato tried for innocent, but failed miserably.

Lydia shifted. "I just gave Thornton shit for his inappropriate relationship with Ed. Do I have to give you the same speech?"

Mickey's brows shot together. "I'm a grown-up. I can make the decisions about what is or is not appropriate in any adult relationship I choose to embark upon."

"Ah, so there is something." I grinned. "Canadians...like, birds of a feather stick together?"

They glowered. No other word for it—a full-on scowl.

Lydia shut the laptop. "I'm happy for you, Mick. Just…" She eyed me. "Well, when we started this whole adventure, we didn't realize the band had a queer member."

"Not that it matters," Kato quickly quipped.

"Not that it matters," Lydia repeated.

Mickey drew circles on the laminate kitchen table. "Perhaps…"

"Yes," I prompted.

"Well, just…maybe Ed isn't the only person who…goes both ways."

I hooted. "Way to go, Mickey."

They glared.

Only slightly cowed, I tried to sober my expression.

The corners of their mouth turned up.

"Well, on that note…" I rose and stretched. "I've charged up the handheld and am going to head over to the main stage to see if I can catch anything interesting."

"That's sort of my job," Lydia protested.

I placed a kiss to the crown of her head. "Show starts in two hours. I'm sure you've got plenty to do between now and then."

"I do," she mumbled.

"Then we're good."

I slipped into my lighter jean jacket, nabbed my sunglasses, scooped up the camera, and headed out.

The sun was well into the western sky as I headed toward the main stage.

My stomach reminded me I'd skipped lunch.

I'd been so focused on nailing the interview that nothing much else had penetrated.

Hopefully, the rest of my team would eat before rehearsal tonight.

As I made my way over to the food, I caught sight of a couple standing near one of the lighting stands.

Axel was unmissable—from the tall, lanky frame, to the trademark black, curly hair—he couldn't be overlooked.

Feeling a little like a voyeur, but curious where this might lead, I turned on the camera and started filming.

The redheaded man he spoke to was a couple of inches shorter. The man was as broad as Axel was, well, waifish. The spikey red hair shone in the sunlight, and although I couldn't see the man's eyes, I imagined blue or green.

Fancifully, I added gold to that list.

Gold eyes were a thing.

Right?

Axel touched the man's cheek.

The man recoiled from the touch—putting actual physical distance between them.

What the fuck?

Axel stepped forward.

The man backed up.

Right into a trailer.

Axel advanced again.

The man held up his hands.

Axel grasped them.

The man ducked his head.

After a moment, Axel gently placed his index finger under the guy's chin and tipped it up.

Their gazes met.

The emotion passing between the two of them nearly brought me to my knees. Nearly had me turning off the camera.

Nearly.

That look? The one they were exchanging? That was how I felt about Ed. How much I wanted him. Not just physically—although that played a large part—but emotionally as well. Like some kind of spiritual connection.

And even though my rational brain kept blinking huge red hazard lights that danger lay ahead, I still would've done just about anything to get him back into a bed. Or a bunk. Hell, bent over the kitchen table would do.

Me being bent, though? I wasn't vers. Just not my jam.

Time spun out until, finally, Axel grasped the man's cheeks.

Their lips met.

Okay…so perhaps Ed wasn't the only guy on the tour who was bi. And if Pauletta was as well—or at least willing to date someone nonbinary—things were about to get very interesting.

The man wrapped his arms around Axel's neck, drawing him closer.

Axel reached around to grab the guy's ass with one of his hands, and he thrust their cocks together.

I slowly increased the zoom and worked at keeping the camera steady.

This is so shady. So wrong. You should stop.

And yet I couldn't help myself.

A rowdy group of goths in black with white makeup passed by the men. The group didn't appear to notice.

The distraction, though, had Axel and the guy jumping apart.

They stared at each other.

Axel tried to advance.

The man held up his hand.

Axel stopped.

Words were exchanged.

I would've given just about everything I had for a unidirectional mic. I didn't have one, so I tried to focus on their mouths and expressions as much as possible.

Then, it ended.

The man bolted.

I'd have put money on Axel following. But he didn't. He pulled out his cell phone, swiped, and apparently took the call because he started speaking.

Out of curiosity, I held the camera on Axel until he disconnected the call. He continued to stare at the spot where his...companion...had stood. Finally, he slashed his hand through the air and took off in the opposite direction.

I stopped the recording.

Quickly, I cued it up.

As I'd suspected, I didn't get anything but ambient noise from the hive of activity going on everywhere.

I focused in tight on their faces.

Axel's familiar expressions didn't surprise me. A bit of playfulness, a bunch of serious, and then some panic.

The redhead, though? He never cracked a smile. His earnestness and concentration were evident in the furrow in his brow. A brow with a few wrinkles.

I looked closer.

At first, I'd assumed the men were about the same age.

That wasn't true. The redhead had little lines around his eyes and wrinkles in his forehead. I might've even spotted a little silver in his light beard. Hard to tell at this angle.

No, I'd peg him as early forties.

So...fifteen, sixteen years difference. Made no difference to me, but clearly something was going on.

The burning question, for me, was what did Ed know?

Chapter Twenty-Five

Ed

Fucking Axel.

Pauletta offered to try to track him down herself, but she was also coordinating with Mickey and Lydia on camera positions.

Jenny and Mikhail had all our equipment ready to go.

Songbird, Meg, and Big Mac were doing vocal warmups.

But no fucking Axel.

When Big Mac spoke to him on the phone, almost an hour ago, he said he'd be *right there*. Well, that'd proven to be a lie.

So I'd volunteered to look for him.

Because, as one knew, that's what best friends were for.

I tried all manner of food locations to no avail. For a lithe guy, Axel ate more than any of us.

I tried the electrical set-up crew.

I tried the sound crew.

I tried the lighting crew.

I jogged between all the other band-tour buses.

No fucking Axel.

In desperation, I tried our bus.

As I checked each bunk, I tried to quell both my rising panic and my rising anger. He was probably fucking fine and just fucking off somewhere, but what if he was fucking hurt or something, and who was I to be mad at him?

No luck.

I checked the john.

Empty.

My bladder decided now might be a good time to go.

Fuck my life.

I pissed, flushed, and washed my hands. As I came out, I heard a noise. "Axel?"

"No, it's Thornton."

He moved toward the back as I moved toward the front. We met in the middle.

"Mickey told me to try to help find him. Apparently you guys are on in less than twenty minutes."

"Fuck." I tried to punch the wall.

He grabbed my hand and pulled me back.

"He's never done this before. Yeah, he comes across as flighty. But he's not. Not when it comes to the music."

"You're overwrought."

"I think I have the right."

"You do." He spun me in his arms so we faced each other.

Well, I looked up at him.

"Let me give you a little relief."

I cocked an eyebrow.

He dropped to his knees.

Every argument on the tip of my tongue—and there were many—fled.

He unzipped my jeans, opened my fly, and pulled out my cock.

The cock which had been, just a nanosecond ago, completely flaccid. Now? Oh, perky and very interested.

"Thornton, we can't do this," I hissed.

He grasped the base of my cock and ran his tongue along the crown.

My cock hardened and protested my...protestations.

"All right, but fast, okay?"

He hummed his approval as he drew me deep into his mouth.

Rational thought fled as I flexed and thrust myself deeper into him.

This. This. This.

I wanted it. Wanted him. Never wanted him to stop, and yet needed it to end.

He sucked. He raked his teeth along my length. He grabbed my balls and slowly squeezed.

Lights exploded before my closed eyes as I arched into the orgasm. I didn't have time to warn him as I spurted cum into his mouth. Holding on to his head, I sought to find breath. To find my center. To find equilibrium.

"Holy fuck."

"Next time." He kissed my deflated cock. "Now, let's go find your frontman. I have a video I want to show you."

My scrambled brain struggled to process. "You want to show me a video? Now?" I almost asked why the blow job, but I couldn't find the strength.

You don't want him to think you're having second thoughts.

If we didn't find Axel and make the stage on time, I'd forever question the sanity of a blow job on the bus.

But I'd never regret it.

I hope I don't regret him.

As I zipped myself up, he showed me the video on his phone.

I struggled to make sense of what I saw. I recognized both men. No doubt in my mind. But why that guy was here, at Rocktoberfest, and why— "Holy shit."

Thornton looked over. "I know, right? I mean, I thought Axel was straight—"

"He is."

"But then he's kissing some guy—"

"It's a mistake." My mind whirled.

Thornton made a noise low in his throat. "I'd say that wasn't a mistake. They certainly look like they know what they're doing."

"But..." I couldn't find words.

"You know the guy." Thornton met my gaze. His amber irises were almost eclipsed by the blown pupils.

I glanced down. Yep, and he still sported some wood. Returning the favor flitted through my mind, but, as I checked the time on his phone, I swore. "Fuck it. We'll just have to go on without him."

"Who is he, Ed? Who's the guy?"

Given Thornton was a genuine journalist, I didn't figure it'd take him much time to figure it out. "That's Hugo Treadgold."

Even as realization dawned in Thornton's eyes, my cell buzzed.

"He's there." My clumsy thumbs typed out a response, and I barreled toward the front of the bus.

"Ed."

I spun back. "What?"

He held up the phone. "What does this mean?"

"I wish to fuck I knew." I met his gaze. "But I need your word you won't use it. Won't show it to anyone else. Even showing it to me...that was a huge breach of privacy, of ethics. That was wrong, man. Promise me you'll keep Axel's secret. You're gay, you *know* how important this is."

"Yeah." Thornton met my gaze. "That's not why I filmed, and not why I showed you and yeah, I probably shouldn't have. I won't out him."

But if he hadn't filmed, I wouldn't have any clue what was going on. I nodded. Without waiting for a response, I vaulted down the stairs and hotfooted it all the way to the main stage.

Jenny and Mikhail were setting up amps while Songbird hooked up her keyboard and Meg organized her drums.

Axel and Big Mac had their heads together as they reviewed some chord progression.

I grabbed my guitar from Pauletta—who glowered—and I rushed onstage.

Lydia stood to one side with her camera, and I spotted Kato in the audience with another.

The stagehand gave us the thumbs-up.

Before I could even contemplate cornering Axel, we had to begin.

Given the chaos of the last hour, I expected...chaos.

I didn't get it.

The rehearsal went off flawlessly.

The stage crew at Rocktoberfest were truly the best I'd ever worked with.

They choreographed everything to the minute.

And we nailed every single one of those minutes.

Then we were cleared, and all our gear was stowed before I even had time to process all that'd happened.

Lydia and Kato waved as they trudged off, laden with gear.

Pauletta and Mickey made some kind of excuse and headed off toward Pauletta's rental car.

Jenny, Mikhail, Meg, and Songbird headed toward the food.

Big Mac, correctly reading the room, said he was going to go watch some other rehearsals.

That left Axel, me, and Thornton.

"Yeah, look…" Axel gazed at Thornton.

"I can go."

"No." I turned to him. "Let's go inside the bus. I want you to show him the video."

"What video?" Axel turned to Thornton. "You shot part of rehearsal, right?" He turned back to me. "Was there something wrong with my performance? Because I thought I nailed that son of a bitch."

"Oh, you nailed it all right." I pointed to the bus. "Now, Axel. Don't fuck with me."

His grin dropped. "Yeah, okay."

As he mounted the stairs, Thornton caught my arm. "I can just give you my phone and get it back from you later. I don't have to be here."

Which was an incredibly generous, if not foolhardy, offer. In this day and age, no one should *ever* offer their unlocked phone to anyone.

"Look, you don't have to stick around for the fallout."

He eyed me. "But you want me there."

I drew in a deep breath. "Look, I'm hurt he didn't tell me, even though he didn't owe it to me. Just…I thought he trusted me. I didn't think we had secrets." *Although aren't you keeping a big one from him?* "And then he's going to get defensive. And then I'll get more aggressive. Then he'll throw shit back in my face and…" I patted my chest. "I don't have the energy to do this right now. Tomorrow is the biggest night of our lives. If I thought I could put off this discussion until we were home in Vancouver, I'd totally do it. But we can't. Because obviously Mr. Threadgold is here—"

"And obviously Axel knows it."

"Right." I let out a sharp breath. "Now I just need to find out why."

Thornton gave me a quick nod, and then followed me as I got on the bus.

I made my way over to Axel. He sat sipping a can of cola, and he'd put out two cans of ginger ale.

Ah. So he knows he's done something wrong.

Well, almost missing the show definitely counted as wrong. I shoved aside the fact I'd nearly done the same damn thing and grabbed a ginger ale. After handing it to Thornton, I took a seat next to Axel.

Thornton sat next to me. He placed his drink on the table. Without prompting from me, he queued up the video.

When he hit play, I watched Axel.

Recognition clearly hit him within about five seconds. "You son of a bitch. You had no right—"

"Probably not—" Thornton began.

"Doesn't matter," I interjected. "We can leave the ethical and moral debate for another day." I tapped to pause the video just as Axel pressed Mr. Threadgold against the trailer. I didn't need to see the rest again. "He's our teacher, Axel. This is all kinds of wrong." I drew in a breath. "Was this going on in high school?"

"What?"

If I'd had a moment's hesitation, Axel's genuine horror at my question confirmed that this—whatever this was—was new. "Well, for that, I'm glad."

"I can't believe you thought—"

"The man's almost twenty years older than you, Axel. And, try to deny it all you want, you were a vulnerable kid. Hurting. In a lot of pain—physical and emotional."

He shot me a *shut the fuck up* look.

But I was on a roll. "And it would've been very easy for someone to take advantage of you."

"Well, you too." He tried to bluster.

I saw right through him.

"And, anyway…" He tapped his finger on the table. "He's only fourteen years older. I'm an adult. He's…a slightly older adult."

"How long has this been going on?"

"What?" Again, another look of horror. "There isn't a *this*." Axel scratched his scalp. "Like he saw me and called me over."

"What's he doing here?"

"I honestly don't know." His jaw ticked. "Do you want to hear this or not?"

Gesturing, I indicated he should continue.

"And, like, we got to talking. Just talking." He punctuated each word. "And I thought about how great having him here was. And how we'd just been talking about him this morning and, voilà, here he is. I mean, that's great, right?"

Obviously catching my unimpressed expression, he continued. "And, like, we got to talking. And reminiscing."

"Like about when you were his student?" I didn't bother to hide my cutting tone.

"Sure." He eyed me. "But like more about our career. He's followed us closely. And even been to a couple of concerts. He was at the PNE last week. Isn't that cool?"

I pursed my lips. "No, not really cool. More like stalking."

"It's not like that, Ed. I swear."

"You don't know what it's like, Axel. You had your tongue down his throat within five seconds of seeing him again. Hell, not that it fucking matters, but I didn't even know he was gay." I arched an eyebrow. "Or that you were."

AXE TO GRIND

And maybe that omission was the crux of my pain. I'd shared my bisexuality with my best friend almost as soon as I'd had words to explain it. Being different—and knowing it—made me question everything.

Axel'd been there to hold my hand. To tell me everything would be okay. Even to encourage me to explore my attraction to other men.

Never—not in a million years—had I considered Axel might be anything other than straight. A small part of me was relieved he'd obviously never felt that way toward me. Talk about catastrophic.

Axel looked over at Thornton. "You shouldn't have taped me. You had no right."

Thornton shrugged. "Maybe. Maybe not. Regardless, you're going to be onstage at one of the biggest music festivals in the States. Hellsbane was barely known last year. Look at them now. If you nail your performance tomorrow night, you might just hit that level of stardom." He held up his hand. "Now, I don't care about your sexuality. You might've noticed I'm not exactly out—I don't want it to be the focus of my work. I don't want to be the *gay* documentary filmmaker."

This took me aback, because I hadn't thought of it like that. He was mostly behind the camera. He didn't have the same intrusive media who might chase him around like they did big rock bands.

"What are you trying to say?" Axel glared. "I'm not gay."

I blinked.

Twice.

"But—"

"That was...just a kiss. You know, like..."

"You seem to be saying *like* quite a bit during this conversation. Being articulate has never been a problem with you, Axel, so I'm worried." I tried to grasp his hand.

He pulled it back. "I have to go."

"Go where?"

"Somewhere other than here." He rose, then met my gaze. "You just don't get it." He pounded his fist on the table. "You are both so far out of line. Filming me." He pointed to Thornton. "And confronting me." That finger jabbed at me. "Fuck you both."

I wanted to ask him what we didn't get, but before I had a chance, he stomped down to the front of the bus and disappeared out the door.

Chapter Twenty-Six

Thornton

Well, that went well.

What did you expect?

Honestly...I don't know.

Which was why I sat back in silence and covertly watched Ed as he ran through a gamut of emotions—all of which crossed his face. He might be the stoic one of the group, but he also felt things very acutely. If someone was in pain, he felt it. If someone was happy, he rejoiced with them. If someone felt betrayed, he was right there as well.

I retrieved my phone from where he'd put it on the table. I'd uploaded the video from the camera, and that'd made things easier. "I should go."

"Was I wrong to confront him?"

"Was I wrong to video him?" I wasn't certain I wanted the answer, but I also needed to make Ed understand why I'd done it—if he hadn't already figured it out.

He rubbed his forehead. "Yeah, you were wrong." He tisked. "Except if I hadn't known, then I couldn't have confronted him." He turned to me. "I didn't want to...but he was so reckless. He's usually better than that. I mean, the ADHD can manifest in different ways, and sometimes he does things without thinking through the consequences. But all people do that, right? Especially young guys."

I started to speak, but he continued.

"I figured once we made it to our early twenties—in one piece—that we were golden. We'd survived. No car crashes. No disastrous events—" He winced.

"What?"

He swallowed. "Nothing. Just...nothing."

Push or withdraw? Every bone in my body screamed to push. Was he thinking about my sister? Was he about to admit his complicity in her death? Was this the moment I'd waited for? Eight years was a long time, and I could taste victory. My fingers curled around the chain in my pocket.

Even as I had those thoughts, Ed curled into my side. He threaded his arm around my waist.

Mechanically, I put my arm around his shoulder.

He tucked his head against my neck. His breath tickled my skin. "I can't believe that just over an hour ago, you were blowing me."

My cock perked up. "Care to return the favor?"

He sighed. "Not tonight. I just...want to crawl into bed and forget this whole day."

"The interview went well—"

"I outed myself."

"Not going to argue with that. You all pretty much did. Except Big Mac."

"I should've pointed out he snores."

"That probably wouldn't have hit the same level of revelation."

"No. But it would've embarrassed him."

"You could've pointed out he's suffering from unrequited love." I said the words in jest, trying to lighten the mood.

As I'd hoped, Ed chuckled. "Yeah. He really needs to give up once and for all. The band has to come first. Like you said, we're on the verge of something big. His childish feelings could ruin that."

"You think his affection is childish?"

"I think it's an infatuation. Meg's beautiful. She's charming and smart and a lovely person. I mean, who wouldn't be attracted to that?"

"Have you ever been?"

He shook his head. "Nah. I saw a talented drummer. Just like with Songbird, I see a talented keyboardist. I don't want to screw every attractive woman I meet. Or, for the record, every woman I meet. I've met guys like that—any willing body. That repulses me."

"But you'd consider every available man?" I didn't want to think I didn't mean something to him, but better I find out now rather than waiting for something that might never come.

Once you expose him, it'll all be over anyway.

Well, there was that rather salient point.

Ed pulled back to meet my gaze. "No, it's not like that. I haven't dated *that* many people."

"But you've done hookups."

"Well..." He scratched his nose. "A guy's got needs."

"I'd expect that line from Axel—not from you."

He winced. "Yeah, okay, not at my best." He cleared his throat. "I'm assuming you haven't been a choirboy."

"No." And since I didn't want to examine my past relationships, I leaned in for a kiss.

Just a gentle pressing of lips, I told myself. Just a confirmation that, for the moment, we had something. Just a sealing of a promise that'd end very soon.

Guilt churned in my gut. Guilt that I had yet to avenge my sister's death and guilt that I was leading Ed on to think there might be more.

There could never be more.

"Hey…oh shit."

We drew apart at Meg's exclamation.

"Guys, we weren't exactly quiet." She dropped two hot dogs onto the table before us as well as a small pile of condiment packets. "Veggie." She pointed to Ed's. Then she dropped into the seat across from us. "I'm fucking exhausted."

Songbird and Big Mac made their way over to seats as well.

"Oh, I caught sight of Lydia and Kato grabbing food." Songbird grabbed her omnipresent pile of cards. She held them up.

Meg, Ed, and I all shook our heads.

Big Mac sat up straighter. "Yeah. I'm feeling lucky."

"Well, then, you're crazy." Meg snagged her sketchbook and opened it.

Ed gave me a sheepish look before dumping three packets of mustard on his dog.

"Hey." I tried for offended.

"What?"

"You took them all."

"You snooze, you lose." His eyes twinkled. "And you seem like a relish kind of guy. Or something hoity toity."

Damn, he had my number. I slathered my dog in relish and added a thin line of ketchup. "Thanks for this."

Meg waved her pencil in the air, but didn't look up.

"Hey, it was my idea." Big Mac looked downright affronted.

"Did you see Mickey and Pauletta?" Ed asked the question casually, then took a bite, full lips stretched around the hot dog.

I imagined him nibbling on my cock. Which was so wildly inappropriate—given everything that was going on—but my imagination often wandered away without permission.

Ed brushed his leg against mine.

"Where's Axel?" Songbird picked up the cards she'd dealt and smiled.

Big Mac did the same and groaned.

A good poker player, he'd never be.

"He, uh, needed some fresh air."

Meg's gaze snapped up as she honed in on Ed.

When he gave her nothing, she pivoted her gaze to me.

"Yeah, not my place to get involved."

Songbird smirked. "But you'll do Ed?"

"Hey," Ed protested.

"I'm amazed you haven't gotten into each other's bunks at night." She wrinkled her nose. "God, I hope you haven't—"

"We haven't," I rushed to assure her.

"Well, I don't have a problem with it." Big Mac played a card.

Songbird grinned at it.

"Fuck my life."

"I thought you said you were *feeling lucky*." Meg didn't look up from her drawing.

"I am." He spread his arms expansively.

Giving everyone a view of his cards.

No wonder he was claiming to be fucked.

"I'm here," Big Mac continued. "At the most fabulous music concert. With my favorite people." He eyed me. "And a journalist who isn't as bad as I thought he'd be."

"I'm flattered."

"You should be." He played another card.

Songbird, with great glee, laid her hand of cards on the table.

Big Mac groaned. "I never stood a chance."

"Nope." She scooped up the cards. "Again?"

"Yeah, why not." He glanced over at Meg.

She didn't appear to notice.

"Don't have anything better to do."

No doubt of what he meant by that. I pressed my thigh to Ed's.

He yawned, gave me an apologetic smile, and rose. "I'm going to bed."

Songbird started dealing cards.

After a moment, I shrugged. "Deal me in?"

She smiled, nodded, and started to divide the cards between the three of us.

Ed leaned over to plant a kiss to my lips.

Big Mac whooped.

Meg groaned.

Songbird hummed as she picked up her hand.

I waited, my attention held by the man behind me, until Ed had wandered to the back of the bus. Sadly, wanting to crawl into his bunk with him and actually doing it were two different things.

I sat and checked my cards.

Fuck my life.

Chapter Twenty-Seven

Ed

As I stepped onto the stage and faced sixty thousand fans, exhilaration ran through me. The electricity arced between the audience and the five of us.

And I was so glad to be sharing it with Thornton.

I sensed his presence.

He stood with Pauletta, just offstage.

Axel strummed his guitar.

The loud crowd hushed.

"Hey." He offered them his trademark grin. "We're Grindstone. All the way from Canada."

A holler came from somewhere in the sea of concertgoers. "Ah, a Canadian. Since we all know each other, I'll grab a Coke with you later."

Laughter rippled across the crowd.

He pointed to Lydia, who crouched before him with the camera pointed at him. "So, don't mind the documentary crew. If you cheer loudly enough, you might make the cut."

The audience roared.

Obligingly, Lydia pivoted and took a wide pan of the insane number of people.

"And on that note...." He gave Meg a look.

She pulled out a quick rhythm.

We were off.

At Pauletta's urging, we started with "Desperation". As predicted, that got the crowd going.

I even spotted a few people singing to the lyrics.

Wow, cool. Maybe they were fans or, just as likely, they'd picked up our album when they heard we'd be performing.

Axel hammed it up for Lydia.

Somewhere in the massive crowd, Mickey also had a camera.

I was glad we'd have the concert to watch later because, as sweat ran down my brow, I felt overwhelmed.

Meg rocked her drum solo.

We transitioned into "Day's Pay for a Day's Labor" with our traditional rock'n'roll sound.

I glanced over at Thornton, who wore a huge grin on his face.

Slipping, I nearly missed a note.

Focus, fuckwit.

Right.

We sang "Immortalized" as good as we'd ever done before. The song that tore at my heart every time. Then we shook it up with "AI", which got fans stomping their feet and cheering loudly.

Once the applause died down from that song, we moved together as a group and harmonized our way through "Calling for Help".

Despite nearly sixty thousand people watching us, I could've heard a proverbial pin drop. This song was where Songbird got to shine. I'd never connected that she'd contributed much to the lyrics—and that probably some of her life experience was in it. I just thought she had a good imagination.

Now I knew differently.

And good god damn, we hit every note perfectly.

As the last reverb of Axel's voice trailed off, the world exploded in sound.

I hoped that translated into both sales and the sharing of a song that meant so much to the five of us.

We launched into "Sunrise". Clearly this was new material and, as Axel's vocals slowly made their way through the sound system, I snuck a peek at the audience.

Some fans swayed, while others looked a little confused.

My heart sank.

Why? Why weren't they getting it? This was such an important song to me. To Axel. We'd poured our hearts and souls into this song. We'd poured eight years of pain into this song.

I tried to push Kyesha from my mind.

Then, however, as I came in with the chorus, some fans started holding up lighters and phones.

Cause we've got nothing but time to our name
Oh, no money, glory, or fame
But I don't need those to love you
All I want is to hold your hand
So, take me to our promise land
That's all I need to love you

They got it. They really got it. The audience was slowly getting into the song.

We played our hearts out.

Moving fast

Though I want this night to last

So, I'm taking a deep breath

Let my worries go to rest

As I take your hands

"Do you think this night will end?

Or will the sun leave us alone?

And the night become our home"

As I share this thought with you

The sun rises, and damn, what a beautiful view

The song ended, and the applause was thunderous.

Phew.

Finally, we launched into "We Need to do Better", and Big Mac rocked his solo, as always.

The audience enjoyed the upbeat tempo of the song, and some even sang along with us.

Three minutes later, the entire thing was over.

The roar deafened as we took our bows. Due to time constraints, we couldn't do an encore. Still, we waved repeatedly as Jenny, Mikhail, and some of the other stage hands removed our equipment.

Even as we hit the backstage, I spotted the next band. I'd done some research on Blind Faith. Musically they were good, but what saved them from being ordinary was their lead singer who was clearly born to be a front man. Also, I'd heard rumors about them fusing classical and rock, and I was curious to see what they were going to do. I was about to wish them luck when Scotty, the lead singer, I thought, spat out, "And just this once, could you not offer me your ass?" The tall blond man in the blinding-white shirt looked fit to be tied with a flush of anger crossing those gorgeous cheeks.

Songbird caught my eye as hers widened.

Yeah, I don't want to be here for this either.

Scotty noticed us as the entire backstage went suddenly still.

The buzz from the crowd filtered to us, but the noise was just background to the drama unfolding before me.

"Oh my God, you're Ed." He bolted forward to shake my hand. Then he grabbed Axel's. "You're, like, brilliant. And that new song? Sunrise? Blew me away."

I almost said something else was apparently blowing him away, but that felt rude and uncouth. "We're following your career, and I think tonight will be amazing for you." I glanced over his shoulder at Kel. "And whisper has it that your playing is divine. Can't wait to hear it myself."

Kel slowly nodded.

Okay, did I just stick my foot in it, or did I help?

I assumed, if they all took the stage and performed brilliantly, that I'd helped. If they bombed, I might just blame myself.

Scotty saluted me, then moved back to Kel.

Songbird poked my shoulder. "Was that...?"

"Yeah."

"And did they just...?"

"Yeah."

"Holy fuck." She nudged me. "We need to go."

And go we did. En masse we loaded everything into the van.

Jenny and Mikhail had slept for most of the day, so they were ready to hit the road despite the late hour. She had family in Sacramento, so they'd decided to take off early and spend a day there before meeting us down in LA.

We bid them a safe journey and then, collectively, let out a deep breath.

"Amazing." Pauletta grinned wider than I'd ever seen her. "Seriously."

I noticed Lydia still filming us but, as Pauletta'd suggested I would, I barely noticed her.

No, I had only eyes for Thornton, who stood beside Mickey.

I wanted to drag him away from everyone so I could have my wicked way with him. I wanted to channel my energy, mix it with my sexual frustration, and fuck him well into the night.

"We're going to watch the next band." Meg snagged Axel's hand. "And then, isn't Embrace the Fear playing?"

Damn.

"Yeah. Oh, and then..." His voice trailed off as he, Meg, Big Mac, and Songbird headed out to where they could watch.

Lydia shut off the camera. She signalled to Kato, and they wandered off in the opposite direction.

I glanced over at Thornton and was about to speak when Pauletta held up an index finger on one hand while yanking her phone out of her back pocket with the other hand. As she read, I tried to catch Thornton's attention. Surely, in this massive, sprawling, created town, there had to be somewhere we could go. Even a quickie hand job—

"Holy shit."

The reverential tone in Pauletta's voice caught my attention.

Thornton held up his hand. "Do you want me to film this?"

Mickey nodded their approval.

Pauletta held the phone against her chest as she waited.

Within a moment, Thornton had the phone pointed at Pauletta.

She beckoned me over.

I read the text.

Then I read it again.

My vision blurred.

She grabbed me and held on.

I shook.

Grand Central Records. The fucking text was from Grand Central Records. They wanted a meeting in three days when we were in LA.

The feeling of elation washed over me, soon followed by panic. What if we blew the meeting? What if they wanted something we couldn't give? What if they wanted us to leave Vancouver?

Mickey snagged Pauletta's phone and held it up for Thornton to film.

Surreal.

"Well, we should probably go find the others." Mickey grinned. "I'm assuming you'll want to tell them."

Pauletta pulled back and regarded me. "I'll keep them busy for the next thirty. Just get on with it." Her fierce whisper likely didn't carry to our guests.

"But—"

"Go, Ed. Take it for the gift it is. We'll be back after the next band. If you're not done—"

"We'll be done. We'll be done."

I caught Thornton's attention.

Pauletta grabbed Mickey's hand and dragged them into the sea of people.

Thornton stopped recording.

"She said we've got thirty minutes or so." No way was I risking us getting caught.

He grinned. "Then we'd better get busy."

We nearly sprinted to the bus. We were up the stairs and heading to the back before reality set in. "Grand Central Records wants to meet with us."

Thornton halted. He advanced toward me and, when he was within touching distance, he took my cheeks in his hands. "Fuck yes, Ed. That performance..." He let the word hang. "I want to use inspired, but that feels clichéd, you know?"

"But it's not a cliché." I grasped his hands as they gripped me. "I felt it. Like nothing's ever been like that, and nothing will ever be the same again. It may be premature, but I feel like today's the beginning of the rest of our lives."

"There'll be more premature action if you don't get naked in the next thirty seconds." He pressed his hard cock against mine. "I need you, Ed. Because I felt that electricity as well. I'm amped up, and God, I'm ready to explode."

I slid my hand between us to palm his erection through the jeans he'd donned for the concert. "Shower?" I was pretty rank, but he likely didn't care. And the others would all want showers as well, but they needed to party out their high first.

"Yeah. But we need to be organized."

I cocked my head.

"We should put our dirty clothes away and grab fresh nightclothes. Then we can just chill after you fuck me into the wall."

"Yeah, that makes sense." Regretfully, I pulled away from him. I went to my bunk and organized both my toiletries and clothes to wear after. Part of me resented the extra time I needed in order to get things organized. The rest of me was impressed Thornton'd put that much thought into it.

I discovered him naked and stepping into the shower by the time I made it to the bathroom. After locking the door and dropping my clothes on his, I stepped in behind him.

He turned and grinned down at me. "Grateful Vera got the water tank restocked, but we should probably be quick." He knocked his elbow. "This is so fucking tight."

"This is the deluxe model. Most of these only fit one." I winked. "This is going to be interesting." Then, holding up the condom and lube, I grinned. "I'll glove up while you wash my back."

"What about your hair?"

"I toweled off after the concert. Just don't get it wet, and we'll be fine."

Which would prove easier said than done, but I was far more concerned about getting into him than I was about what might happen to my hair.

In other words, fuck first—practicalities later.

Thornton's fingers raking down my back with the cascade of warm water had me fumbling with the condom. The sensation of closeness intensified with the intimacy of the water. Showering was something ritualistic—and I was always the first in the shower after each concert. I needed to cleanse and rid myself of the stress.

A bite to my neck brought me out of my reverie. Thornton snaked his arm around my waist to palm my sheathed cock. He nuzzled my neck. "I don't need prep. I just need you to fuck me."

Sounded good in theory, but that wasn't how I rolled. "Turn around."

He obeyed, then spread his legs, and he bent his knees to give me just the right angle.

The right angle to admire.

The right angle to fuck.

I squeezed lube onto my fingers.

He flexed his perfect ass.

My mouth dried.

With the fingers not covered in lube, I dragged them down his back, using my blunt fingernails.

He whimpered.

I squeezed his ass.

He moaned.

Holding my hand at the small of his back, I nudged my lubed fingers to his entrance.

"Now." He panted the word.

"Not yet," I shot back. "I control this."

He snickered. "Or so you tell yourself."

I let go of his back. "We don't have to do this—"

"Fuck." He hit his head against the stall. "You're in control. You're in charge. You decide everything."

"Better." I put my palm on his ass as I slid my finger into his entrance.

He sucked in a breath.

I added a second finger.

A whimper escaped him.

Ducking my head, I spotted his impressive erection. Yeah, he wanted this.

Not that I'd really doubted—but I preferred confirmation.

I scissored my fingers, slowly working him open. Reno felt like a million years ago, yet it'd only been three days. How I'd lived while living on the razor's edge of pleasure, I wasn't certain. I twisted my fingers and hit his spongy spot.

He grunted. "Going to come."

"Go ahead."

"Want you in me."

That might've come out as a wail.

Prolonging this, under other circumstances, would've proved amusing. But limited water was a thing and time was running short. I slathered my cock with lube and lined myself up.

He lowered farther, trying to press back against me.

In one long, steady, slow stroke, I entered him.

His groan went straight to my balls.

The rest was just doing what came so naturally. I pushed into him with ever-increasing thrusts.

He pushed back, all the while clawing at the stall.

The sound of slapping skin reverberated in the small space.

My balls tightened, and as I gripped his hips, I fought to maintain purchase. "Jack yourself."

His only response was to nod frantically. Then, a moment later, his hand disappeared, and soon his arm worked frantically.

Finding a rhythm that worked for both of us took a few tries, but soon we were clearly on the same trajectory—chasing the same goal.

He got there first.

As he spasmed around me, I gave three more sharp thrusts before tumbling over the edge myself. I gripped his slick back as I flew through the air with the intensity of the orgasm. The feeling rivaled how I'd felt tonight.

Performing in front of sixty-thousand people.

Giving my all for this one man. In this one perfect moment.

A pounding on the door caused me to pull out of him rather indelicately.

He grunted.

"Leave us some hot water and, for fuck's sake, trash the condom."

Thornton groaned at Axel's admonition.

"He's obviously not worried about how I represent him in the doc."

I laughed. "Uh, no." I slapped his ass. "Wash off fast." I glanced at my waterproof watch. "That fucker. We had at least another eight minutes."

Thornton laughed. "I don't know about you, but I needed that shot of adrenaline. I was pretty much a pile of putty before he rudely, uh, roused me."

"You're such an easy lay."

He grabbed my cheeks in his hands and pulled me up for a bruising kiss. He was panting when he pulled back. "This wasn't just about sex."

I startled. "Yeah, I get it."

Or at least I thought I did.

We rinsed off, shut the water off, disposed of the condom and wrapper, then set about drying off and getting into our sleep pants. Once the bathroom was set to rights, we emerged and headed toward the living area.

Axel sat on a seat with his feet on the table.

I knocked them off.

He chuckled. "Oh, did I interrupt?"

"Fucker."

"No, that was you." He turned to Thornton. "I'm right, aren't I? Because he's always been a toppy guy and—"

I whacked him on the arm.

Hard.

Thornton sat, wiggled his butt, then sighed. "I am a satisfied man."

"Ew." Axel wrinkled his nose. "TMI."

For a rock star, his odd prudishness struck me sometimes.

"But discussing Ed's topping preference isn't?"

"Hey, I waited until I was pretty sure you'd both come." Axel dusted his shirt with the back of his hand.

"Bravo." I dug into the freezer and came out with three ice-cream treats—another post-show ritual.

Axel caught his deftly, but Thornton bobbled his—and nearly dropped it.

"Uh, thanks."

I unwrapped my chocolate-and-vanilla sandwich. "You're welcome. That might or might not be Big Mac's." I shrugged. "Serves him right."

"What did he do?" Thornton examined the treat as if debating, then he shrugged, unwrapped it, and bit into the chocolate ice cream.

"He let that fucker come back early." I pointed to Axel.

My best friend shrugged. "All's fair in love and war."

I wasn't certain which *love* and which *war*, but it didn't matter. I held out my hand for a fist bump.

Thornton chuckled.

Everything in the world was right.

Chapter Twenty-Eight

Thornton

We stayed until the last act of Rocktoberfest.

Lydia and Kato had gotten some background, including a chat with Brody North, the versatile wind-instrument player from Corvus Rising.

Mickey and Pauletta vanished at one point, missing some of the biggest acts.

On Sunday morning, when we heard that a drummer from a band that performed the night before had died of a drug overdose, I watched Ed and Axel closely for a reaction. Word spread like wildfire, explaining the sirens we'd heard the night before.

The two men were quiet for a bit, but they appeared to rally, and we watched Hellsbane and Blade as well as some others, on Sunday evening.

Fortunately, Vera had organized her sleep so we were able to get on the road overnight once the finale of the festival concluded. We could've stayed to schmooze, but we had LA and Grand Central Records in our sights.

The rest of us crashed and slept right through the drive to LA.

Part of me wished I could've been awake and watched the scenery for the six-hour drive. The rest of me was so exhausted, I couldn't keep my eyes open. In fact, I'd been the first to crash—much to my horror.

About an hour later, Ed crawled in beside me.

I tried to rouse. The single bed was a ridiculously small space, and I wasn't good at not being able to stretch, but Ed being squished against me felt so damn good that I didn't care.

He kissed my neck. "If we do anything but sleep, I'll be banished. Just...sleep, okay?"

Being totally exhausted, I had no problem nodding, gathering him in my arms, and promptly falling right back asleep.

In the morning, I awoke to a demanding bladder.

Serious shuffling was involved, but eventually I made it to the bathroom.

Since Ed hadn't gotten up, and I didn't want to disturb him, I meandered down toward the front of the bus. I snagged an orange juice, put the coffee on, and took stock of my surroundings.

We appeared to be at a campsite near a beach, and the sun was rising behind us.

Pauletta'd left the concert early to fly to LA in preparation for the meeting with the record executives this morning.

Ed had wanted everyone in the meeting.

Songbird, Meg, and Big Mac all balked at the idea and claimed they needed to get set up in the venue for tonight's concert. Mikhail and Jenny were to arrive shortly.

Axel tried the same schtick, but—much to his horror—both Pauletta and Ed had put their collective feet down.

He needed to attend.

The record executives were aware of the filming, and had offered to let Lydia sit in their lobby and film us going in and coming out. Hopefully with a contract.

Pauletta'd put her foot down on that as well.

Obviously she intended to negotiate. Or at least wanted to take time to look over whatever the record label was offering.

I was out.

As I sipped my juice, Axel trundled in.

He slapped me on the back, winking in Ed's direction. "Thanks for not...you know."

I snickered. "Boning your friend while the rest of you slept two feet away?"

"Uh, yeah, something like that." He eyed the coffeemaker, then turned back to me. "Wait, aren't you the bonee?"

"TMI, Axel."

"Sure. But Ed's very particular."

And I had a dozen questions about that—none of which would I actually ask Axel.

"Did someone say *bonee*?" Songbird made her way over to the coffeepot. "You make this?"

She directed the question at me.

"Yeah."

"We should keep you around. As long as we're not discussing boners." She poured half a cup, put the kettle on to boil, and flopped down in a chair. She pulled her knees up to her chin. "That was intense."

Axel cocked his head.

"Rocktoberfest." She waved her hand. "You know what I mean."

"I still can't believe you're making me go to the meeting this morning." Axel pouted. "I think Songbird, Meg, and Big Mac should have to as well."

"Put on your big-boy shorts and get over yourself." Ed joined us.

First, he pressed a kiss to the top of Axel's head, then he turned to lean over me to give me a full-on tongues-included kiss.

"Mmm. Coffee." He grinned.

Songbird waved. "We'll see the contract before everyone signs. I trust Pauletta. We'll discuss it when you guys get back."

If they came back with a contract.

Within thirty minutes, Axel and Ed were showered and dressed. By the time they'd eaten the breakfast Songbird prepared, Pauletta was cooling her heels.

"Why is everyone up so early?" Axel might've whined that.

"It's nearly ten." Pauletta pointed to her watch. "We're their first appointment for the day." She paused. "I think."

"Is that good or bad?" Ed tried to straighten his tie.

I helped.

"Let's choose to believe they're eager." Pauletta gave Axel a once-over. "You'll do."

He grinned. "You love me, baby."

"Only reason I do this," she shot back as she exited the bus.

Axel followed.

Ed gave me another kiss before doing the same.

Meg collected the breakfast dishes.

I tried to help.

She waved me off. "What are you up to this morning?"

"My crew are in a motel across the way. We're going to review footage and start figuring out what we'll use. Mickey likes to edit on the fly whenever possible."

"Efficient." Songbird pulled out her cards.

Meg finished the dishes. She walked back to the bunks and returned a moment later with sunglasses. "I'm going for a walk on the beach."

Big Mac began to rise.

"Alone."

He plopped back down.

Songbird dealt him a hand.

I followed Meg outside.

Once the bus door was closed, she turned to me. "Can I ask you a question?"

I suppressed the snippy response that she just had. "Of course."

"How do you see us?"

I blinked. "As a band?"

"Sure." She waved her hand. "Or as a disparate group of clueless musicians—either works."

Ah.

Shit.

"Well, the depth of talent is enormous."

She waved for me to continue.

Right.

"I think, with Rocktoberfest, that you got the right songs in front of the right people. The request for the meeting with the record label today proves that."

She continued to stare at me.

Although, with her sunglasses, I could only see my reflection. "I think the interpersonal dynamics are fascinating. I always do. That's why I love my job."

"What have you seen?"

"I'm not sure—"

She held up her hand. "I don't want to see the final documentary and be shocked." She tilted her head. "I might be recovering from surgery or something."

Oh. So, no-holds-barred dirty tricks this morning, huh?

Fair enough.

"I know several of you are hiding secrets. Important secrets."

"We just told you all that, and—"

"Look. I saw someone with someone that no one seems to know about and whose existence would change things."

"What are you talking about?"

"And I see that some of you regard each other differently than the other might perceive."

She tilted her head. "Am I the clueless one?"

Fuck. "Maybe…?"

"Does this have to do with me and Big Mac? He's been such a jerk lately—"

"Possibly because he's half in love with you."

Her mouth dropped open. After a moment, she sputtered. "Uh, no. He's got plenty of women. Lots of girlfriends. Getting lots of action."

"Is he, though?" I replayed the last almost two weeks in my mind. "Because I haven't seen a single thing that leads me to give credence to that statement."

"You're nuts." Yet she said the words more slowly.

"I'm heading over to the motel. Do you want to join me for the walk?"

She shook her head and, instead, pointed to the beach. "But, thanks." She inserted her ear buds and stalked off.

Did you just do the right thing, or are things going to blow up in your face?

I honestly didn't know.

So, instead of trying to figure it out, I headed over to the fast-food restaurant across the way. I loaded up on muffins, donuts, breakfast sandwiches, and 4 extra-large coffees.

Mickey answered their door with a weary smile and very sleep-rumpled. And still wearing their pajamas. "Sorry, just got up."

We'd planned to start an hour ago, but I'd figured they might want to sleep in.

"Kato and Lydia?"

They shrugged, then pointed to the next door.

"Okay. Do you need more sleep?"

They shook their head. "I'm good." They scooped up a coffee. "I'll be over in twenty."

"Take your time. We don't need to be at the venue for a couple of hours."

"When is the meeting?"

"With the executives? Starting shortly."

"I want you back over there when the three return. They might share their news over the phone, or—more likely—they'll wait to give it to the group."

"That's going to be an incredibly personal moment."

"Look, if I thought we could get away with it, I'd send Lydia as well. It's going to be a pivotal moment—either way." They sniffed. "Hell, they might want it memorialized."

Leaving me standing in the doorway, they moved back into the room and snagged their phone. "I'm going to text Pauletta."

"She might be in the meeting already."

"So she'll ignore the text. Hopefully she sees it before they head back, and she can give me the go-ahead to send you and perhaps Lydia."

"Or she might put a kibosh on the entire idea."

"Well, at the very least, you need to be there. If she chucks you out, then we'll deal with it."

Mickey was right, of course, but this felt intrusive.

Like being boned by the lead guitarist isn't?

The image should've brought shame, but instead, brought a goofy smile to my face.

Mickey was in the process of waving me off when their phone buzzed.

"Well, hot damn. Yes to having both you and Lydia. Even if the news is bad, she wants it documented. She said, 'two hours'." They put their coffee on the table and headed into the bathroom. "I'll be over in fifteen."

They made it in twelve.

I sat at a little dining table in Lydia and Kato's room. I tried not to notice that only one bed appeared to have been slept in.

Lydia was neat, I told myself. Likely she just remade the bed.

Then why are both pillows disturbed?

Yeah, I needed to remind myself their relationship—whatever it was—was none of my business. Apparently, this tour was proving more interesting than I ever could've imagined. Because, no matter what I told myself, I hadn't planned to get sexually involved with Ed. Hadn't foreseen that getting to know the other band members would make me think twice about my plans.

My phone vibrated with an incoming text. I checked. Bonita, the eldest of my three remaining sisters.

—*Are you okay?*—
—*Why would you ask?*—

I forced down the panic. Maybe she had bad news, and she wanted to make sure I was okay before she shared it. Then I dismissed the idea. If this was bad news, she would've called.

—*It's Kyesha's birthday, and I thought you might be sad.*—

My lungs contracted as all the air whooshed out. How the fuck had I forgotten? I *never* forgot her birthday. Or the anniversary of her death. No matter what was going on in my life, these dates never escaped me. As I drew desperately needed air into my lungs, I tried to get the shaking under control. I fingered the chain in my pocket before typing out a response.

—*Thanks for remembering. I'm okay. How are you?*—

A long time passed before she answered.

—*Busy. Looking forward to seeing you at Thanksgiving, if not sooner. I love you.*—

—*I love you too. I'll see you before November, I promise.*—

Because I'd need to discuss the documentary with them. I should've before embarking on this, but revenge had been my only goal. Until this moment, I hadn't considered that my family might be collateral damage.

Fuck.

Bonita signed off with her signature flurry of heart emojis.

I jolted back to reality. I had all the incriminating evidence in a false bottom of my go-bag. Figuring out the perfect moment to unveil it was proving challenging. However, I was nothing if not creative.

I'd find a way to bring Ed and Axel down once and for all.

Damn the consequences.

Damn the repercussions.

Damn my heart.

Chapter Twenty-Nine

Ed

The ride back to the tour bus in Pauletta's rental nearly proved to be my undoing.

By mutual agreement, the three of us didn't speak. Oh, we had plenty to discuss. Just we needed to be together as a group to do it.

I still questioned why we couldn't have had everyone in the meeting.

Pauletta reminded me the other three felt more comfortable stepping back and letting us handle it.

"Is this real?" Axel grabbed the back of our seats and pulled himself forward while we stopped at a red light.

I glanced back and glared. "Are you wearing a seat belt?"

He rolled his eyes. But he also sat back and buckled the damn thing.

With great restraint, I held back the litany of reasons why seat belts were important. Not least was the legality—the last thing we needed was for the cops to have an excuse to stop three Black foreigners in a fancy luxury SUV.

I certainly wouldn't have chosen something so…conspicuous.

Pauletta claimed she'd felt lucky.

Maybe that claim had merit.

We stopped at a high-end restaurant that offered takeout, and I passed the food back to Axel since my leg kept jiggling.

"Ed." Pauletta snapped the word as we stopped at another intersection.

"I don't think—"

"Good. Don't think. Let me do the thinking."

Wow. Part of me really resented that statement. All my life—at least in my relationship with my mother—she'd told me to shut up. To be quiet. To behave. To be unobtrusive. Those words had stung back then. And as often as I told myself I'd moved past them, they still had the ability to wound.

Axel's disapproving tone broke into my reflection. "I don't understand why you got pasta in mushroom sauce."

I caught Axel's horrified face in the mirror.

"Because I like mushroom sauce," I said, glad of the change of topic. "Because the option was one of the few vegetarian choices." I shrugged. "Given how health conscious everyone out here is supposed to be, I was kind of disappointed in the selection."

Pauletta turned left on the advance signal. "We can find somewhere else. If the food gets cold, we can always reheat it."

"I didn't say I wasn't happy," I snapped. "I really like mushroom sauce. If there'd been twenty vegetarian options, I'd have still picked it."

"You're being bitchy," Axel nagged.

I turned my head to glare at him.

He merely shrugged.

After a moment, I sat back in my seat and huffed.

At yet another red light, Pauletta laid a hand on my thigh. "Five minutes. Ten, tops."

I glanced out at the sea of cars. Fricking cars everywhere. Vancouver had traffic, but this LA stuff was brutal. And we weren't even in LA proper anymore.

But I couldn't remember where we'd wound up. Closer to the venue.

"Are Jenny and Mikhail setting us up? We're good for the rehearsal at four, right? And what are sales like? Did they pick up after—"

"We're sold out, Ed." Pauletta executed the right turn the NAV system directed her to take. "We comped the executives." She took another left, and soon I spotted the trailer park where we'd taken up residence. "Now, Thornton and Lydia are going to be there. Why don't you text and make certain everyone else is as well."

Since the most expeditious way to do that was to text Songbird, I did. We had a group text, but that often got ignored.

Maybe because you're always bossing them around.

Well, if they didn't act like children—

Nope. No sassy comeback to that one.

Songbird sent me a text confirming they were all present. The other reason for not sending it to group text was I often just got thumbs-up emojis...which often told me precisely nothing. Perhaps an acknowledgement the text had been received—but rarely any concrete and helpful information.

"Maybe we should leave the food in the car." My leg continued to jiggle.

"Like, why?" Axel's brow furrowed.

"Well, Lydia will probably have the camera rolling when we come in, and Big Mac might want to eat before we even tell the news. Then the food'll become the thing rather than the news—"

"Uh, you're kidding yourself that anyone is going to look at Pauletta's face and not know."

"Hey." She eased into the parking spot, put the car in park, activated the parking brake—even though we were on flat ground—and shut off the engine. "You know, you're far worse than I am."

"Moi? I can totally keep secrets."

My gut clenched as I thought of Kyesha. The one secret the three of us kept from the world. The one our bandmates would never—could never—know.

"Ed?" Pauletta rested her hand on my knee, steadying it.

"I just...our lives are about to change. Forever."

"We'll still be us." She offered me the warmest, most genuine smile—pure Pauletta. "Axel, grab the food. We've always been about food before—might as well stay on brand."

Our food was piled in paper bags on a substantial cardboard tray. In the end, it proved easier for Axel to hand it to me.

Then he slid out of the SUV and shut the door.

Pauletta used the remote to lock the vehicle and set the alarm.

We made our way over to the bus.

Big Mac stood at the door and, as predicted, grabbed the food. Thereby intimating that Axel couldn't carry it up the stairs himself.

I wasn't impressed, and shot Pauletta a look.

She offered me what I termed her *enigmatic* smile. She'd plucked Big Mac from an obscure—and frankly horrible—garage band. In the process, she convinced me to give the guy a chance. Ninety-nine percent of the time, I didn't regret that decision. But if he didn't get his head out of his ass and fix things with Meg, I might lose my shit.

I was the last to mount the stairs and was greeted with organized chaos. Ah, Lydia was at the back of the pack, filming us.

Thornton was trying to stay unobtrusive.

Pauletta, however, had the clever idea of labelling everyone's food so there wouldn't be any debate. Or, worse, opening up other people's food before deciding it wasn't theirs. God, I detested that.

Thornton managed to tuck Lydia's aside—a spaghetti dish that could easily be reheated—and joined the mêlée.

By the time we'd sorted our food, drinks, and were actually seated, things felt...anticlimactic.

Meg took a sip of her seltzer water. Then she glanced at the three of us.

Pauletta sat on the end, Axel next to her. I sat next to him with Thornton on my other side.

"Well?" Her impatience wasn't hidden.

"I think we should eat first." Axel poked his steak.

Great. More burned flesh.

I turned my head to find Thornton had ordered eggplant parmesan.

He winked.

Despite my best efforts to stay annoyed—or at least neutral—I smiled.

Then I glanced across at our three bandmates.

All three watched me like hawks.

"What? I'm the least likely to give up a secret."

Songbird pointed her fork at me. "Which is why we noticed the goofy grin." She indicated Thornton subtly.

Warning me how it looked for the camera.

Shit.

"We've been offered a deal."

Pauletta's revelation didn't bring the cheers I expected.

"What does that mean for us? Grand Central is one of the biggest labels on the west coast—but they don't have a branch in Vancouver. Most labels don't have a presence in Vancouver." Big Mac pushed his T-bone around the plate.

"They want us to come to LA to record the album." Pauletta cut into her chicken cacciatore. "And the touring schedule they're suggesting once they release the album is pretty daunting." She glanced at everyone. "But they're offering us a chance in the big leagues."

"How long would we be away from Canada?" Meg worried her lips.

"As long as your dog has a vaccination certificate, she'll be allowed into the States. They would give us the use of a luxury house—that permits dogs."

Pauletta hadn't made many demands, but that'd been one.

"Also, perhaps, we can incentivize your ex to move on from you. Find another dog. Join a dating app. Get out of your life for good."

Big Mac held up his bottle of craft beer that we'd brought. "I'll drink to that."

Meg toyed with the label on hers. "That's a big step." She eyed the camera, considered, then took a deep breath. "The relationship wasn't a healthy one."

After a moment, Big Mac dropped his knife and fork so he could wrap his arms around her. He pressed a kiss to her temple, while Songbird took her hand.

"Sorry." She blinked several times, but a tear streaked unheeded down her cheek. "This is overwhelming." She met Pauletta's gaze. "When you found me, I didn't think I could ever make a living as a professional musician. And now…everything feels possible."

"Because it is," Pauletta assured her.

"How long do they figure we'll be in LA?" Songbird poked at her shrimp linguini.

"If we write the songs and do the hard work in Vancouver, then we can probably lay down the tracks in just a few weeks. Depends on how much time you want to spend seeing the sights—"

"Like maybe once or twice." Songbird indicated Thornton. "No offense, but this isn't our favorite place to be."

"None taken. I'm not from LA."

"We were...touring is one thing, right? We get to meet fans and do events. But day-to-day living in the States feels like it'd be exhausting. Personally, I like boring."

"Don't we all," Meg murmured.

"How will this fit in with her surgery?" Big Mac looked from Pauletta to Meg and back.

"Whatever timetable we can work out. We can either do the songwriting while she recovers or record the album first and let them do post-production while she recovers."

"*She* hasn't decided yet," Meg pointed out.

Big Mac gently tipped her chin toward him. "I looked at the statistics. Your risk, with that genetic sequence is almost twentyfold more likely to get the disease. That's like..." He waved one of his hands in the air. "That's like...practically a guarantee."

"You looked that up?" She blinked at him. Several times.

"Yeah, of course."

Then, as if realizing the implications, he waved his hand around. "I'm pretty sure Ed looked them up as well."

"On my list of things to do..." I offered a smile. "It felt intrusive."

"I shared with you."

"Which we appreciate." Pauletta pointed to our cooling meals. "No worries about working out the details—that's what I'm for."

"If we sign," Axel countered.

"Why wouldn't we?" Songbird furrowed her brow.

"It means giving up an element of creative control." Axel gestured to everyone. "We've always had the final say in everything we do. We've always agreed as a group. This would change that dynamic."

"Yeah," I said wryly. "But think of all the money."

Everyone laughed.

Including Thornton.

But I didn't miss the shadows that passed through his eyes. I wanted to ask, but as soon as we finished our meals, Pauletta dug out the contract.

Lydia shut off the camera and settled down to eat, while we went through the nitty-gritty, the words on paper that would change our lives.

My questions for Thornton were quickly forgotten.

Chapter Thirty

Thornton

The concert that night went off without a hitch.

To top it off, the record executives made their presence known to Mickey, who was handling the wide camera at the back. They did a quick interview with the team from Grand Central—Tessa, Judith, and Bryan—before filming what proved to be a nearly flawless performance.

Standing next to Pauletta backstage, I cheered nearly as loudly as she did.

The band did three encores.

"They're going to run out of songs," she commented.

I laughed.

After the show, they showered before the meet and greet with fans.

I positioned myself, as unobtrusively as possible, near the record executives.

Tessa noticed me and gave me a *you think we're that dumb* look.

I shrugged sheepishly.

She broke away from the other two and approached me. "Impressive show."

"Yeah, I thought so."

"How's the doc going?"

"It's taking shape." No way was I giving more than that while we were still shooting.

"That's good." She indicated where Lydia was filming Songbird having an intense conversation with a group of young women who looked very much like her. "They have a lot of appeal. Huge potential fan base."

I wanted to demand that they not exploit the group of people who I now considered friends. Until I realized it didn't matter what the executives did. I wouldn't be around for any of it.

My only decision was whether to confront Ed or Axel or both. And whether to do it in Portland after their concert or if I might be better off waiting until we got to Vancouver.

Logically, I should consult with Mickey to get their opinion.

But I wouldn't.

No, I had to hold this secret in until the last possible moment.

Which made me want to explode.

I pressed a finger to my forehead.

Tessa cocked her head. "Headache?"

"Yes, a bit." *Chickenshit.* "I think I'm going to head back to the bus."

She smiled. "I was surprised to hear you were embedded. I mean, maybe I shouldn't have been, but that was quite a risk Pauletta took."

You have no idea.

"I think I'm a pretty safe bet. I'm always fair."

Liar.

"True. And I appreciate the publicity you're going to give the band." She tapped her chin. "If I can match them with the right production team, I think they have unlimited possibilities."

"Yeah. You're right. If you'll excuse me." I offered her a wan smile as I departed.

I made my way over to Mickey and made my excuses.

They offered a sympathetic smile and said we'd touch base in the morning. With only one driver, we couldn't do the entire trip to Portland in one go. Our plan was to drive to San Francisco overnight. The band wanted to do some sightseeing.

Mickey, ever looking for an opportunity, was sending Lydia with a still camera to nab some candid shots we might be able to use.

No one even considered that I wouldn't be going. I'd become almost one of them.

Almost.

Pauletta had no interest in any of this. She was scheduled to spend another day in LA nailing down the incredibly favorable contract, then she was flying to Portland where she'd meet us the day after next.

As I mounted the stairs to the bus, the headache swamped me.

Goes with the guilt.

I sauntered to the back, stopping to grab my sleep clothes before I headed to the bathroom. I had a quick shower to wash off the...whatever...before I donned my sleep pants and T-shirt. Finally, I brushed my teeth.

To my noted cowardice, I didn't look in the mirror

Back at my bunk, I pulled out Kyesha's chain and my go-bag. I rooted until I felt the false bottom. After hesitating for a moment, I got into the bunk and pulled the curtain. I flipped on the light, then settled with my legs crossed. I had to duck my head a bit, but that didn't matter.

I pulled out the worn file folder and put it on the bed before me. And stared.

Why are you doing this to yourself?

I knew what the folder contained. Had looked over the contents hundreds of times over the past eight years. Most of what was contained within I never should've been able to obtain. Knowing I hadn't actually bribed anyone didn't make the feelings of guilt abate. If not illegal, my methods had been definitely unethical.

The ends justify the means.

Or so I'd told myself a million times the last almost decade.

I couldn't do it.

With shaky hands, I returned the folder to the bottom of the bag and zipped it up. I fingered Kyesha's chain. It'd been returned to us with her possessions after she died. I'd asked for it, and my parents agreed. I carried it in my pocket as a talisman. A reminder for what needed to be done. I tucked it back into my pants pocket where it always remained. Finally, I grabbed a couple of painkillers, downed them with some lukewarm water, and crawled under the covers.

When I awoke, hours later, I had a headache hangover, but the pain was gone. Slowly, I eased myself from the bunk.

My feet hitting the cold floor felt good. I padded toward the front of the bus.

We were on a highway, as far as I could see. Were we still on the 5 or had we hit the 580?

I advanced slowly.

Vera caught sight of me in the mirror. "Hey, can't sleep?"

"Not really."

"Well, join me. We're about forty minutes out of San Fran."

For the life of me, I couldn't orient myself. I held up a finger, then backed up until I got to the fridge. I grabbed an apple juice, then headed back to a seat at the front.

Vera grinned.

"You want something?"

"Nah. But thanks. So tell me, how'd you get into journalism?"

"I was going to ask you about bus driving."

She waved me off. "I drive just about everything. I like working for myself and being able to travel at the drop of a hat. I'm lucky when Mr. Magnum calls me for this gig. I love the folks in the band. Good people, you know?"

My stomach dropped. "Yeah, good people."

"So…journalism?"

"Boring story."

"I've got time."

"Fair enough." I launched into an explanation of how I'd gone from college right into wilderness photography. I waxed on about all the exotic locations I visited—making certain to gloss over all the horrible parts of the experience. As curious as Vera seemed, I didn't figure she'd want to hear about some of the disasters I'd endured.

The dark-skinned woman was quick with a smile, asked incisive questions, and her brown eyes sparkled.

In the light of oncoming headlights, I spotted grays threaded through her black hair. I was ashamed I hadn't really paid attention to her before now. Like Jenny and Mikhail, she was part of the machinery. Part of what made the band so successful. I supposed they could've driven their own camper van and hauled their own equipment, but having a crew to do those things allowed them to focus on what was important—the concerts, the music, and the fans.

While Pauletta ensured everything ran smoothly.

We arrived in San Francisco just as the sun rose and the residents hopped into their cars and began their commutes.

Vera pulled onto a side street. "When everyone's awake, I'll drive over to Orphan Andy's."

"Another diner?"

She grinned.

"We didn't do one in LA."

"Too many to choose from? Not close enough to the beach? Who knows?" She winked. "I've learned to never ask."

"If I made a coffee, would you drink it?"

She waved me off. "I need to sleep as soon as you all are off to your sightseeing."

"You don't find this shifting around sleep to be disruptive?"

Another flick of the hand. "I can sleep anywhere. Anytime. Just like I can drive anywhere. Anytime. Comes from my time in the military."

My eyebrows rose to my hairline.

She snickered.

We spent the next hour talking about her time in the service.

I was utterly entranced. She'd done two tours in Afghanistan with the Canadian Forces as well as a peacekeeping tour in Haiti. We lamented the current political quagmire the country found itself in these days. Then we talked about her time in the far north. Even above the Arctic Circle.

"That's nuts." I laughed the comment after a particularly harrowing story about landing a Hercules in a snowstorm in Iqaluit, Nunavut.

"What's nuts?"

Ed ruffled my hair from behind.

I turned to look up at him with a huge grin. "Vera used to be in the armed forces."

He smiled down at me—rather indulgently. "I know."

"Yeah, but—"

He swept down to press a kiss to my lips.

Vera snickered. Then she turned the bus back on. "Hang on, Ed. We'll be at Orphan Andy's in about twenty."

"Great. Everyone except Meg's up. I'll nudge her." He caressed my cheek before heading to the back.

As Vera pulled out into traffic, she sighed.

I hesitated.

She signalled and maneuvered us into a left turn lane. She glanced over at me. "I just want to see that man happy long-term—you know?"

That lead balloon was back in my stomach. "Yeah, I know."

The atmosphere at Orphan Andy's suited the band's mood. Everyone was upbeat and grinning.

Meg ordered French toast, while Songbird chose omelettes.

Big Mac ordered Huevos Rancheros, and Axel settled on the New York steak.

Ed winced, then selected banana pancakes.

I wanted to do the same—in solidarity—but bananas weren't really my thing. I opted for chocolate pancakes and, before I could say anything else, Axel ordered me a side of bacon. I frowned.

"Bacon is like, nectar of the gods," Axel told him.

"Actually, it's the flesh of some poor pig," Ed grumbled.

Meg caught my gaze. "I'll be thrilled to divest you of some of your bacon. Oh, I hope it's crispy."

And so the meal went. I always struggled with whether Axel made the meat jokes to aggrieve Ed or whether he was truly clueless about how his best friend felt.

As Ed sliced into his pancakes, he caught my notice. "I worked in a poultry factory. For a day. The pay was amazing...and now I know why. I swore to never eat meat again."

I was so horrified, I didn't know what to say.

Songbird surreptitiously nabbed my side of bacon and passed it over to Meg, who put it on the far side of the table.

Axel bit into his steak and moaned.

I eyed my meal with trepidation. Oh well.

We did a bunch of touristy things in San Francisco.

What if they become famous? Will they always be so carefree? Able to do whatever they want?

I didn't have simple answers for that. Surely there'd be people who'd have no idea who they were. But how did one find those people? How did one know where to go to be left alone? All five band members were distinctive and memorable.

Okay, maybe not Big Mac. He could just pass for a skinny, white, short dude. The rest, though, had uncommon—and stunning—looks.

As we trudged onto the bus, and Lydia bid us farewell, I took a moment to really look at each person. Each was excited—about the day? About the contract? About the upcoming Portland concert? It almost didn't matter. Aside from the odd moody moment, these were—generally—five healthy, happy, and well-adjusted people.

Which brought me back to my sister.

I railed that Ed and Axel could be living life to the fullest while my sister's ashes had been spread down a rock face and into the Pacific Ocean. She'd barely been a baby, and her life had been snuffed out. And maybe expecting Ed and Axel to suffer every day was unfair...but I wanted some kind of acknowledgement of what they'd done.

Anyway.

With the help of a reservation, we chowed down at Gary Danko. They didn't have a ton of vegetarian options, but Ed managed to get a solid meal with a fabulous dessert.

This time, my crew joined us, and no one complained when I picked up the tab.

As we got back on the bus, Ed tried to question me about it. I tried to pass it off as a business expense.

Clearly, he didn't buy it.

I was *not* going to tell him about my family money. I rarely touched it, but I never had to worry about money drying up.

Contented, we made our way to bed in various groups. Finally, after Ed bid me goodnight, I remained in the lounge with Axel.

I met his gaze, and casually asked, "So, any regrets?"

"About today, about the tour, or about life in general?"

I shrugged.

"Yeah, I've had a few."

I sat back to listen.

Kyesha's name never crossed his lips.

Chapter Thirty-One

Ed

Vancouver was my physical home.

Seattle was my spiritual home.

Portland was my metaphysical home.

I just felt happy in this town. Oregon was a nice enough state, but being in Portland settled me. She'd welcomed us when we were just starting out. She gave us venues and packed them in with fans—making us feel like we might one day make it big.

As I did the sound check, I caught sight of Thornton sitting in the audience.

I'd panicked last night when I heard him ask Axel about regrets. In fact, I'd almost left my bunk and sought some excuse to go out and sit with them. In the end, though, I had to trust my best friend. He hadn't consumed any intoxicating substance that might loosen his tongue. He wasn't tired like I was. As he'd talked about some of his misspent youth and then lamented some things we'd done as a band back in the beginning that maybe hadn't been the brightest, I'd closed my eyes. Eventually, the sound of his voice and the vibrations of the bus had lulled me to sleep.

This morning, I'd been the first out of bed.

Vera had stopped in Eugene for a break, but she was determined to hit Portland before rush hour.

As Thornton had yesterday, I joined her up front.

"You got questions?"

I smiled. "Yeah, a few."

My knowledge about the woman who drove us with such care had increased exponentially—and I felt guilt at never having asked these questions before. I was normally a courteous person, but I supposed I also believed in privacy. If someone wanted to share their life story, they would, right?

Wrong.

I still knew almost nothing about Thornton, yet he knew just about everything to do with me.

Almost everything.

Yeah, I still held secrets. Ones I'd carry to the grave.

Three hours later, we pulled up to Grits'N'Gravy.

We piled out, and I coaxed Vera into joining us. Jenny, Mikhail, and Pauletta soon piled in and we took up a significant part of the back corner of the diner. I carefully positioned myself at the end of the table—next to Thornton.

Oh, how life has changed.

Yeah, well...he orders vegetarian just so I don't have to smell his meat.

But you like his meat.

Ugh. So tacky.

But true.

We hadn't had time for even a hand job since leaving Nevada.

You'll be home soon.

True...but how long would Thornton stay in Vancouver? His assignment had been focused on Rocktoberfest. The added concerts were a bonus. His mission had been to get inside our heads—my words, not his—and I felt he'd done a pretty good job at that. I knew more about the people in my life than I ever had before. Even Axel. Given we'd been friends for over twenty years, that feat impressed.

"That French toast not to your liking?" Thornton scraped some chunky hash browns onto my plate.

He knew me so damn well.

"No...I just..." I met his gaze.

Those amber eyes shone bright.

"How long are you staying in Vancouver?"

Slowly, he nodded. "Mickey wants another couple of days of filming. Pauletta said you'll have some downtime before heading back to the studio. Is that where you do your song writing?"

"Nah. We do most of that at our condo. Studio time's too expensive not to use it for rehearsing or, when we can, recording. Pauletta said we sold out of all the CDs we brought to Black Rock and that our downloads spiked. We need to do whatever we can to sustain that before recording the next album."

"Are you happy about the contract?"

I glanced at Pauletta, who only had eyes for Mikey.

"It's an incredible opportunity."

"That's not what I asked."

I shifted in my seat. "I'm a Canadian boy at heart. Things aren't perfect at home, but they're a damn sight better than other places. I don't mind touring, but I don't want to spend extended time in other countries."

"They said they'd record the album as quickly as possible."

"Right." I fingered my paper napkin. "But I'm a perfectionist. So's Paulie."

"And the others?"

I smiled wistfully. "Yes, to some extent. I like that we'll be able to bring Meg's dog, Wren. A bit of normalcy, you know?"

"I can't imagine the six of you in a vast house in, like, Malibu."

Grinning, I speared a chunk of potato. "Oh, you can't, can you? Well, it'll only be five. No way Pauletta will crash with us. She'll have a place of her own."

"Does she always hold herself apart like that?"

I cocked my head. "Not in the way you're thinking. She's got a head for business like no one else I've ever met. She leaves most of the artistic stuff to us. Oh, she's got an opinion—on everything—but she likes to give us free rein at times."

"Or enough rope to hang yourself."

"What?" His comment startled me. "That's wrong. Pauletta looks out for us—she's always looked out for us."

"Even in the days of your misspent youth?"

"Especially in those days. She's the reason we're clean." I winced. "No, that's not right. I do it for myself...for the people I hurt. I owe it to them to live my best life. For me, that means being clean. Means the same for Axel as well."

"Who did you hurt?"

He asked the question in a quiet and earnest voice.

I almost—almost—gave in and told him everything.

Instead I turned my focus back to my French toast and devoured it.

Vera drove us to the Arlene Schnitzer concert hall, then headed off to sleep.

We might've been early, but the stage manager and her assistant were there to greet us. We helped Mikhail and Jenny move all the equipment in while Pauletta and Mickey spoke in a corner of the cavernous room.

The concert hall sat nearly twenty-seven hundred people. To date, this would be one of our bigger indoor shows. As I gazed up to the upper balcony, my stomach dropped.

I nudged Axel, wanting him to note the vast expanse and rows of seats.

He strummed his guitar. "I think Pauletta wants us to try a different playlist tonight."

"Not a new song."

"Nah, nothing like that. Just a different order."

Whatever Paulie thought was best would work for me. Occasionally she did audience testing—to see which songs connected. Sales gave that information as well, but Paulie liked to hear directly from fans.

Meg wandered over, drumsticks in hand. "Heard we're sold out."

I gazed out again over the space. "That'll be cool."

"That'll make the bigwigs happy."

Before she could step away, I snagged her arm.

She stopped.

"Are you guys okay, with having bigwigs in charge?"

Songbird caught sight of us and headed over.

Big Mac was still tuning his guitar.

Meg hissed his name.

His head popped up. Spotting the impromptu meeting, he headed our way.

Axel stuck his chin out at me. "You having second thoughts?"

"No."

"About what?" Big Mac's dark-brown eyes were almost black in the dim light.

"He's wondering about having corporate bosses." Meg eyed me. "You think it won't be a good change?"

"I'm not saying that." I pressed a hand to my sternum. "It's an amazing opportunity."

"But you're thinking we should wait until the documentary comes out to see if we can get a better offer?"

Songbird's suggestion shocked me. "No, I hadn't been thinking that at all. But clearly you have."

She shrugged. "I've had lots of thoughts. I think the opposite is true. If we can have the studio album completed and ready to go when the documentary comes out, that might be the boost we need."

Meg tapped her sticks on her thigh. "She makes a good point."

Songbird stood a little taller.

"You've always got good points." I dipped my head in acknowledgment. "As long as we're in agreement. We...haven't really had time to talk about this." Out of the corner of my eye, I caught sight of Lydia.

Crouched.

Unobtrusively filming us.

Fuck.

Axel slapped me on the back. "I know you don't want to be a corporate shill."

"I'm not implying we'd be defrauding anyone—"

"You know what I mean. And I know what you mean." Axel pressed a hand to my chest—over my heart. "But if you have doubts—"

"I don't."

I tried to shrug away from his hand, but he held steady.

"It's just...added scrutiny. You know?"

My bandmates all looked at each other in confusion.

Axel stared right at me.

He understood.

"Let's take five." He looked at everyone. "We just need to grab a water, and then, if we can pry Pauletta away from her new paramour, we can regroup and find out what she has in mind for tonight."

No one moved.

Finally, I put my guitar on the stand. "Yeah, I just need five."

At that comment, the others dispersed.

Axel snagged my hand, and we started to move offstage.

Lydia made to follow.

Axel gave her the slash across the throat.

Slowly, she stood.

I watched as the light on her camera flickered off.

She gave us a smile and headed down toward where Pauletta and Mickey were still deep in conversation.

Axel grabbed two bottles of water and practically shoved me out the back door of the venue. The venue hadn't been particularly warm, but the cool air hit my skin, and I sucked in a breath.

"Fucking fall."

"Yeah, and winter comes after." He handed me a bottle. "Fucking circle of life and all that shit."

I took the bottle.

"Why are you harping on about the past?"

My gaze cut sharply to him.

"I know what you're thinking about. Or rather, who you're thinking about. Eight years is a fucking long time, Ed. I don't think she'd still want you to be…whatever this is…over her."

"You can't say what she'd want. You didn't know her that well."

His wounded look—with the hurt eyes and the downturned mouth—got to me. But I couldn't relent. "You know what I mean."

"No, I don't. Even you admitted we were kindred spirits."

"Sure. And you both liked cocaine. That didn't help you spiritually in any healthy ways, Axe." I never used his nickname because he truly hated it. And he'd never gotten out of his parents whether he'd been named after the singer, the car part, or if the name was some far-distant family member.

Truthfully, it didn't matter.

Well, for sure for me...and I was pretty sure it didn't matter to him either.

"Ed."

At his stern admonition, I stopped fidgeting. "What?"

"Do we need to go to a meeting? See the counsellor again? Because I thought we'd finally moved on."

"Is there any moving on, Axel? Really?"

"Okay, well, I'm going to project. If I'd been the one to die, I wouldn't want Kyesha—or you—to be still mourning me eight years later. I mean, it'd suck if I were dead, but I wouldn't enjoy the idea of you moping around. I'd wish you the best and hope you were making the best of your second chance. Which is what I'm doing. My God, Ed, all she wanted was for us to nab a record contract and to make it big. Would I prefer that she be alive? That she be here to share it with us? Of course. But she's not. And grieving her doesn't show how much we cared about her."

How much *he* had cared for her.

Shame heated my cheeks. At first, it'd been nice to have a genuine fan who followed us around. She'd seen our first show in Portland and had eventually followed us up to Canada. As she ingratiated herself, though, I sometimes found her irritating. But then she'd started to bring around party favors, and I'd been too naïve and stupid to realize the dangerous road we were traveling down.

Now Kyesha was dead.

And we were on the cusp of something that could either be huge or could be a total bomb.

Maybe the doubts stemmed from that—the fact we could fall on our faces and be a complete failure. If we continued on, limping through the indie world, then any success or lack thereof fell entirely on us.

Axel held open his arms.

Ah, we're going to hug it out.

I couldn't say we'd actually resolved anything, but then I realized that hadn't been the point.

Of course, I was going to agree to the contract. Of course, I was going to write the best songs and play my heart out. Of course, I was going to try to forget Kyesha and those early years.

After all, did I really have a choice?

No. No, I didn't.

I stepped into his arms and let him embrace me. His warmth enveloped me, and I settled into the comfort I always got when we hugged it out.

Then we went back inside and fucking killed it.

Chapter Thirty-Two

Thornton

The Schnitz was bigger than both the venues in Park City and LA, with a completely different vibe. The elegance of the hall gave a boost, I felt, to the band. Elevated them.

And their fans still stood and danced during several numbers.

Lydia again filmed from the stage.

Mickey had a camera at the back of the orchestra section.

I stood backstage next to Pauletta as we tapped our feet.

The opening band was local, and I was apprehensive that they might get a warmer reception than Grindstone.

I needn't have worried.

Even as I scanned the audience, I noticed quite a few Rocktoberfest T-shirts. Whether the fans had bought the ticket before or after that show, clearly they were enthusiastic about this performance.

Again, the band wound up doing three encores.

Fans ate it up.

The team showered, then headed to another fan meet and greet. While Ed seemed a bit lighter than before, Axel kept glancing around the room. As if he expected someone.

Portland was my home, of course, and I longed to drop by my condo. We didn't have time, though, and soon we piled back into the bus. I expected at least someone to stay up—adrenaline and all that—but everyone called it a night and headed to their bunks. Hitting the road just after midnight meant we'd hit the Canadian border just after sunrise. I supposed they all wanted to be coherent for that.

Not feeling sleepy—perhaps because I hadn't spent my afternoon rehearsing and my evening delivering a high-voltage, nearly three-hour rock concert—I sat at the table and pulled out Songbird's cards. As the miles sped by, I played hand after hand of solitaire while occasionally scribbling notes on my phone. I needed to have all the filming done by the time we had the ultimate confrontation.

I'd just begun my eighth—or maybe ninth—game when Ed appeared.

He stood next to me and curled his body around me, tugging my head against his chest. "Come to bed."

"Uh—"

"Just to sleep. This might be our last chance and...I just want to hold you."

"Well, how can I refuse an offer like that?" Truthfully, because of my size, I was always the big spoon. "That bunk's a tight squeeze."

He ruffled my hair. "So we'll get close. Like we did before."

I angled my head back, and he lowered his mouth to mine.

The kiss lingered, heated, then backed off again.

My cock stiffened. "I don't know..." I said the words as he tugged me to my feet.

"Blue balls never killed anyone." He palmed my erection.

I strained in my jeans.

He squeezed.

The sparkle in his eyes stole my breath.

"I can't..."

Immediately, he released me. "Of course, sorry. I didn't mean to push—"

"No." I shook my head. "I...meant something else. You...me...now... Yeah, that I can do."

"You can't promise me tomorrow."

I nodded.

"I'll take whatever you can give me." He went up on his tiptoes and grazed my cheek with his lips. "No expectations, okay?"

In so many ways, I knew this was going to end in disaster.

Still, I grabbed my nightclothes and headed to the bathroom to change. After brushing my teeth—again not looking in the mirror—I headed back to the bunks.

For some reason, I'd expected we'd cuddle in Ed's bunk.

Instead, he was in mine, plastered up against the wall. He'd brought his pillow and had tucked himself under my blanket.

I stowed my clothes and crawled in, maneuvering so I faced away from him. I pulled the drapes closed.

He snapped off the light.

I pulled the blanket over myself and settled in as he tugged me closer.

The fit wasn't perfect, given the size difference, but the feeling of comfort invaded me.

"You okay?" His breath whispered across the sensitive skin under my ear.

I shuddered. "Uh, yeah."

He threaded his arm under mine and pressed his hand to my sternum. "Breathe, Thornton."

"Uh, yeah."

His erection poked my lower back.

I sucked in a breath.

"Blue balls," he whispered, even as he stroked his fingers up and down the center of my chest.

"I don't think—"

"Don't think. Just sleep, okay?"

I nearly laughed out loud, but worried that might wake the others. Sleep? Like this? My cock strained and my balls felt heavy.

Yet, as we rolled toward Canada—and my destiny—I did relax.

Vera's voice over the loudspeaker, warning us we were near Blaine, dragged me out of the most erotic dream.

Ed nuzzled my neck. "Too early."

I chuckled. "Yeah, something like that."

"Hey, Ed." Axel's voice raised. "Where the fuck are you?" Unceremoniously, he threw open my drape.

Bright light flooded into the tiny space.

"Aw, shit. I'm never sleeping in that bunk."

"Get your mind out of the gutter, Axel." Ed snickered. "All we did was sleep."

Axel sniffed the air. He wrinkled his nose, then sniffed again. "Yeah, okay." He met my gaze. "So much for professionalism." Then, "The lineup isn't long. Like, ten minutes to the border."

Axel's prediction was off by about twenty minutes, but soon we'd made our way through Customs.

I had to say, on the whole, Canadian border guards tended to be a lot friendlier than American ones.

Not that I'd admit that to anyone.

Within a short period of time, we were through inspection and on our way.

As we sat around the table, Axel's stomach growled.

"We can all come back to our place and do takeout," Ed offered. He didn't look all that happy about the possibility.

"Sure," Big Mac began.

Meg smacked him on the chest.

"Oh, right." He cleared his throat. "That's a very generous offer. But we're all tired and need to, uh, recuperate." He glanced sideways at Meg.

She nodded her approval.

"Right. But we're all getting together tomorrow, right? At the studio?"

While no one said so outright, general nods of agreement rippled through the group.

Suddenly, the bus lurched.

Ed slammed into me.

Meg landed in Big Mac's lap.

Axel held out a protective hand for Songbird.

"Sorry," Vera yelled.

"Everything okay?" I was the first to find my voice, although it shook a little.

"Yeah, nothing to worry about," she called back.

Ed continued to press against me. Whether because he was still unsettled or because he was just taking advantage, I couldn't be certain.

And I didn't care.

We crawled in rush hour traffic, again going through the tunnel under the Fraser River.

I marveled I'd done this two weeks ago in such a different mood.

How much has changed.

How much has stayed the same.

That reminder had me sitting up a bit straighter.

Ed started to shift away.

I pressed my hand to his thigh, under the table.

He stilled.

Songbird caught my eye. Her gaze lowered, then raised again. A small smile crossed her face.

Approval? Did she assume we'd done more than just sleep last night? Or was she giving her blessing for whatever might come next?

If she only knew...

Yeah, that was the point, though, wasn't it? They couldn't know.

We began the drop-offs with Songbird.

Meg was next.

Big Mac moped until we got to his street and he had to get off.

Vera drove the rest of us downtown to the guys' condo.

Axel eyed my go-bag as we made our way to the front of the bus. "You coming up?"

"I—" I sought Ed's gaze. "—hadn't given it much thought."

Liar.

I'd thought about nothing else since we hit the border.

A room awaited me at Hotel BLU. My SUV was in their parking garage. In other words, I didn't have an excuse to stay.

Axel slapped me on the back. "You have to see the bachelor pad." He patted Vera on the shoulder, then hauled his suitcase down to the street.

Ed met my gaze. "Your call. Vera's happy to take you wherever you want to go."

"What do you want?"

He blinked. Twice. "Uh, you. I'd have thought that was pretty obvious."

"Maybe." I hedged. "But what if we are only a fling?"

After a moment, he poked my chest. "You're American. I'm Canadian. We both have demanding careers." He waved his hands around. "This might only ever be a fling." His hand flicked between the two of us. "But it's our thing. So we might as well own it."

"Okay." I grabbed my bag, he secured his suitcase, and we descended the stairs. We both waved to Vera.

She returned the gesture, then pulled into traffic.

The height of rush hour was apparently past, but many vehicles still littered the street. Even as I had the thought, a gust of wind blew down on us.

I eyed Ed's suitcase. "That wasn't all your stuff..."

He shook his head. "Jenny and Mikhail will do a sweep of the bus. They'll organize laundry and dry cleaning for the stuff we left behind."

As we stepped into the lobby of his building, I wrinkled my nose. "Not a fun job."

He shrugged, waved to the concierge, then led me to the elevators. "They're paid well. And they can always say *no*. I know they have other jobs they go back to, but I suspect it's not as lucrative as being roadies for us."

"Or as glamorous," I said dryly.

He chuckled. "Sure, there's that."

Just before we stepped into the elevator, I glanced back at the opulent lobby. When had I become so accustomed to the grandeur that it didn't even make an impression? "This is quite a place."

"Yeah, we shouldn't have been able to afford it. Long story, but Pauletta arranged some kind of financing, and the real estate market was still recovering from the recession. The timing just...worked."

He swiped a fob and selected the third floor from the top.

I whistled.

"Yeah, yeah, I know. But we work our asses off. The thing is more than half paid off and we've never missed a mortgage payment. Helps there are two of us."

"And you keep Axel on track."

"Well, there's that." He rubbed his eyes.

"You tired?"

"There are days when I always feel tired."

"Ed, you're twenty-seven. That's not normal."

He managed a small smile. "Weight-of-the-world shit, not actual physical weariness. Put me on stage in front of thousands of people, and I feed off their energy. Give me a less-than-ideal night's sleep and I'm a wreck."

My ears perked. "Because of me? We didn't—"

"Not because of you."

The elevator door swept open, and we stepped out.

"Well, not entirely because of you. You might've already guessed that I don't share a bed often—and that was the first time I shared a bunk."

We'd slept entangled the entire night.

"Are you tired?"

His hand poised on the doorknob, he hesitated. He gave me a long, lingering, up-and-down examination. "Shower, then fuck, then sleep." Again, his hand hovered. "Your crew expecting you?"

I shook my head. "They're in Portland until tomorrow morning. They'll be up in time for the afternoon rehearsal."

He went up on his toes to press a kiss to my cheek. "Fucking brilliant."

Finally, he opened the door, and we stepped inside.

Chapter Thirty-Three

Ed

I snagged Thornton's hand and dragged him to my room.

We abandoned our luggage near the front door.

Apparently my equivalent of a sock on the knob.

Axel was nowhere in sight, but his shower was running, Although the cleaning crew would've put his laundry away and changed his sheets, his room—seen through his open door as we passed—was still...cluttered.

Mine wasn't. Not a single thing was out of place. Sometimes I wondered if my obsession with organization was a coping mechanism to deal with Axel's continual chaos.

My accent wall was slate-gray while the other walls were white. Blinds covered my floor-to-ceiling windows, casting the room in shadows. The doors to my walk-in closet, and the ensuite bathroom beyond it, were closed. Although the room was fresh, it had a feeling of disuse.

Thornton nuzzled my neck from behind. "Fuck first, tour later?" He pressed his erect cock against my ass.

I pushed back against him. "Need you. Need to be in you." Important to clarify, lest there be any confusion. That being said, if he wanted to fuck me, I wasn't sure I'd have the ability or wherewithal to say no.

He snagged the hem of my sweatshirt and, with my help, dragged it over my head.

Holding myself still, I waited as he removed his button-down shirt and dropped it to the floor.

It's going to wrinkle.

OMG, that's what you're thinking about?

Fair enough. Point made.

He pressed his chest against my back—warm skin against my already cooling flesh.

"You're going to fuck me, right?" He slid his hand down to cup my already perking cock.

"Yeah. You need a shower?"

"Oh, we'll have one after. Right now, I want to make you sweat."

I had no problems with that idea. I spun in his arms, grabbed the back of his neck, and dragged him down for a kiss. A kiss that went on and on and on. He kissed me with a desperate ferocity that matched my own. I wanted him. Needed him. Hoped this would never end—all the while knowing it had to.

He snagged the button of my jeans and tried to get it open while sticking his tongue down my throat.

The results were...less than ideal.

"You do you. I do me. Lube's in the drawer."

His eyes glinted with mischief.

Yet removing our footwear forced us both to slow down.

I didn't want slow. I wanted action. I wanted…so very many things. Things I couldn't have.

Stop wallowing.

Yeah, I needed to focus on the present. I had a naked man on my bed with his legs spread wide as he fingered himself. Stretching himself open to accommodate my cock.

I finished undressing, organizing all our clothes on an oversized reading chair I particularly enjoyed using on rainy days. Then I meandered over to the nightstand.

"Jesus, Ed, I'm so ready here and…" His eyes fluttered shut, a look of absolute bliss overtook his features, and his cock jerked.

Ah prostate.

Not wanting to make him wait more than necessary—okay, much—I donned a condom, slathered myself in lube, and crawled onto the bed to position myself between his legs.

Legs he opened wide, giving me the most perfect view of his hole.

"What are you waiting for?" Said through gritted teeth.

"I'm savoring."

He let out a long wail of frustration.

Yet still, I held myself back. I remembered Reno. I remembered the tour bus in Black Rock. And I'd remember this time as well. But those had been rushed couplings—knowing someone waited. This was…our time. I wouldn't have anyone steal the pleasure from me.

Thornton opened his eyes.

I read the plea in those amber orbs. Deciding I'd made him wait long enough, I lined myself up. I entered him gently, but once the crown of my cock was buried within him, I thrust in.

He clawed at my back, urging me on.

Repeatedly, I withdrew, then pushed in.

Repeatedly, he made noises of pleasure.

I pushed him higher and higher as I chased my own orgasm. Although I needed this to go on forever, that was impossible.

Just as I was about to lose my mind, he grabbed his cock and gave it a couple of hard tugs. That tumbled him over the precipice.

The contractions around my cock were enough to push me over the edge as well. I flew over the cliff and plunged down to the ocean as waves of pleasure crashed over me.

As my arms gave way and I landed on him, the monumentality of what we'd done sank in. Not that we'd had sex—we'd done that before—but that I really could love this man. And that was all kinds of fucked up. Because, in my heart, I knew he had an agenda. I'd known that from the very beginning—and nothing had changed.

Also, he didn't know my secrets. The stuff I held close to my heart. The stuff that ate away at my soul.

Thornton murmured, "I just want to stay like this forever."

Attributing Thornton's words to, like, sex hormones and shit, I merely smiled into his shoulder.

He stroked down my flank. On this meandering journey back up, he grazed my ribs.

I tried to pull away.

His eyes widened and his lips curled up. "Ticklish?"

"No."

"Oh, you're such a liar. I can always tell when you're lying."

"You can not."

"I can."

"How?"

"If I told you that, I'd lose my advantage."

"I don't believe you." Yet I continued to smile at him.

"Doesn't matter what you believe—it's what I can prove."

"Well, you have your tell as well."

His eyes narrowed.

I considered telling him about the eye twitch—which I'd only spotted a couple of times since the first time we'd met. Generally, he didn't lie to me.

Or at least, if he did, he hid it well.

But *generally* wasn't never.

Chapter Thirty-Four

Thornton

Leaving Ed's was tough. We lounged over a mandarin-orange salad he made. He served me a tuna melt on the side and had a grilled cheese for himself. I could almost pretend we were just a normal couple.

Until Axel appeared, left the condo, and reappeared five minutes later with a very attractive—and very young—blonde on his arm.

The woman—really just a girl, although probably legal—gave us a cute wave before following Axel into his bedroom.

He shut the door.

My conscience took a knock. Was this how it'd been with my sister? They hadn't lived in this condo, but where they had been...had she just been one in a line of groupies? Had she meant so little to the men?

Which led me to the dilemma of Ed. He seemed like a really great guy. But he carried an underlying...sadness? Vulnerability? Whatever it was, I didn't like to acknowledge it. That he might have deep feelings.

That he might reciprocate the care I was coming to feel for him.

Lights and sirens flashed and blared in my mind. *This way lies madness and danger.*

I rose, snagged both our plates, and headed to the kitchen.

Ed followed. "Sorry about that." He swept the crust he hadn't finished into the compost container. "Awkward."

"Must happen frequently."

His gaze snapped to mine. "Not as often as you might think…" He swallowed. "But more often than I'd like."

"Ever the same girl?"

Eyes narrowing, he took a breath. "Sometimes. He's not a man whore."

"I don't like the term applied to women either. How about player? Playboy?"

He hesitated. "The few times he tried something long-term, it never worked out."

Part of me wanted to demand what my sister'd been to these two men or—worst of all—if they'd shared her.

I couldn't bring myself to ask. "You bring a lot of women home? Or men?"

He shook his head. "Nah. That's not my jam. As you know, it's mostly men these days. And we always go back to their place or to a hotel." He swept his hand across the living space and to his bedroom. "I like my privacy."

Pointing to Axel's room, I said, "Not much with that going on."

After a moment, he moved his hand in a *so-so* gesture. "He's got everything he needs in there. If I'm around, he tends to stick to his bedroom. I haven't hung out with most of the women. I don't want to be a third wheel."

Way more was going on below the surface, but I didn't want to push. There'd come a time for that.

"I should be going."

His look of hurt was transitory—but no way could I have missed it.

"We can do something later."

He pressed himself against me. "I want to do something now."

I laughed. "Seriously? Two orgasms weren't enough?"

"Good things come in threes."

Axel's door opened. He sprinted, shirtless, over to the fridge. He grabbed two bottles of water, nodded to us, and went back to his room.

I stepped back from Ed. At least we'd put our clothes back on after our showers. I held his gaze.

His eyes flashed hurt.

I bent to kiss him. "Later, I promise."

"Yeah, okay."

After a hesitation, I headed to his room to collect my shoes. I put them on, then came back into the living room.

He stood by the balcony door.

I wasn't sure what the right move was. "I'll call you?"

He waved without turning around.

I donned my coat, grabbed my bag, and left.

All the way down the elevator, I kept replaying the scene in my mind. Should I have stayed? What was there left to say? Should I have invited him to join me at my hotel? What was there left to do?

Let him fuck you until you can't stand up straight.

My stupid subconscious. Pushing to the fore with all the thoughts I had but wasn't willing to contemplate.

I hit the street. The crisp autumn air invigorated me. I was pretty sure the way back to my hotel, but I took a moment to check on the map.

Yep, I was right.

As I headed down Robson Street, marveling at the lack of tents everywhere, I thought about the documentary my sister Bonita was nagging me to make about tent cities. Oh, Vancouver had homeless people. They had rows of tents. Just not here, in the more expensive part of town.

I could only begin to guess what Ed and Axel's condo was worth.

Well, I could check to see other real estate listings in the building, as well as recently sold units. Apparently they'd bought years ago—back when Vancouver was a livable city. These days, the town was one of the most expensive in the world. Toronto and a few other Canadian cities were creeping up as well.

I thought about the documentary I'd seen recently about San Francisco's homeless population. How people were drawn there because of both the services offered as well as the cheap drugs. Did Vancouver have the same problems? Although it could get cold in the winter, it was definitely warmer than most of Canada. And, on top of that, huge numbers of unhoused people here were Indigenous and racialized.

Society continuing to fail them at every turn.

I made a note to scour Canadian news sites to see what was being said about homelessness in Canada.

Two hours later, I shoved my laptop away in disgust. Yeah, same problems, same platitudes, same inaction. A local news had told the story of a guy who'd been moved when the tents had been taken down. He'd found an electrical room he could stay in. Then it caught fire, and he died.

Not only was that a horrible way to die, but it felt so unnecessary. Like somehow, he should've been offered another choice.

You're getting off track. Yeah. After the stunt I was about to pull, no one in their right mind would let me do any kind of documentary or interview again. I'd be lucky to be relegated to Antarctica to photograph the penguins.

Right now, that didn't sound so bad.

The people I really didn't want to hurt was my parents. Bringing my sister's death to prominence would open old wounds. Would they understand? That this'd been my mission for the last eight years? That everything I'd done to this point had been for this? Why hadn't I thought about this before? From their perspective? And, while I was asking stupid questions... What was going to happen to my relationship with Ed?

Seriously? What relationship? You're going to destroy his life, and you think he'll ever want to speak to you again? You're a fucking idiot.

Yet I still yearned.

To fix the guilt, I moved to the bag I'd carelessly tossed onto the second bed. As I withdrew the worn folder, I careened into the mental space where nothing mattered but the wrong inflicted upon my family by two of the most selfish men on the planet.

Yet... They weren't selfish at all. Axel might be flighty—although his diagnosis which he revealed explained a bit of the...inability to focus. Well, and to hyperfocus when it came to music.

And Ed? Somehow, I pictured him being remorseful over what happened with my sister. He seemed like a guy with a conscience.

Or he was the best fucking actor north of Hollywood. Had I been taken in by a con man?

As I eyed the contents of the minibar, I considered further.

I'd always considered myself a decent judge of character. I'd never have hooked up with Mickey, Lydia, and Kato if I hadn't trusted them. And they'd never let me down.

But I was about to let them down.

That makes you a shitty douchebag.

Well, yeah. Hashtag truth.

A knock sounded at my door.

Since Lydia and Kato weren't due until tomorrow—and Mickey had something tonight—I was confused.

I checked the peephole, and my heart soared.

Then sank.

Slowly, I opened the door.

Ed stood on the other side with a bouquet of spring flowers, a bottle of what I assumed was non-alcoholic wine, and a shit-eating grin on his face. That grin faltered when he saw me. He didn't look over my shoulder, but he did ask, "Is this a bad time? I should've called. Right."

He tried to shove the flowers and bottle into my hands.

"I'll just go. I mean, you probably have—"

I used my grip on each to tug him into my room.

This time, he did look around.

I didn't miss the look of relief on his face.

God, he thinks I'd just...hop into bed with someone else? Does he not know me?

Huh. He knew I had secrets.

We both had secrets.

I put the vase of flowers on the table and held up the bottle.

"Nah." He rubbed his forehead. "But you go ahead."

I placed the chilled bottle in the fridge. "What's going on, Ed?"

He moved toward me, stopping just short of my personal space. "I missed you."

"Missed me...or worried I might be in here with someone else?"

His dark-brown eyes flashed. "I'm not like that. If you want to have someone over—"

"Then why did you look so relieved when you saw I was alone?"

He winced. "You saw that, eh?"

I cocked my head. "Kind of hard to miss. You're pretty predictable in some respects and, in others, I can't get a read on you at all."

His gaze scanned the room. He pointed to my laptop. "How's the footage looking?"

Letting out a long breath, I gave him a once-over. "I haven't looked at any of the Portland stuff yet. The rest looks good, Ed. I...think it'll make a good doc."

He spun, his face tilting as if asking for clarification on my hesitancy.

"See, you say stuff like that..." He rubbed his forehead. "I know you." He winced. "Well, I don't *know* you."

"Oh, I'd say you know me pretty well. How many times has your dick been in my ass?"

Another wince. "That wasn't what I meant."

"I know it wasn't." My gaze shifted to the folder, then quickly back to him. "You think I've got some ulterior motive. I don't."

"Your left eye just twitched."

I furrowed my brow. "What?"

"Your left eye twitched. It does that whenever you're lying. Oh, it's so subtle that most people wouldn't notice. But I've noticed. Every time we start to talk about the documentary, you get squirrely. You become evasive."

"I haven't—"

"Oh yeah, you have." He pressed his thumb and index finger to the bridge of his nose.

Is he getting a migraine? Should I offer him something? "Look—"

He took in a deep breath and let it out slowly. "I need to know, Thornton. I need to know. Whatever you're hiding. Whatever you plan to pounce on me with during the final interview."

His gaze hit me squarely in the chest, robbing me of breath.

"I'm going to insist it just be me. I can't have you ruining Axel as well. Whatever it is that you think you have, drop the bombshell on me. I'll deal with the fallout."

"You don't know—"

"Oh, but I do. You've dropped several broad hints. You're not as subtle as you think you are. You've got something on us. And you're planning a big reveal. Well, fine. Reveal it to me. I can't have you ruining Axel's life."

"But ruining yours is okay?" I didn't want to know.

And yet I needed to.

His dark eyes flashed. "I'm protective of what's mine. Axel is a brother to me. He saved me more times that I can count—"

"I thought you saved him."

He bit his lip, and pain radiated off him and hit me like waves. "We tell that to people—because that's who we are. That's the persona we've created." He blinked rapidly several times. "He saved me, Ed. From something horrible—" His voice cracked.

Jesus, was he about to admit about my sister?

"You can talk to me." I beseeched him in my best calm voice. The one I used to coax skittish interviewees into revealing everything.

What are you saying? If he confesses now, you lose everything.

And if I waited until the interview to reveal everything, I'd lose any chance of a future with him. And that's what I wanted. More than anything. Despite all the obstacles—and plenty existed—I wanted us to find a way to be together. I glanced at the folder again. Could I do it? Could I walk away from vengeance? Could I betray my sister like that? And still look myself in the mirror?

Not that I'd been doing that much lately. I'd even grown scruff because I didn't want to face the man I'd become. The liar. The fraud.

The monster.

Ed faced me. "What's in the folder, Thornton?"

He said my name with an icy tone I'd never heard.

Do or die.

I cleared my throat. "Why don't you look for yourself?"

He held my gaze for what felt like an interminable amount of time—but was likely only about thirty seconds. Then he snagged the folder, sat at the table, and opened it.

His leg immediately started jiggling.

My heart leapt into my throat.

You need to calm down.

No, I needed a drink. But, out of respect for the man in my room, I wouldn't consume one. Instead, I dropped to sit on the bed.

Ed took forever to read the first page.

The media report.

He flipped to the second page.

The coroner's report. That report was voluminous. Then the news clippings—from Vancouver as well as Portland. Finally, the photographs. The ones seared in my memory for eternity. The reason I kept fighting.

Time limped along as Ed continued to read. From what I could tell, he wasn't skimming. He was reading—as if this was all new to him. Well, he might not have seen the reports before, but he bloody well knew what had happened.

I rose.

He didn't take his eyes from the papers.

I began to pace.

He continued on as if I wasn't in the room.

Resisting the urge to mark time by looking at the clock radio proved impossible. And as each increment of time passed—one minute, ten minutes, thirty minutes—I thought I'd lose my mind. I fingered the chain in my pocket, seeking both strength and patience.

Finally, just as I was about to completely lose my shit, Ed looked up.

He didn't meet my gaze.

"Who is Kyesha to you?"

"My sister."

Chapter Thirty-Five

Ed

In my heart, I'd known this moment would come. Had I known it would be Thornton to resurrect the specter of the young girl who'd died so senselessly? So needlessly? So idiotically?

No.

Well... I hedged. I'd known he had *something*. I just hadn't realized he had this. That he had *her*. In all my catastrophic thinking, I'd thought we'd kept this secret. And that if he had this, he would've brought it up long before now.

"You don't have the police report."

"Not for lack of trying," Thornton spat out.

"There are...facts beyond what you think you see."

"I know what I see. I see a young woman who was plied with drugs. A young woman who died of a drug overdose. I see two young men who got away with murder."

My gaze shot to his.

Breathe.

"Neither Axel nor I killed Kyesha." I tapped the closed folder. "The medical examiner had it right—she died of a drug overdose."

"You gave her the drugs."

Of course he thinks that. Two Black kids. What else might we be good for?

Was there a point in arguing? In pleading my case? Our case, I corrected myself. Because clearly Thornton was hellbent on bringing down both Axel and myself.

Slowly, I rose. "You don't have all the facts."

"So tell me." He spat out the words. "Spin all your pretty lies and explain to me how you didn't kill her."

"I...feel responsible for her death."

His eyes flashed in triumph.

"But I didn't cause her death. I didn't give her the drugs. Axel didn't give her the drugs. I...think you need to do more research." I started to move toward the door.

He barred my exit. "You think I'm going to let you leave like this? Without getting some accountability?"

Breathe. Suddenly, I felt the need to command the autonomic function. "I need to talk to Axel. Obviously you're going to go public. I wish you'd collect all the facts before you do...but I can't force you to do proper research. But I can protect what's mine." This time, I knew my eyes flashed. "He...doesn't know the complete story. Bringing up Kyesha again is going to devastate him. He needs to hear the truth from me."

"What truth?" He spat out these words as well. "If there's something I don't know, why don't you tell me?"

"I recommend you speak to Detective Tyson McGillvary of the Vancouver Police Department. He wasn't a detective back then, but he'll know the people that were. He'll know the case. He…" I drew a breath. "He was the first on scene." My gut churned. "I'm surprised you don't have the police report."

"Not for lack of trying. I filed a privacy request and was told the report would be mostly redacted—to protect my sister's privacy. Which is such bullshit."

I didn't know anything about privacy requests. I wasn't certain I understood why Kyesha needed protecting—but maybe if he'd known what was in the report, none of this would've happened. He likely wouldn't have come to see the band and to do this sham documentary. He wouldn't have felt the need to ambush Axel and me.

I would've never met him.

That thought hit me square in the gut.

Did I regret him? And even if he didn't splash our story across the screen, could I ever trust him? "Did you seduce me to get information about Kyesha's death? Or just to set me up?"

"I think the seduction was mutual." His amber eyes flashed. "You seduced me to keep me away from time alone with Axel. Were you worried he'd spill the beans?"

"Axel doesn't talk about Kyesha." I kept repeating her name so he'd know I didn't just think of her as disposable. "Pauletta doesn't either."

"Pauletta?" His voice bit.

Oh shit.

Yet she'd never shied away from the God's honest truth. On occasion, she'd bring up the incident if it looked like Axel or I was considering stepping even a toe out of line. One reminder of that horrific night—that horrific month—and we'd fall right back into line. We'd do whatever she wanted. I didn't like to think that she had our balls in a vise—but she kind of did.

We were okay with that. Fame might be a steep climb—but we did it with the ropes Paulie'd set out for us. She forged the path, and we followed in her wake. She did the tough shit so we could focus on the music.

And on staying sober.

"Will you..." I drew in a deep breath. "Will you let me talk to Axel? To warn him? I mean, if I tell Pauletta, she'll likely try to pull any future interview." I rubbed my forehead. "And I don't know if we've said anything incriminating—"

"So you admit criminal liability."

My gaze shot to his. "That wasn't what I said, and you know that wasn't what I meant. You need..." My mind flashed back to that awful night and my stomach heaved. I just didn't have the strength. "Talk to the police officer. If you still have questions, then come and find me."

"I have hundreds of questions." Still with the icy tone.

"I know you do." I waved at the file on the desk. "But until you've heard the entire story from a neutral third party, you...won't have all the facts." My chest squeezed, and I fought for breath. "There's a lot you have no idea about. And if I tell you, you're not going to believe me."

"You don't know that. I might."

Hope flared in my chest.

Then I met his gaze, and that ember died.

No, he didn't have an open mind and a willing heart. Whatever I said was going to be scrutinized and disregarded. Because not only did it exonerate Axel and myself, but it damned Kyesha. The truth made her look bad—and I couldn't be the one to taint the memory of his sister. No, best leave that to the professional. Detective McGillvary would be gentle. I knew that from the depths of my soul. I knew it in my heart. And he'd empathize with Thornton—give the man the respect he deserved.

I couldn't understand why Thornton hadn't already gone that route. He'd been so meticulous.

They wouldn't give him the report.

Right. And maybe he had scruples. Maybe he knew pushing that boundary wouldn't earn him any favors. Hell, maybe he'd planned to speak to the police after interviewing Axel and me. To verify the veracity of our statements. Or to prove us liars once and for all.

Could go either way.

I hadn't removed my coat, so I had no excuse to linger. "I'm so sorry Kyesha died. I know it sounds trite...but I would've exchanged my life for hers. Life doesn't work that way though, you know? I lived, and she died."

He appeared to take a physical blow at my words.

More guilt swamped me.

"Axel and I have tried to honor her memory in our own quiet way."

"Do you talk about her?"

I bit my lip. Was this one of those times when a lie would soften the blow? Or, perhaps, the truth was what he needed to hear.

"We never mention her by name. But she's always with us. She's the reason we stay sober. She's the reason we wrote "Sunrise"."

His eyes widened in evident astonishment. Yet, he didn't have the right to be surprised. He had the medical examiner's report. He knew her cause of death. And, if the person doing the autopsy had been even vaguely competent, he would've known she was a regular drug user. Hell, how had he not known before she left Portland and came to Canada?

Or maybe he'd been oblivious. Sometimes we didn't see what was right before us. The truth. The god-awful heart-stoppingly painful truth.

"I'm going to go." In reflex, I patted my back pocket.

The phone sat where it always did.

"You have my number, and you know where we live. The next move is up to you."

I didn't wait for a response. Instead, I pivoted away from him and headed to the door.

As I opened it, he said, "I'll find out the truth."

Without looking back, I answered, "I hope you will."

With that, I left his room, easing the door shut.

God, what had I been thinking? I'd wanted a booty call. I'd wanted to take him out to dinner. I'd wanted to spend more time with him—out from under the weight of the documentary. Just the two of us. Like it'd been in Reno—before Big Mac cockblocked us.

Before Axel'd brought a woman home and had, essentially, cockblocked us.

Every time we'd started to get close on an emotional level, something had come between us. I'd seen tonight as an opportunity to start over.

I arrived at the lobby, having no memory of the descent in the elevator. *I should go home.*

Yet as I walked down Robson Street, I couldn't quite bring myself to do it. Instead, I went into the library.

Although the Carnegie Library—at Hastings and Main—had been closer to my house, I'd always dragged Axel here.

The security guards sometimes gave us a second look. Just as often, they'd be people who looked like us.

We'd go up to the sixth floor and sit at desks across from each other and study.

He'd fidget and lose focus.

I'd gently guide him back and silently demand he put his mind to his work.

If we managed to get everything done, I'd take us to McDonald's, and we'd split a strawberry sundae. In the end, we'd graduated from high school. I wanted to go into a music program, but everything was too expensive. We got jobs, played gigs, and sank into a life I would now know to call pathetic. And dangerous.

Kyesha's death pulled us back from the brink of total self-destruction. Of annihilation.

That and Paulie's insistence we get clean. She'd threatened to walk away.

Axel might've been willing to let her go, he was so far into his addiction.

When I threatened to walk as well, though, he'd had that come-to-Jesus moment when he realized he'd lose everything.

We both pledged sobriety and had stayed that way.

Some days we held on by our fingernails.

But we held on.

After touring the sixth floor, I took the escalators back down to the main floor. I headed back onto Robson Street and stopped by the Starbucks for an Americano.

I contemplated buying something for Axel. In the end, I snagged a lemon square. Tucking the little paper bag into my pocket, I then turned westward and headed home.

To my relief, I found him alone.

He sat in the living room with the news playing in the background as he scrolled on his phone. When he spotted me, he sat up. "I didn't expect you back tonight."

I handed him the lemon square, put my coffee on the counter, and removed my coat. After hanging it up, I snagged my coffee and headed back into the living room.

Axel folded up the empty bag and put it on the coffee table. He eyed me. "That bad, eh?"

I eased myself down into the chair across from him. "Worse."

He cocked his head and, after a long moment, grabbed the remote and shut off the television. "I'll kill the bastard."

"It's not—"

"No." He held up his hand. "I'll fucking kill him. You're, like, the most amazing guy in the world. He's lucky you give him the time of day, and—"

"He's Kyesha's brother." Might as well lay it all on the line.

The shock on Axel's face might've been comical—jaw dropping and all that—if this situation hadn't been dire.

"Kyesha was Black."

"I know."

"Kyesha's last name wasn't Graves."

"I know."

His eyes narrowed. "So how do you know he's not bullshitting you?"

My breath caught in my throat. I'd never thought to question it. Mixed-race families existed. Maybe one of them had been adopted and kept their original family's name. Maybe Kyesha'd been married, and we hadn't known.

"Ed."

Axel's sharp voice had me straightening.

I let out a long breath. "I didn't ask for proof. I didn't need to." I gazed down at my rapidly cooling coffee before meeting his gaze. "There are...things you don't know."

"I know everything—"

"No, Axel. You really don't. And I wish I didn't have to be the one to tell you. I could call Pauletta and ask her to come—to tell you and to back up my version of events—but we don't have time." *And this isn't Pauletta's mess to fix.*

"What do you mean *we don't have time*?"

"I...suggested Thornton talk to the police."

"He hadn't already?"

"Seems weird, I know, but he seems to think he knows everything that happened. He doesn't." I met my best friend's gaze. "And neither do you."

Chapter Thirty-Six

Thornton

Detective Tyson McGillvary, of the Vancouver Police Department, was a damn handsome man.

I hated myself for noticing...but I would've had to be blind not to see the man's beauty. Well, or rugged handsomeness. His close-cropped, steel-gray hair spoke of age, but his face had few lines. If I had to guess, I'd say early thirties. His dark-brown eyes, though, spoke of wisdom beyond those years.

To my surprise, we sat across from each other at his kitchen table.

"Sorry," Tyson said, as he pointed to a chair. "My dad's not well, and my wife..." He let the words trail off.

I could fill in the blanks with a dozen viable ideas, but I chose the simplest. Clearly, she wasn't here. I heard wheezing with occasional fits of coughing coming from the other room. "I'm sorry to bother you."

He waved me off as he placed two mugs of coffee on the table. Reluctantly, I took the milk and sugar he offered. I didn't want to disturb him any more than necessary, but he replicated my actions.

To make me feel comfortable, or because that's how he takes his coffee?

Could go either way.

"It surprised me you called." He pointed to his laptop, which sat closed. "I pulled up all the case notes from the file. Truth is, though, I remember the case vividly."

"One of your firsts?"

He shook his head. "Nah. I wasn't a rookie at that point. Was well on my way to becoming a detective. Had a fire in my belly back then—I wanted off patrol."

"You were the first one on scene?"

He nodded. "Me and my partner, Ginny. The call came in to 911, so we hustled our asses. But..." He winced. "Clearly, she'd been dead for a while. The young man-" He gazed upward. "—Ed. He called it in. He was trying to do CPR. I mean, the guy was frantic. But I eased him off and pulled him aside as Ginny checked her over. I'm sorry to be so blunt—she was cold. Clearly had been gone for a long time.

"Ed...was beside himself. Like, genuine anguish. At first, I assumed they were a couple."

"They weren't?" I knew this, but I wanted it confirmed.

"He said not...and I believed him."

"He can be a convincing liar."

Tyson arched an eyebrow. "Well, that might be true. We found evidence, though, that she was involved with someone else."

"Axel Townsend?"

"Yeah." The man nodded slowly. "I would've chosen to interview him, but he was up in rehab at Eternal Springs in Hope. That's a couple hours away."

I didn't understand. "He wasn't there that night?"

"No one was."

I furrowed my brow. "But…"

"Ed said he drove Axel up to Eternal Springs. The medical examiner pinned her approximate time of death to when they were on the road." He cocked his head. "Look, I'm sorry you didn't get the report. The privacy laws up here are pretty strict."

Waving my hand, I urged him to continue.

"We traced Kyesha's movements in the hours before her death. We found surveillance footage where she bought the drugs—"

"She bought the drugs?" I didn't try to keep the incredulity from my voice.

"Yeah." He hesitated. "We have her making a large cash withdrawal that afternoon and, a few hours later, buying the drugs. When Ed returned home, he found the door open. Kyesha's bag—and whatever drugs there might've still been—were gone. We took fingerprints and quickly identified the guy. Not too bright, that one. He kept her cell phone, and we were able to track it."

"I got the cell phone back. But the thing was locked and I could never unlock it."

"We had the same problem. But finding it on the guy was good enough for us. Plus, he admitted the whole thing—only he claimed she was already dead. Again, the timeline fit. I'm sorry to say, but it looks like she shot up alone. And died alone."

My chest tightened. I'd known about the drugs in her system—but I'd assumed Axel and Ed had given them to her. I assumed they hadn't even tried to save her. It'd never occurred to me that they hadn't been there at all. I pulled out the worn folder and put the pictures on the table.

Tyson picked them up. "Oh, yeah. Some local reporter. Honestly, that was unusual. I think they caught on that she was an American teenager." He pointed. "That's me. That's Ginny. And that's the detective who took over the case—Lou Hobson. He passed a number of years ago. Heart attack. Turns out he had a bad ticker and it was just a matter of time."

I'd tried to track him down but had hit nothing but roadblocks. Tyson's words went a long way to explaining things.

"Anyway, Ed was as helpful as he could be. He admitted the three of them had done drugs in the past. He said he'd recently stopped—and had finally talked Axel into doing the same."

"And no one questioned Axel?" This didn't make sense to me.

"That would've been Lou's call. I saw a notation that he called Eternal Springs, and they said Axel was in isolation for seven days. I mean, I'm sure he could've pushed, but he had a soft spot for people trying to get clean. His..." He trailed off. "Privacy. But he had someone close to him who'd gotten clean. He believed in the power of a good rehab—even if relapse was always possible." After a moment, Tyson handed the photos back. "I don't see that either Ed or Axel have had any more run-ins with law enforcement."

I hadn't been positive about that—but it fit with the two men I'd met just over two weeks ago. With their every interaction, I'd felt the sobriety. The drive to do good. And yes, Ed had been hiding something from me. Something important. But he hadn't known about my family's adopting Kyesha. He hadn't known she meant something to me. "Anything else you can tell me?"

Tyson tapped the table. "Not really. Although your sister's case is tragic, it's also not uncommon. Drug use...anyway. Her death was just before fentanyl became a thing in the Vancouver drug supply.

Everything starts here and then sweeps across the country. You're from Portland?"

I nodded.

"Then you've probably seen a similar situation. Vancouver decriminalized small amounts of drugs—hasn't made a lick of difference. The addicts still use, the drug dealers still make money, and suffering still continues. We don't have enough rehab beds. But, even if we can get someone into treatment, keeping them clean for the rest of their lives is a tremendous challenge."

His words cut deep. "I didn't know she had a drug problem."

"Ed told Lou that she'd mentioned doing drugs in Portland before following the band to Vancouver. He...was distraught over her death. Blamed himself—"

"So he is to blame."

Tyson held up his hand. "I didn't say that. Ed blamed himself for not being there—but he was legitimately on the road. And could he have saved her even if he'd been there?"

I thought back to the medical examiner's report. "Tainted drugs."

"That hit was far more potent than she probably realized. We had a string of overdoses and deaths that week. More than usual. Higher-ups considered issuing a warning, but the numbers leveled off. Whatever'd been in the supply had worked its way through, and there didn't seem to be a point to riling people up."

"Would it have made a difference?" I needed to know.

"I doubt it. Kyesha was the second death we traced back to the supply. There wouldn't have been enough time between the first person and hers to issue any kind of warning."

Slowly, Tyson reached out his hand to place it over mine.

"I get that you're angry and you want to blame someone. The dealer got five years but wound up dying in prison—of a drug overdose.

Even drugs make their way into our correctional institutions. They're pervasive and, frankly, I don't know that we'll ever find a solution. So we do the best we can and we keep trudging along."

His words hit home. Hard. I hadn't known about Kyesha's use in Portland. And I hadn't thought to trace her credit card while she was in Canada. I'd made a series of mistakes and assumptions during this *investigation*, and I wasn't proud. I'd blundered my way into a pile of assumptions—some of which had clearly been wrong.

Tyson regarded me. "Ed's really sorry."

I tilted my head.

"He called me. Gave me the heads-up that I might hear from you. Asked me to be as honest as I could."

Tyson squeezed my hand.

I considered pulling away.

But I didn't. I needed the comfort he offered. I needed to know I'd survive this.

"He still blames himself. That kind of guilt..." Tyson inclined his head. "I've followed his career. He and Axel have done a lot of charity work. A lot of good deeds and paying it forward."

"And you'd hate to see that all brought down by my actions."

He appeared thoughtful. "You do what you need to do. I suspect..." he trailed off. "No, I hope, that Axel and Ed are strong enough to withstand whatever comes next."

"You're worried they'll start using again."

"I'm always worried every former addict will start using again." His eyes softened. "But something tells me that you're not going to try to destroy them."

I yanked my hand back. "I was never out to *destroy* anyone."

Liar.

He continued to regard me. "If you say so. Kyesha might be a cautionary tale. About using drugs. About using drugs alone. About tainted drug supplies." He scratched his stubbly chin. "The world has changed a lot since she passed."

I knew what he meant.

"But other things haven't. We still don't take care of those who need our help the most. We still judge others before we've walked a mile in their shoes."

Compassion came off him in waves. He wasn't just talking about Kyesha, Axel, and Ed. He was also talking about me. About how he hadn't been where I sat but that he saw my pain.

"I need to go." I rose jerkily.

He steadied the two virtually untouched cups of coffee before rising as well. "I'll see you out."

From the other room, a terrifying bout of coughing reached me. "No, please, take care of your dad. I'm sorry to have bothered you."

"I..." He cleared his throat. "I don't know how much longer we have."

Born of an instinct I didn't understand, I grasped his hands. "So treasure every day. Be there for him. Let him know he's not alone."

Tyson blinked several times. "Yeah. I can do that."

I released his hands, grabbed my folder, and bolted.

Chapter Thirty-Seven

Ed

Four days had come and gone without word from Thornton, Mickey, or the crew.

Four days of waiting.

Four days of tamping down panic.

Pauletta, that first morning, had known something was amiss. She'd pulled me aside when the documentary team hadn't shown up. "I'm not going to hassle them—but you're going to tell me what's going on."

And so I had. Every wretched detail.

In the end, I wasn't certain who was more devastated.

Well, Axel, of course. That was a given.

But Pauletta and I'd protected him for eight years. Back then, it'd been because of his fragile sobriety. Then it'd become a habit I hadn't known how to break. Sometimes he could be mature, and I'd think he was ready to know the truth. Then he'd do something childish and irresponsible, and I'd worry the truth would send him to a dark place. We needed him clean, sober, and clearheaded.

But now?

Maybe, Paulie had admitted cautiously, eight years was long enough for him to be able to face the truth.

I wasn't convinced.

I watched him like a hawk.

And, after four days, he told me off.

Big time.

Part of me worried he was still angry that I hadn't told him the entire truth eight years ago or at any point since then. Keeping a few critical details to myself had felt like the right move, back when he was fragile, but that omission loomed large now. Part of me worried he might relapse. And, a small part of me worried he might seek out Thornton. To what...? Set the record straight? Tell his side of the story.

I just didn't know.

We managed to write one song.

The band met to try it out, as well as to solidify "Sunrise". The record executives wanted that to be our first release. And as much as I worried about the overlords, nothing bad happened. In fact, they considered our counteroffer. Instead of us coming to LA to record the album, would they consider sending a producer north? Several studios in Vancouver had equipment that rivalled the best studios in LA. We'd be more comfortable on home turf. They wouldn't have the added expense.

That particular argument had been waved away—as if money were no consequence.

I didn't feel that way. I still wanted to pinch every penny. We might not ever be able to pay back Mr. Magnum for his generosity over the years, but it'd be nice to be able to pay our own bills.

All those things happened in a blur, though.

Each night I went back into my room and remembered how I'd felt when I'd been inside Thornton. How it'd felt so damn right. How I couldn't believe things were really over.

Dozens of times, I pulled up his contact information.

Dozens of times, I held my fingers above the keyboard.

Dozens of times, I put the phone away.

Detective Tyson McGillvary had called. Ostensibly to update me on his meeting with Thornton—and he had provided some details. Mostly, though, I had the sense he wanted to be certain Axel and I were doing okay. Way above and beyond the role of a police officer, but he'd always seemed like a super caring kind of guy.

Nearly a week after I'd seen Thornton for the last time—although I hadn't known it was going to be the last time when it'd happened—Axel and I sat in the living room, two pizza boxes on the coffee table.

His meat lovers was nearly demolished.

My vegetarian Greek was barely touched.

He glanced over at me. "Man, you can't keep moping."

I whacked him with a throw pillow. "I'm not."

"Dude, you didn't even look at Irene."

I tilted my head.

"Cassie's roommate."

Part of me wanted to ask who Cassie was.

Most of me didn't give a shit.

"You're not going full-on gay, are you?"

I sighed. "I'm not full-on anything. And that's, like, so inappropriate. Bisexual is a thing." I sniffed. "In fact, I think I'm giving up sex altogether."

Axel moaned. "Dude, you're like, my wingman, and it's Halloween night. How is it that we're not at a bar and partying?"

Because I don't think you being around alcohol right now is a good idea?

Perhaps because I didn't think I should be around it either.

I rose to grab the pizza boxes.

Axel swung the pillow and hit me on the ass.

I pivoted.

He grinned. "About the only ass action you're getting these days."

"You have no idea what you're talking about."

"Oh, you've had a pile of hook-ups and I've not noticed?" He snickered. "You haven't left my sight—"

"I have."

"Yeah, sure. To piss." He made a disgusted noise deep in his throat. "You think I don't know you're sleeping on the couch so you can make sure I'm not drinking?"

"My bed is too soft these days. I need a new mattress."

"No, you need to forget about that douchebag, and you need to stop worrying about me."

A knock sounded at the door.

Axel and I stared at each other.

"Kids trick-or-treating?" His suggestion.

"They never have before." I shrugged.

The knock sounded again.

Axel popped off the couch. "Cassie said she was working tonight. Maybe she changed her mind."

Well, if she'd made it past security, I'd have words in the morning with the building manager. No one was allowed to come up to our door except Pauletta. Even Big Mac, Songbird, and Meg had to be buzzed up.

"I'm not sure—"

Axel swung open the door. "About time, you fucker."

"Hello. Nice to see you too, Axel."

I froze at the all-too-familiar voice. The voice I heard every waking moment. The voice that haunted my dreams.

"May I come in?"

Axel held the door open and made a sweeping gesture.

Thornton entered slowly. Cautiously.

When he caught sight of me, he stopped his forward momentum.

My heart caught in my throat. I'd spent the last five days telling myself our time together hadn't mattered. That Thornton hadn't been *that* gorgeous. That I'd move on.

That I didn't love him.

Lies. All fanciful lies.

"Do you want something to drink, or are you here to dump and run?"

He swallowed slowly, stepping far enough into the room so Axel could at least close the door. "Ginger ale, if you have it."

Axel snickered. "I just figured you'd been trying to impress him that night. Who the hell drinks that shit?"

"I do."

"Me."

Thornton cracked a little smile as he and I spoke at about the same time.

Axel grabbed his arm and dragged him into the living room as I poured two glasses of ginger ale with ice. *Food? No food? Am I trying too hard? Am I not trying hard enough?*

Why is he here?

Okay, I was deluding myself with that question. Tyson and I had had a long conversation after Thornton left him. Didn't give me any idea where this man's head was at, but at least I'd had a bit of closure with the officer who'd seen me at my worst.

Steeling myself, I headed into the living room.

Axel sat in the chair.

Leaving me to sit next to Thornton. On the couch.

Fucker.

Axel. Not Thornton.

Who held a flash drive in his hand.

Okay, maybe he was a fucker too.

I handed him the drink.

He took it with a small smile, linking his index finger over mine for just a moment.

How am I supposed to interpret that? Is he sending me some kind of signal?

And, in my befuddled state, was I even capable of interpreting it?

I didn't know.

Appearing as nonchalant as I could pull off, I sat next to him on the sectional—keeping a decorous distance, of course.

He frowned for a moment, as if he didn't understand my reticence. Then, as if remembering himself, he smiled.

That dazzling smile that lit my insides.

God, I was *so* confused. We'd said our forever goodbyes. Hadn't we? And we were never supposed to see each other again. Except—

"Why are you here?" My voice might've been low and harsh, but I didn't give a fuck. The guy was up to something—he was always up to something. He'd had ulterior motives from day one.

He tapped the flash drive with his index finger. "Rough cut."

Axel and I exchanged glances. *What the fuck* glances.

"That was...quick." Axel took a swig of his cola out of the glass bottle. For some reason, he swore cola tasted better out of a glass bottle.

Meg had tried to call it nostalgia.

I pointed out we were *all* children of plastic.

She'd merely smiled and gone back to her sketch pad.

Thornton sat a little straighter. "We haven't got the sound fixed up, or the tracks overlaid. The narration is...rough."

"Yeah. So you said." I eyed him. "Do you really think we're buying what you're selling?"

To my surprise, Axel held up his hand. "Maybe the man deserves a chance. Maybe we should see what he has to say before we judge him."

"Oh, like he gave us a chance? Like he didn't come into this whole clusterfuck with preconceived notions? About all of us, I might say. He doesn't care who he destroys, just as long as he gets—"

"Ed."

Axel snapped my name.

I halted my tirade.

Thornton held my gaze. Finally he ventured, "Why don't we watch the video and then hash things out?"

"And you'll leave it we ask you to?"

He winced. Then, slowly, he nodded. "Of course I'll leave if you ask me to. I'd never stay where I wasn't welcome."

I arched an eyebrow.

He held my stare.

Warmth heated my cheeks. That stare always did things to my inside. Made my stomach clench. Made my heart flutter. Made my cock stir. *Oh, for fuck's sake, not now.*

My body fought mightily but, after a moment, it complied.

Thornton licked his lips.

Fucker.

"Fine. We'll watch your video."

Before I could move, Axel leapt out of the chair, snagged the thumb drive, and headed to the entertainment system. The irony of my life was that although I understood mixing boards and computer composition programs, I was clueless about the functioning of our entertainment system. I could, if pressed, muddle through.

After loading the thumb drive, Axel moved back to the couch.

He nudged Thornton over toward me.

"Axel." I didn't try to hide my frustration.

"What?" He looked over Thornton to me with that innocent face I didn't buy for even a second. "I want to sit looking straight ahead."

Like he wasn't capable of swivelling the swivel chair.

I started to rise.

Thornton put a restraining hand on my thigh.

Of course, I could've gotten up. He wasn't actually holding me down. In strength, we nearly matched each other. In fact, I might've been able to take him...were we to brawl.

I didn't want to brawl. I wanted to drag him back to my room and fuck him until my dick chafed and his ass was so sore, he wouldn't be able to sit comfortably for a week.

Axel pressed play.

Despite my better judgement, I resettled.

Thornton kept his hand on my thigh. I felt his fingers tremble, and that comforted me, that this meant something to him too."

The video began.

Chapter Thirty-Eight

Thornton

I couldn't remember a time I'd been more nervous. Which said something, because not only did I have an excellent memory—I also had been in some harrowing circumstances over the years.

None of them had anything on this moment.

Axel sat forward, his leg brushing mine. Tension radiated off him, despite his attempts to be nonchalant.

Not for one moment did I believe he wasn't...worried? Curious? Well, something that caused tension.

Ed was nothing less than a basket case. In the *holy shit, I don't know what's going to happen, and it's freaking me out* way.

I knew him. Yes, it'd only been three weeks since we'd first met. Yet I knew the man. Not just biblically—although we did in that way, of course. But I knew his soul.

Or at least, I believed I did.

He also sat forward, riveted to the screen.

I knew the video intimately—having lived and breathed it for the past five days. Mickey and I'd worked sixteen-hour days trying to get some kind of rough cut. Lydia and Kato'd contributed, but hadn't put in nearly the same number of hours. Instead, they'd taken jaunts around the city—getting some background footage. They wanted to do more shots of the band working on their new songs, but I'd made up excuses.

None of my team bought them. Even for a second. But, by the same token, none of my colleagues called me out on my prevarications.

Mickey took me aside and tried to talk to me.

I maintained the best thing we could do was to get a rough cut put together.

Being tactful—or having a sense of self-preservation—I hadn't mentioned I was aware they were in constant contact with Pauletta.

Our one blowout had happened tonight—as we'd copied.

Mickey'd assumed we'd be showing it to Pauletta first.

I dropped the little bombshell that I was going to Axel and Ed's.

They lost their shit.

To compromise, I suggested they take a copy to Pauletta's condo and give her a private showing. Given I'd kept them away from their *secret* paramour for five days, the offer was the least I could do. By making the suggestion, I was also confirming I didn't have a problem with their relationship. Of all of us, I was the least in a position to cast stones.

All this played through my mind as I watched the screen. I tried to figure out what was going through everyone's mind. Not just Ed's and Axel's, but Pauletta's as well, watching at her place. Would she regret letting me in?

And how would she feel when I asked for the final interview? More importantly, how would Mickey react? I hadn't told them about my sister. I doubted they'd ever forgive me that omission.

The fifty-nine-minute doc ended with a full shot of the six of them when Pauletta told them about the contract. We'd covered from the first rehearsal to each of the concerts, to Rocktoberfest, to the individual interviews.

When the screen went dark, I snagged the remote from Axel and turned the machine off. I didn't need to retrieve the drive—we'd made several copies, plus we had everything on the computer backed up to the cloud.

Ed cleared his throat.

But didn't speak.

Axel rose, slowly. He snagged the remote from my hand and headed for the entertainment system. The very impressive system.

"I don't need it back. It's just a rough cut—"

He pivoted back to me. "You didn't mention Kyesha."

To my credit, I didn't wince. Instead, I glanced over at Ed.

He continued to stare at the blank screen.

Clearly, this wasn't what he expected.

"Yeah." I turned my attention back to Axel. "I don't think it's finished."

Ed stiffened even further.

I continued to rest my hand on his thigh.

Truthfully, it stunned me that he hadn't removed my touch.

After a moment, I drew in a breath. "I'd like to interview you." I glanced at Ed. "Both of you."

He flinched.

"I know talking about her brings up bad memories—"

"You have no fucking idea what you're talking about." Ed growled the words—low enough for only me to hear, despite the ringing silence in the room.

"Ed—"

"No, Axel. This isn't up for debate." More growling—only this time, louder—in response to the man's attempt.

Axel strode from the room.

Ed shook off my hand. "I think you need to go."

"But—"

He rose and turned to face me. "We were just—and I mean just—starting to come out of the...chaos...that you've created. Axel plays a good game, but I warned you that he could be fragile. I—" He winced. "Axel never knew."

I didn't understand. "That Kyesha'd died? How'd you keep that from him?"

"Not that she'd died." He rubbed his fingers against his forehead. "That she died while I was driving him to rehab."

Oh shit.

Then I repeated the words out loud. "Oh shit."

"Yes. Shit. Really bad shit. He's been in a tailspin since I had to tell him. I'd never—" He winced. "I'd never lied to him. When they let me visit him, after a couple of weeks, I told him that Kyesha had died. But I didn't give him the details. Like the fact she'd died in our living room. Or share the detail that we'd been on the road when it happened, that it was just hours after he left her behind to save himself. He was already wracked with guilt. Can you imagine how he'd have felt? He blamed himself. That would've intensified. Instead, Pauletta and I stood by him while he got clean. She arranged for this condo, and we moved in. We never spent another night in that house.

"Slowly…things got better. Pauletta got us better gigs. We started making payments toward paying her dad back. We…put our lives back together."

"And Kyesha?"

He met my gaze. "We never talked about her. No matter what you think, I cared about her. Axel loved…" He winced yet again. "I shouldn't—"

His vague apology non-apology was cut off when Axel returned. He held a photo envelope in his hands. "I keep meaning to put these in an album. But…that'd be like an irrevocable act, you know? Like admitting she was never coming back."

"Axel." Ed's pain-laden voice hit me.

"No, Ed." Axel held out the envelope to me. "He needs to see."

I took it—with no small amount of trepidation. The envelope was well worn. Likely eight years old, if I didn't miss the mark. My hand shook as I sat, the paper vibrating in my grip.

Ed grabbed Axel by the arm and bodily shoved him toward Axel's bedroom, leaving me sitting alone.

"You don't have to go." My voice wasn't as steady as I would've liked.

Ed looked at me with some emotion darkening his eyes. Compassion? Fear? I couldn't read it.

"Just a few minutes. Maybe call us when you're, uh, done?" With that, he manhandled Axel out.

Who caught my gaze just before he disappeared.

No missing the pain in his eyes. Because I held his precious memories, or because he had more he wanted to say?

I didn't know.

I was beginning to understand Ed, despite the damaging mistakes I'd made in prejudging him, but Axel was still a mystery.

One you're not going to solve if you don't rip the bandage off.

The bandage over the gaping wound from when my sister'd died. The one I honestly didn't know if I'd ever heal from. I'd been on my first overseas assignment.

She'd run off to Canada.

I hadn't even known before she was already lost. Taking a deep breath, I pulled out what had to be about twenty-five photos.

At the first one, my breath caught and, unwillingly, my eyes watered.

Axel and Kyesha—side by side. With huge grins. With their heads pressed together, and the widest smile I could ever remember seeing on Kyesha's face, they appeared happy. Like, really happy. Both pairs of eyes were clear and sparkling.

Honestly, I couldn't ever remember seeing my sister so joyous.

Every subsequent photo was the same. Some were of Kyesha alone. Others with Ed, Axel, and my sister. Pauletta was in a couple of shots—but I had the sense she'd been the one behind the camera.

Did she know that I was Kyesha's older brother? Had Axel and Ed informed her?

Mickey hadn't said anything, but they might've wanted to keep things on an even keel while we finished the rough cut.

The rough cut.

My clumsy way of...apologizing? Offering an olive branch? I just didn't know.

The last picture was of Kyesha. She wore her favorite yellow dress.

I scrutinized the picture.

The dress hung loose. Her bare arms appeared painfully thin. She smiled, but it didn't reach her eyes. Her dull eyes.

Why did he keep this picture? At the bottom of the pile, to be sure. Still, like all the others, it showed signs of repeated wear.

He'd looked at these many, many times over the years.

"Sunrise" played over and over in my head.

Oh, sweetheart, why didn't you call me? I would've been here. In a heartbeat.

Knowing Kyesha, though, with her stubborn streak a mile wide, she likely hadn't seen herself as needing help.

Clearly, Axel had fallen far enough for him to be in the right mental headspace for Ed to convince him to go to rehab.

Had he planned to try to convince Kyesha? Why hadn't he called my parents?

Because she'd been nineteen. Legal here. Well, legal in some things in the US as well. Different drinking ages. And pot hadn't been legal in either place back then.

But pot and alcohol hadn't done this to her.

Meth.

The coroner's report had said meth.

And Tyson had mentioned a tainted supply of illegal drugs.

In the end, I could blame Ed and Axel for not helping her.

I could blame the drug dealer who'd sold her the lethal shit.

Or I could blame Kyesha for taking the drugs. She'd made the choice. Not just to take drugs, but to take them alone.

Or I could accept this was just one of those things and not lay blame at all.

Slowly, I slid the pictures back into the envelope. I needed to find the courage to ask Axel if I could get copies made. Or, even better, if he had the negatives or digital copies so I could print out ones for myself. The first few I'd share with my parents.

My folks still grieved for Kyesha, but not with the single-minded intensity I did. Having so many other children to raise didn't give them time for self-flagellation. I couldn't judge how often they grieved for her when they were alone, but to the rest of us kids, Dad repeatedly pointed out Kyesha'd been old enough to make her own choices. He and Mom asked us to be smart, to be safe, to come to them if we needed them, but her tragedy didn't seem to consume their lives like it had mine.

I rose, stretched, and made my way over to Axel's door. I had no idea what to expect—or even what I was going to say—but I needed to speak to the two men.

Chapter Thirty-Nine

Ed

The knock wasn't unexpected, but I still startled.

Axel rose, from where he sat next to me on the bed and headed to the door. He met my gaze.

I nodded.

He opened the door.

A very uncomfortable-looking Thornton stood on the other side. "May I come in?"

Ever the polite guy.

I propelled myself off the bed, turned him gently around, and shoved him out the door.

"Hey." Axel sounded baffled.

"Right, like I'm going to let him hang around in your room." I grimaced.

Said room didn't smell—but likely because I'd opened a window. And, even on this mild evening, the calendar still read October thirty-first, so that fresh air held a chill.

"Let me close the window," Axel tried.

I propelled him out just as quickly. "Let the room breathe." I didn't add that if he just put his laundry in the hamper, the room wouldn't be so...stale.

He huffed.

Thornton, to my surprise, smiled. "God, you two really are like brothers."

Intuitively, I understood he didn't just mean the skin color. We fought like brothers. We did everything together.

Well, almost everything.

So when he'd loved someone, she felt like my sister.

I'd truly seen Kyesha as a sister. As a kindred spirit. As a young woman, our age, who loved music as much as we did and maybe loved my brother-of-the-heart.

Thornton held the envelope out.

Axel took it.

"I'd love to get copies of those photos."

After a moment, Axel glanced at me. "Yeah, I've got them on a CD. I can get it burned or—"

"Yeah, that'd be great." Thornton was quick to speak. "Thank you."

A gesture? Of forgiveness? Of understanding? An attempt at a truce?

Not that there'd ever really been a battle. At least not between the two most important men in my life.

I still didn't know where I stood with Thornton.

He cleared his throat. Then scratched his chin. Then clasped his hands. "I would still really love to interview you." He met Axel's gaze before sliding it to meet mine as well. "Both of you."

"You might not like what we have to say."

I watched him closely for his reaction.

Axel offered, "We can keep it light—"

Thornton held up his hand to cut Axel off. Not unkindly, I didn't think, but clearly, he didn't want to go down that path.

"I'm okay with the truth." He ran his hand through his hair—as he'd already done several times, if his slightly disheveled appearance was any indication. "You're going to tell me hard truths. But..." He faltered. "She was this vivacious person." He hesitated. "Yet...she always felt a little sad. I wondered if she might have had undiagnosed mild depression. Looking at some of those photos...I just don't know. Was it all drugs and partying?"

Before I could answer, Axel dropped the photo envelope onto the coffee table, then snagged Thornton's hands. "I'm going to tell you a hard truth right now. Something Ed doesn't know. Something I think would hurt your parents...so I won't repeat it on camera."

Thornton appeared startled, but he continued to hold Axel's hands.

"Your sister loved your family. She talked about them all the time. And she probably mentioned an older brother Thornton—and I probably should've remembered that name. But I've shoved those memories down, you know? As a way of coping."

"Yeah, she called me Tony." He let out and abrupt laugh. "Use to drive me nuts. He cleared his throat. "You were saying...?"

"But she wasn't always happy." Axel gazed at me briefly before turning his attention back to Thornton. They were both so tall that they met gazes straight on. "She didn't feel like she belonged anywhere, not in her adoptive family, not outside it. She wanted to know more about her roots. That's part of what she was trying to get from Ed and me."

"I don't—"

"Basically, she hadn't spent a great deal of time around Black people."

Thornton took a step back, as if he'd received a physical blow to his chest. "She never..."

"No, she wouldn't."

Axel released the man's hands when he tugged them away.

They both glanced at me. As if I could somehow conjure up with the right words.

I couldn't.

"She didn't love you any less." Axel drew Thornton's attention. "But she needed more than just what she could get from your family. Our music..." He squinted, as if thinking back. "She said it spoke to her. She leaned so hard into some of the lyrics, trying to hear who she was in the words we wrote. We hardly sing those songs anymore because we associate them with her."

"I wondered why she sometimes seemed so distant..." Thornton took a couple of steps toward the sliding glass door.

"It'll be cold," I warned.

He shrugged.

I caught Axel's gaze.

Just him and me.

Axel nodded. He picked up the photo envelope. "I'm just not sure what else to say."

Thornton's gaze shot to him. "Sorry."

"Don't be. I'm here when you're ready to talk." Without another word, he went into his room and shut the door.

In the confusion of his arrival, Thornton hadn't taken off his shoes, but no way was I going out on the balcony without mine.

He waited while I shoved my bare feet into running shoes. With no small sense of self-preservation, I grabbed my bomber jacket as well.

As I walked back through the living room, I snagged his hand. When I didn't get any resistance, I laced my fingers with his and made my way over to the sliding glass door. I unlocked it, then slid it open.

A brisk wind hit me.

Undaunted, I stepped over the little doorsill and encouraged Thornton to do the same.

Once we were both on the balcony, I closed the door.

He continued to hold my hand.

A firework went off in the distance. Down near False Creek, if I had the orientation right. It might be a school night, but Vancouverites took every opportunity possible to light fireworks. Why not on Halloween?

After I'd let the silence linger long enough, I tugged Thornton to the railing. As I pushed him against the glass of the balcony, I tucked my smaller body into his side. I laid my head on his shoulder and placed my hand over his where he gripped the railing. Finally, I lightly gripped his waist with my other arm.

Offering unspoken support.

Maybe taking a bit for myself as well.

I'd adored Kyesha. Her death hit me hard. Differently than Axel, of course. He'd loved her in the romantic sense. I'd seen her as a sister and friend. Someone who understood our struggles—all of them.

Thornton leaned into my touch.

The wind whipped his hair.

He sighed. "I had no idea, Ed. You have to believe me. I thought..." He sighed again. "I don't know what I thought. That we could just make her life as easy as possible and everything would work out? I believed—in my heart—that love was enough. No one could love her as much as we did. All of us. I adored her. Doted on her. The younger kids looked up to her."

His body shook.

Whether from the bitter wind or some memory, I wasn't sure.

"I got word a couple of days after she died. I was overseas. Despite racing home, I missed the funeral. But I stayed."

He flexed his fingers under mine.

"I stayed for almost two months. Everyone was engulfed in grief. I tried to help, you know? Just being there and talking to the kids." He shuddered yet again. "Well, Bonita was in undergrad and Pietro was almost finished with high school. But the twins were only seven. They didn't understand."

As he hadn't either, I presumed. So how did one explain something to a child that one didn't understand oneself? "How many of you are there?"

He nodded. "Uh, I'm the only biological child. Then...my parents just started adopting kids. Bonita and Pietro are siblings. She's a nephrologist, and he's a nurse." He paused. "Uh, she's twenty-eight, and he's twenty-six."

"Bonita and Kyesha were about the same age?"

"Yeah. They were both nine, and Bonita had been with us three years when my folks adopted Kyesha. And then came Ayala and Abigail. Preemie twins. Chaos incarnate. I was just heading to college when they arrived. God, Kyesha loved them so much. She was a mature twelve and wanted to be involved in every aspect of childcare. I always thought..." His voice broke. "I always thought she'd make the most amazing mother. Just that she had to find herself first, right? She said she needed a gap year. A year before she started college. My parents mentioned she'd come to Canada for some opportunity, and I thought that was a good thing."

This time, I winced. I'd known virtually none of Kyesha's background, except that she'd been adopted by white parents. I hadn't asked. Just blithely assumed if Kyesha wanted to talk about her family that she would. Or assumed she, like Axel and myself, had shitty parents and didn't want to go there. Honestly, it'd never occurred to me that she had a truly loving family waiting for her to *find herself* and then come home.

I had no words of comfort to offer.

Another gust of wind nearly blew us over.

"I'm ready."

Not entirely certain what he meant, but happy to assume he meant we could go in, I led him back inside.

The condo's ambient temperature sat at a comfortable level, but cold still penetrated my body.

I moved to flick on the gas fireplace. I hated using it because the thing wasn't environmentally friendly, but it'd take too long to jack up the heat.

Thornton waylaid me. "Can we just…"

Meeting his gaze, I read the pleading in those amber eyes. "Sure, sweetheart, whatever you want."

I didn't know how he'd take the endearment, but it slipped out.

Those amber eyes softened, and a small smile crept across his face. "Am I? Your sweetheart? I thought—"

I pressed my index finger to his lips. "Don't think. Just…come with me." I snagged his chilly hand and gently tugged him toward my bedroom.

Once inside, I turned on a bedside lamp that cast a low glow in the room.

Since I wasn't Axel, the room wasn't a disaster. In fact, the cleaning crew had come earlier in the day—fresh sheets, scrubbed bathroom...everything perfect. "No aroma-du-sweat-socks," I joked. They'd cleaned Axel's room. And he'd promptly made a mess.

Thornton chuckled. "You guys really are opposites."

"Yeah."

He snagged me around the waist and pulled me close. "Thank you." Then he lowered his lips to mine.

I'd planned a seduction. Or at least to find a creative way to make him forget the emotional pain he'd just endured. And, to a certain extent, that was what happened. Instead, I moved the teddy bear I always kept with me—the one Kyesha'd gifted me in one of her lighter moments—to the nightstand, and I pulled back the covers.

We explored as we stripped each other down to bare skin. A touch here. A caress there. A nip or nibble.

All leisurely. After all, we had all night. Or so I told myself. The truth was, I just didn't know.

But as he lay on my bed and I deep throated him, I prayed this wasn't goodbye.

After he'd come, he wanted to reciprocate.

Honestly, I rarely turned down blow jobs.

Tonight, though, I did.

As I held him, he slipped into an exhausted sleep, and he remained unmoving and dead to the world until I finally sank into slumber.

In the morning, he was gone.

Chapter Forty

Thornton

I wrapped up the final moments of my interview with Ed and Axel in the studio, trying to stay professional. Axel looked more relaxed than I expected. Although not in a disrespectful way. Ed sat on the edge of his seat, not meeting my eyes.

"Thank you for the interview. And for speaking so candidly about Kyesha." I offered my hand.

Axel shook first.

Ed took my hand as well, but cocked his head.

Ah. I ran my hand through my hair. "You were expecting more."

Axel glanced back and forth between us, then pointed to Mickey and Pauletta.

I nodded.

He made a beeline for them, clearly not wanting to stick around.

Not that I could blame him.

Ed motioned to the farthest corner of the studio.

Lydia and Kato were packing up equipment, but Ed didn't appear convinced he might not still be recorded.

I followed him.

He stared up at me. "That whole interview, and you didn't once say she was your sister."

"Yeah..." I ran my hand through my hair again. "I'm going to do a voiceover to briefly touch on her life before meeting you guys. I'll add the photos Axel gave me—he signed a release—"

Ed waved me off. Clearly copyright violations weren't the issue.

What does he want from me?

Those fathomless dark-brown eyes gazed up at me. I expected anger for the way I'd ditched him, but I read concern and compassion.

Or I hoped I did. "I'm okay, Ed. Really."

He stared at me.

Give him more.

"I flew home to talk to my parents at the crack of dawn."

"And left Mickey to arrange all this." He waved around to indicate the studio.

Shit. "I'm sorry. I should've said something—"

"You don't owe me an explanation. I mean, it's not like we're in a relationship or something. Or that we mean something to each other."

"I left a note."

He yanked the apparently offending object from his back pocket. "*I'll be in touch*. That's...what? How was I supposed to interpret that? Then you go radio silent—"

"Hey, you didn't call or text—"

He slammed the paper against my chest. "I assumed this was a kiss-off."

Oh. "I didn't mean it like that. I just..." *How can I explain this to him?* "I had to talk to the family—to get their take before this last interview. To tell them I was working with you and Axel, and find out what they wanted me to do." I scratched my nose.

He continued to stare.

"I'm going to be honest…it opened a lot of wounds."

He winced.

I held up my hand. "Shit that should've been dealt with years ago. And…I shared what you and Axel said. About Kyesha's unhappiness. Which opened up a discussion with all my siblings, none of whom are white. That wasn't just a bomb I could detonate and then walk away from."

After a moment, he blinked.

"All good. None of the other four feel the way she did."

"And you believe them?"

His question had me taking a step back. "Are you suggesting they might be lying?"

"No." He drew a deep breath. "I would never accuse someone I don't know of something like that. Just…kids often say things so their parents won't feel bad. Maybe the other kids saw how Kyesha's feelings affected your family, and they didn't want to do the same."

"We discussed that. Bonita and Pietro are certainly mature enough to be able to speak up. Both assured us they didn't have an issue." *Although, yes, both of them were generous kind souls who might hesitate to rock the family boat. I made a mental note to leave the door explicitly open, so they could tell me if they ever wanted to talk more.* I hesitated. "The discussion with the twins was…more delicate. Ayala said she didn't give a shit—her word—and Abigail kept demanding to know why I hadn't gotten your autograph. She's followed you guys because of Kyesha's connection. There was a CD of your songs in the stuff of Kyesha's that we were given. Abigail found it in Mom's room, and got hooked on your music."

"You mean Axel's autograph."

"Uh, no. My fifteen-year-old sister has a massive crush. On you."

Despite his coloring, I couldn't miss the darkening of his cheeks. "You didn't…" He made some odd gesture.

I grabbed his hand. "I didn't tell her that you fucked me. But I might've left the impression I'd grown close to you. And the other band members," I quickly added.

His gaze narrowed.

"Yeah, Bonita gave me that look. I think there might be an invitation to Portland in your future." I swallowed. "If you still want to, you know…" I replicated his odd gesture with my free hand.

He snagged that one.

We stood there, holding hands, gazing into each other's eyes.

A wolf whistle had Ed stepping back from me.

I hung on tight and pulled him closer. "I want this. Whatever this is. If you can forgive me for leaving suddenly—"

"You needed time."

"—and returning unceremoniously when we had no chance to talk privately—"

"You do need to learn to pick your moments."

I brought our joined hands to my lips and kissed Ed's knuckles. "Give me a chance?"

He held my gaze. "You live in another country. We live divergent lives."

"I believe we can make it work." *Please, trust me.*

"You're serious?"

"What's the expression? As a heart attack? Yeah, and all that. I want to know you're in my life. I might have to go away for work. And you'll go on tour—"

"We hope."

I cocked my head. "Problems with the contract?"

"Nah, nothing like that." He gazed up to the ceiling before looking back at me. "What if no one buys the album? Or what if they watch the documentary and decide we're just druggie losers?"

I squeezed his hands. "You know the doc won't show any of that. You're all an inspiration." I smiled. "Meg's going to let us film some of her surgery. Well, not the surgery itself, but—"

"Big Mac finally found the courage to tell her how he feels. Something about not wanting to spend another day miserable like me."

I squinted. "Ed, I was gone four days."

He shrugged. "I might've been a surly bear with a thorn in his paw for those four days."

My giggle escaped unbidden. "Are you going to be a grizzly when I go away if I'm not *radio silent*?"

Those luminous dark-brown eyes shone. "Nah. That'd be okay."

A solid thump to my back had me dropping Ed's hands and turning.

Axel stood there, with a shit-eating grin on his face. "Dude. Dinner. The Georgian. Mickey said you're paying."

"Hey," Mickey called. "I so did not."

Pauletta put her arm around their shoulder. "Axel's just...being Axel."

"I am paying." I inclined my chin to Lydia and Kato.

They gave me a thumbs-up.

Axel snagged his phone from his back pocket. "Great. I might've already told Meg, Big Mac, and Songbird."

I snickered. "And you made reservations?"

He grinned. "They said they were booked, but when I dropped your name, that changed. Interesting, no? Who are you, Mr. Thornton?"

My cheeks heated. "My family knows the owner."

Ed snorted. "What if he'd said no to paying?"

"Well..." Axel shrugged. "He loves you. He's not going to say no." After he dropped that little bombshell, he sauntered away.

Slowly, I pivoted back to Ed.

He blinked. Several times. "Don't mind Axel. He's just talking out of his—"

I bent to kiss him, cutting off the word I knew was coming. Yeah, Axel could be an ass. He was also the best friend of the man I loved—they came as a package deal.

Ed grabbed the back of my neck as I deepened the kiss.

I pulled him flush against me.

Mickey shouted, "See you at the restaurant in twenty."

We kept kissing.

I wanted him to know. That I was committed to the relationship. That I wanted all he could give me—and that I'd keep coming back for more. That I would never grow tired of him.

Finally, he pulled back. "Love?"

"I know, it's crazy, right? It's been a month." I brushed a kiss to his forehead. "My parents knew after three dates. They've been married forty years."

"Married?" He might've squeaked that.

"We're not there yet."

"But..." He blinked.

"Yeah...maybe..." I snagged his arm. "We better go before Axel buys a round for everyone in the restaurant."

"He wouldn't." Yet even as he said the words, he picked up the pace.

I didn't care. In fact, if Axel did it to celebrate, I'd be okay with that. Celebrating the completion of one project...and the beginning of the rest of our lives.

Damn, I was one lucky man.

Epilogue

Ed

Vancouver's unrelenting April showers gave us a break the night of the premiere of the band's documentary. All those folks watching had enjoyed the show without the distraction of wet shoes and clammy pant legs.

Thank God.

I was so fucking sick of the rain.

Since Portland got almost as much as Vancouver, our visit to Thornton's family last weekend hadn't brought a reprieve.

The family who'd welcomed me with open arms.

With the man whose side I tucked myself into now.

We'd just screened the documentary to a full house at the Stanley Theatre, here in Vancouver. Now we mingled in the lobby with other industry professionals. Like, movie people and music people and theater people...

Two weeks ago, we'd been in LA for the launch of the new album.

That night, Thornton had been tucked into my side, and I'd been the one in the spotlight.

I was happy to turn the tables on him tonight. Truthfully, I was still pretty raw from what played out on that big screen. I'd seen the final cut of the doc with his family last weekend.

My choice.

If the documentary upset them—in any way—I wanted to be there. To support Thornton. To shoulder the blow.

I shouldn't have worried.

His family cried and smiled and raved about what a great job he'd done and how proud they were of him.

Bonita took me aside later and confided she'd worried about him for a long time. She confirmed that although the family had grieved, they'd made peace with Kyesha's death. Thornton had been the one who'd never been able to move beyond it. She then thanked me because of the difference she'd seen in her brother since I'd come into his life.

Basically, she'd left me speechless. None of Kyesha's family other than Thornton were here tonight, but they'd all sent their support.

Pauletta handed me a ginger ale. "Hell of a job."

I smirked back at her. "You were right."

She blinked. "Oh, I'm sorry, could you repeat that?"

Thornton, who'd been speaking to someone, stopped to press a kiss to my temple, and told her. "You were right."

I narrowed my eyes. Somehow, I felt ganged up on. Yet, I'd take the higher ground and simply admit defeat.

As I scanned the room, I spotted Songbird, Big Mac, and Meg speaking to a local reporter. Geneva Alvarez? Yeah, that was her name. And if I didn't miss my mark, she had eyes for Songbird.

Well, that'll be interesting.

At least the reporter seemed respectful of the newly-engaged couple. The rock Meg wore on her left ring finger was the equivalent of Big Mac peeing on her leg. But if she was happy, we were all happy.

The wedding was scheduled for next month. By then, Meg would be completely recovered from her reconstructive surgery.

Pauletta clinked her glass against mine. "I just got this week's sales numbers."

"Oh?"

"Climbing fast, Ed."

My stomach lurched. I wanted to know the exact numbers—because that was kind of my thing—but now wasn't the time.

She pointed to my ring. "You guys set a date yet?"

I fingered my ring.

Last weekend, when we'd been at his parents' dining room table for a feast, he'd taken my hand, hidden by the tablecloth.

Touched, I'd clasped his fingers. Then I'd felt something cold against the pad of my ring finger.

He'd slid the ring on an inch, then eased it back nearly off.

Giving me the opportunity to quietly say no without it being a big deal.

I'd slid my finger into the ring, then casually turned to kiss his cheek.

His mother caught us canoodling and beamed.

A few minutes later, when she asked about our future plans, Thornton casually said that he'd have to consult his fiancé.

The table went silent.

I pulled my hand out from under the table and showed off the beautiful platinum band.

Pandemonium had erupted.

I'd been overwhelmed, embraced, and hugged by everyone. Totally overwhelmed.

And now Pauletta wanted us to set a date.

"We were...uh..."

"October." Thornton snagged my hand and kissed the ring. "I'd do it tomorrow, but Ed's still getting paperwork organized."

"Like applying for a work permit?"

He nodded in acknowledgement of Pauletta's question. "Although it'd be faster if we just got married, and then I could apply for my permanent residency—"

"I don't want them to think you only married me to get Canadian citizenship." I glared.

Thornton shrugged. "Everyone knows things are getting bad. Canada's a little slice of heaven."

"Until the other guys get into power," Pauletta pointed out. "The pendulum always swings, my friend." Like Americans, we had two diametrically opposed main political parties. One of which I approved and one that drove me nuts.

Another maddening shrug. "When we're married, we can pick where we live."

I eyed him.

"But it'll be Canada," he quickly added. "I'm looking at hooking up with a production company in the Vancouver area."

"You going back to wildlife documentaries?" Pauletta might've snickered that question.

"No." Thornton again met my gaze. "Social issues. I'm working on one about tent cities in Vancouver, Portland, and San Francisco."

"Hey." Mickey pressed a kiss to Pauletta's cheek in greeting, then hugged me.

I hugged them back. "The doc was great. Thanks for all you did to pull that together."

They grinned. "Some of our best work." They tilted their head. "Who's Axel talking to?"

I glanced over and winced inwardly. "That's Mr. Treadgold. Our music teacher."

Mickey snapped their fingers. "Right." They turned to Thornton. "Didn't you try to interview him on background?"

This time, I stiffened.

Thornton grabbed my hand. "Yeah, before we got started, I approached him." He met my gaze. "And I didn't afterward because Axel begged me not to. I don't usually like subjects dictating who I can and can't speak to..." He blinked. "I didn't want to hurt him."

"I didn't say that." Axel's angry words carried clear across the lobby.

A hush settled as others cut their conversations off mid-sentence.

"Axel—" Mr. Threadgold tried to step toward my clearly agitated bandmate.

"No. You promised."

Before any of us could react, Axel pivoted and stalked out of the room

Mr. Threadgold started to follow him.

Then he stopped.

Finally, he turned to face the gaping crowd.

His cheeks turned crimson, and he headed in the opposite direction—right out of the theater and onto Granville Street.

"I should go—"

Thornton placed a hand to my chest. "Don't."

"I meant Axel."

"Of course." He pressed lightly. "I think he needs to cool off."

"I just..." I eyed Pauletta, Mickey, and Thornton. "He's been off since October. I've tried to talk to him, but I'm just not getting anywhere."

"And you think…" Mickey indicated the door with their chin.

"I've wondered."

Pauletta's phone buzzed.

I glared. "Seriously? Everyone who's anyone is here tonight."

She handed Mickey her glass and fished her phone out of her purse. "Yes, but this is the email I've been waiting for."

As she swiped and did a bunch of other stuff, I gazed over to Thornton.

"We can try talking to him tonight."

I swallowed. "We planned to tell him we're getting a place of our own tonight."

"That can wait. We're not in a rush. Real estate's kind of crazy right now—spring rush. If we wait until early fall then we might be able to get something cheaper."

"Is money an issue?" With the record contract and the money we were getting from touring, I was looking at being able to contribute almost equally.

"Money isn't the issue. You know that. I want you and Axel to—"

Pauletta squealed, cutting Thornton off.

We all turned our attention to her.

She held up the phone. "Rocktoberfest. In October. Headliner."

I couldn't hold in the tremor of excitement. A year ago, we'd barely made the cut. And this year… "Headliner?"

"Yes." She did a little dance.

Mickey threw their arms around her.

They hugged.

Meg, Big Mac, and Songbird, obviously noticing the commotion, came over.

"We're, uh…" I glanced at Thornton.

He nodded encouragingly.

"We're going to Rocktoberfest. We're going to be headliners."

Meg's squeal matched Pauletta's.

Big Mac swept her up against her and spun them around.

Songbird offered her quiet but excited smile. "We need to tell Axel." She glanced to where he'd taken off—back toward the theater.

"It'll keep." Thornton kissed me. "Now, I think it's time for the champagne." He winked at me. "Or sparkling cider."

The monumentality of the moment started to sink in. "I think we can say we've made it."

"It's only going to get better—I promise."

Maybe I should've been wary of such a grandiose promise—but I wasn't. Because I honestly believed, with him by my side, I could conquer the world.

As Pauletta went to find the manager to get the bubbly, I pulled Thornton to me. "This is a forever love, right?" I had that ring on my finger, echoes of his proposal in my ears, but I needed to hear it one more time.

"Yeah, Ed, it really is."

We kissed to seal the deal.

Sunrise

Turn around
see the sun's going down
But I don't wanna go, so let's put on a show
The night is young
There's still so much to be done
As long as I'm with you
Everything feels brand new
So let's dance the night away
Up until the sun brings the next day
Cause we've got nothing but time to our name
Oh, no money, glory, or fame
But I don't need those to love you
All I want is to hold your hand
So take me to our promise land
That's all I need to love you
Moving fast
Though I want this night to last

So I'm taking a deep breath
Let my worries go to rest
As I take your hands
"Do you think this night will end?
Or will the sun leave us alone,
And the night become our home?"
As I share this thought with you
The sun rises, and damn, what a beautiful view
Well, we've got nothing but time to our names
Oh, no money, glory, or fame
But I don't need those to love you

All I want is to hold your hand, so take me to our promise land, That's all I need to love you

All I want is to hold your hand so take me to our promise land That's all I need to love you.

Lyrics by Zeb Fazel https://linktr.ee/zebfmusic

Want Axel's story? Rocktoberfest 2024 is here!
Check out *Grindstone's Edge HERE*

Road to Rocktoberfest 2023!

Each book can be read as a standalone, but why not read them all and see who hits the stage next? Hot rock stars and the men who love them, what more could you ask for? Kick back, load up your Kindle, and enjoy the men of Rocktoberfest!

Check out the other Rocktoberfest books HERE.

Want more Gabbi Grey?

Check out her *Love in Mission City* series, set in beautiful British Columbia.

The first book is

The first book is *Ginger Snapping All the Way*

Also available:

Stanley's Christmas Redemption (Love in Mission City Book 2)

Sleigh Bells and Second Chances (Love in Mission City Book 3)

Love in Mission City: The Boyfriends Duet

Love in Mission City: The Shorts

The Beauty of the Beast

Page Against the Machine

The Lightkeeper's Love Affair

Ace's Place

Marcus's Cadence

Not in it for the Money

The Beauty of the Beast

Hugh (Single Dads of Gaynor Beach)

Anthony (Single Dads of Gaynor Beach)

Xavier (Single Dads of Gaynor Beach)

Love Furever (Friends of Gaynor Beach Animal Rescue)

Husky Love (Friends of Gaynor Beach Animal Rescue)

My Past, Your Future

If Only for Today

Catch a Tiger by the Tail

Solstice Surprise

Valentino in Vancouver

You See Me

Sun, Surf, and Surprises

Love Without Reservations

An Uncommon Gentleman
Caressa's Homecoming (Bound by Love Book 1)
Cole's Reckoning (Bound by Love Book 2)

Audiobooks

Ginger Snapping All the Way
Stanley's Christmas Redemption
Love in Mission City: The Shorts
Page Against the Machine
The Lightkeeper's Love Affair
Ace's Place
Marcus's Cadence
Not in it for the Money
My Past, Your Future
If Only for Today
Catch a Tiger by the Tail
Solstice Surprise
An Uncommon Gentleman
Hugh (Single Dads of Gaynor Beach)

Want a free short story? The story is set in Gaynor Beach, California where there are plenty of single dads and puppy rescues! You can sign up for my newsletter so you can keep up with all the great stuff I'm doing as well as pictures of my own pooches, Ally and Finnegan.
Hemingway's Happy Day

Interested in knowing more about Gabbi?

Sign up for her newsletter
Follow her on Bookbub
Follow her on Instagram

USA Today Bestselling author Gabbi Grey lives in beautiful British Columbia where her fur baby chin-poo keeps her safe from the nasty neighborhood squirrels. Working for the government by day, she spends her early mornings writing contemporary, gay, sweet, and dark erotic BDSM romances. While she firmly believes in happy endings, she also believes in making her characters suffer before finding their true love. She also writes m/f romances as Gabbi Black and Gabbi Powell.

Made in the USA
Las Vegas, NV
29 January 2025